DEATH IN BERLIN

DEATH IN BERLIN

M. M. Kaye

St. Martin's Minotaur
New York

Library of Congress Cataloging-in-Publication Data

Kaye, M. M. (Mary Margaret).
  Death in Berlin / M. M. Kaye.
    p. cm.
  ISBN 0-312-18621-5 (hc)
  ISBN 0-312-26308-2 (pbk)
  I. Title.
PR6061.A945D33 1985
823'.914   85-1733
                                                            CIP

First published as *Death Walked in Berlin* in 1955.

First St. Martin's Minotaur Edition: June 2000

D 12 11 10 9 8 7 6 5 4 3 2

TO
all those Army wives who like myself
have followed the drum

Author's Note

This story is set in the battered Berlin of 1953 — eight years after the end of World War II and eight years before the infamous Berlin Wall went up, cutting off all free communication between the East and West sectors of the city.

My husband's British regiment was already serving in Germany when they received orders to move to Berlin, and within less than ten days of our arrival he himself was suddenly transferred to a new post in England, where there was no immediate accommodation available for his family — myself and our two small daughters. He departed alone, leaving us behind until such time as an army quarter could be found for us, and it was during the following few weeks of waiting that I thought up the plot for this book — largely as a result of long walks through the green, leafy suburbs between the Herr Strasse and the Grünewald where there were any number of ruined, roofless houses in which the Nazi élite had once lived, and wondering what their late owners had been like and what had become of them?

The Berlin I have described here is the Berlin I saw then. For being at a loose end I had plenty of time on my hands, and I spent a great deal of it exploring and taking notes for future use: scribbling down detailed descriptions of the ruined city, where the worst of the devastation was in the sector occupied by the Russians. Making rough sketches of the Maifeld, that vast, pretentious stadium-complex that Hitler had had built in the 1930s for the Olympic Games, and which later became the setting for innumerable Nazi rallies — and later still, after a brief period of Russian occupation, the headquarters of the British sector.

I also made notes on other things besides scenery and ruins. Small incidents that I thought might come in useful, such as the fact that only a few hours after our arrival at the original, ramshackle Families' Hostel, where we had to spend a night or two before moving into our army quarter, I happened to catch a glimpse of the woman who would be allotted to us as our cook-housekeeper. She had, it seemed, dropped in to visit a friend who worked at the hostel.

My husband, Goff Hamilton, says that his own clearest memory of his first brief stay in Berlin is of finding me standing in the dusk one evening beside the big outdoor swimming-pool in the Stadium area, staring down at the dark stagnant water with its 'anti-freeze' criss-cross of heavy straw cables, and replying (when he remarked a shade tartly that he presumed I was busy drowning someone in there?), 'Yes: I've had an idea about that straw ...' The trials of a man whose wife writes murder stories!

Goff was a major at that time, and when, six years later, he returned to command the British sector's Berlin Brigade, we lived in a lovely house complete with a heated swimming-pool and a spectacular view over the Havelsee; and I could barely recognize the city as the Berlin I had described in this book, for by that time most of the ruins had disappeared: from the British sector, at least. The Russians too had vanished from the Rundfunk; though they still mounted a guard on a memorial they had built on the western side of the Brandenburg Gate, and took their turn at garrisoning Spandau gaol, ostensibly to keep an eye on its three remaining Nazi inmates, but obviously because it allowed them to keep a foot inside the West Berlin door! The ruined Kaiser Wilhelm Kirche on the Kurfürstendamm, that had once seemed to me so strangely beautiful, had by now been pared down to a single broken spire which, in the guise of a war memorial, had been incorporated in a new and very modernistic church where it no longer looked like some romantic ruin from Angkor Wat, but regrettably like the stump of a blackened and rotted tooth that should have been pulled out long ago.

A few months before we left, The Wall went up. And with its rise many fond hopes for the future of humanity came tumbling down. I watched it being built: which is possibly why, when I look back, I think that I prefer the battered but more hopeful Berlin of 1953.

Prologue

With nightfall the uneasy wind that had sighed all day through the grass and the gorse bushes at the cliff edge died away, and a cold fog crawled in from the sea, obliterating the darkening coastline and muting the drag of waves on shingle to a rhythmic murmur barely louder than the unrelenting and monotonous mutter of gunfire to the west.

The hours crept by in silence until at last the moon rose, tingeing the fog with silver and bringing with it a night breeze that blew gently off the land and eddied but did not disperse the fog.

Something that appeared to be a bent whin bush moved and stood upright, and a low voice spoke in the patois of that lonely stretch of coast: a man's voice, barely above a whisper. 'It is good. Now we go — but without noise. I go first, and each one will put the hand on him who is ahead. It is better to carry the children. Now——!' There was a rustle that might have been the wind among the bushes and the harsh sea-grass as the little band of refugees, formless and without substance in the uncertain moonlight, rose from the shelter of the whins and began to creep forward along a narrow goat track that descended the low, sandy cliff.

But despite their desperate caution it proved impossible for them to move without noise, for the dry, sandy soil broke under their feet, sending little showers of earth and pebbles rolling and clattering down to the beach. A child whimpered softly, and there was a sudden harsh tearing sound as a woman's skirt caught and ripped on a length of rusty sheep wire. And when at last they gained the shore their stumbling progress across the rattling banks of shingle was a torture to stretched nerves. But at least they had now reached the sea ...

Behind them the wolf packs of hate and destruction howled across Europe, while on either hand the smoke from the pyres of Rotterdam and Dunkirk blackened the sweet May skies; but ahead of them, beyond the narrow sea and the shifting fogbanks, lay the coast of England.

At the water's edge the shadowy bulk of a fishing boat loomed out of the surrounding fog, and despite the darkness it could be seen that the man who stood knee-deep in the creaming water, holding the prow to the shore, was tense and listening. His head was raised and he was not looking towards the stumbling line of refugees, but to the right, where the curve of the bay ran out in a huddle of weed-covered rocks.

He spoke in a harsh whisper and without turning his head: 'I am afraid. Be swift!' Then over his shoulder to a dim figure in the boat: 'Be ready with the sail, Pierre.'

A child began to cry in small gulping sobs: the sobbing of one who would normally have screamed its woe aloud, but who had been reduced by an adult experience of fear to the status of a terrified animal.

'Hush thou!' The whisper was savage with fear as the small figure was lifted over the gunwale. There followed three more children, the last of whom appeared to be clutching a large doll. The man who had been carrying her climbed in after her and turned to pull a shivering woman into the boat.

'Quick!' muttered the man in the water. 'Oh be quick!'

And then, with shocking suddenness, the darkness was ripped apart by a streak of flame, and the fogbanks and the low sandy cliffs that curved about the lonely bay echoed to the crash and whine of bullets, hoarse shouting voices and the clatter of running boots upon rock and shingle.

Without words the man who steadied the prow of the boat, and he who had led the refugees down the goat track, put their shoulders to the laden boat and thrust her off into deep water. The sail, invisible against the night and the drifting fog, rose and took the breeze and, slowly at first, the boat began to move away from the shelving beach. The two fishermen hauled themselves aboard and the remaining refugees, panic lending them strength, flung themselves screaming into the water, clawing at the receding prow, and were dragged on board.

A lone figure ran wildly across the shingle. It was the woman whose clothing had caught on the rusty tangle of sheep wire. She had paused in the darkness to free herself, appalled by the noise of the ripping material and the fear that she might dislodge stones and clods of earth if she dragged at the cloth, and so had arrived late upon the beach.

She rushed into the water, her feet stumbling among the treacherous pebbles as the waves snatched them from under her. But the boat had gone. The fog had closed behind it, and there was nothing to show that it had ever been there. She tried to scream: to shriek to them to come back for her, to save her and not leave her alone on that dark beach. But her throat was dry and her breath came in hoarse gasps.

The vicious chatter of a machine-gun added itself to the noise of running feet, and tracer bullets ripped brilliant orange streaks through the fog around her. Turning from the sea that had betrayed her, she ran back like a hunted animal towards the dark whin bushes, the low sandy cliffs and the hostile land ...

1

Miranda Brand knelt on the floor of a bedroom in the Families' Hostel at Bad Oeynhausen in the British zone of Germany, searching her suitcase for a cake of soap, and regretting that she had ever accepted her cousin Robert Melville's invitation to spend a month with him and his family in Berlin.

There was something about this gaunt building, about the dimly familiar, guttural voices and the wet, grey miles that had streamed past the train windows all that afternoon, that had acted unpleasantly upon her nerves. Yet it could not be Germany, and the fact that she was back there once more for the first time since childhood, that was responsible for this curious feeling of apprehension and unease that possessed her, because she had been aware of it before she had even set foot in the country.

It had begun ... When had it begun? Was it on the boat to the Hook of Holland? ... Or even earlier, on the boat-train to Harwich? She could not be sure. She only knew that for some inexplicable reason she felt tense and uneasy, and ... And afraid!

Yes, that was it: *afraid.* 'Well then what are you afraid of?' Miranda demanded of herself. '*Nothing!* But you can't be afraid of nothing!'

I'm getting as bad as Aunt Hetty, thought Miranda ruefully, and was smiling at the recollection of that neurotic and highly strung spinster when the door burst open and Stella Melville rushed in and slammed it noisily behind her, causing Miranda to start violently and drop the lid of the suitcase on the fingers of one hand.

'*Ow!* What on earth is the matter, Stel'? I wish you wouldn't make me jump like that. It puts years on my life.' Miranda blew on her injured fingers and regarded her cousin's wife with affectionate indignation.

Mrs Melville drew a quivering breath and her hands clenched into fists: 'I *hate* the Army! *I hate it!* Oh, why did Robert have to be a soldier? Why couldn't he have been a farmer, or a pig-breeder, or a stockbroker or – or — oh, *anything* but a soldier?'

Stella flung herself face down upon the bed and burst into tears.

'Good heavens!' said Miranda blankly.

She stood up hurriedly and perching on the edge of the bed threw a comforting arm about Stella's shoulders: 'What's up, darling? — that tiresome Leslie woman been sharpening her claws on you again? Forget it! I expect all those seasick pills have upset her liver. Come on, sweetie, brace up!'

'Oh go away!' sobbed Stella furiously, attempting to burrow further into the unyielding hostel pillow: 'You don't understand. No one understands!'

'Well tell me about it then,' said Miranda reasonably. 'Come on, Stel', it can't be as bad as that. Tell your Aunt 'Randa!'

Stella gave a watery chuckle and sat up, pushing away a wet strand of blond hair with the back of her hand. 'Aunt 'Randa! I like that, when I'm old enough to be your mother.'

'Give yourself a chance, darling. I shall be twenty-one next month.' Miranda hunted through her coat pockets, and producing a passably clean handkerchief handed it over.

'*Twenty-one,*' said Stella desolately. 'Dear God! and I shall be forty!' She blew her nose and sat looking at Miranda; her pretty pink and white face blotched with tears, and the ruin of her carefully applied make-up suddenly revealing the truth of that last statement.

Miranda looked momentarily taken aback. 'Will you? Well I suppose if you'd been married at eighteen I could just—— Look, how did we come to be discussing our ages anyway? What has your age got to do with hating the Army?'

'Perhaps more than you think,' said Stella bitterly. She saw that

Miranda was looking bewildered, and laughed a little shakily. 'Oh, it isn't that! It's — well Robert has just met a man he knows, and — and oh 'Randa isn't it awful? He told Robert that the regiment is going to be sent to Malaya next year!' Stella's blue eyes brimmed over with tears that coursed slowly down her wet cheeks and dripped off her chin, making ugly dark spots on her smart grey dress.

'Malaya? But good heavens, Stella, why on earth should that upset you? If I were in your shoes I'd be thrilled to bits! Sunshine, palm trees, temple bells — not to mention masses of servants in lovely eastern clothes to do all the dirty work for you. Just think of it! No more washing up dishes or fuel economy: *heaven!* What are you worrying about? You don't have to worry about Robert, because he told me once that Malaya was a "Company Commander's war" — whatever that means. And anyway the papers all seem to think that this Templer man has got the bandits buttoned.'

'You don't understand,' repeated Stella impatiently. 'I know *you* think it would be lovely to go there, but I'm not you. People like you think of the East as exotic and exciting, but to me it's only uncivilized and frightening. Perhaps that's because I'm not an exotic or exciting person. I don't like strange places. I love my own bit of England and I don't want to live anywhere else.'

'But you can have it both ways,' urged Miranda. 'You can live in England and in between you can go off and see romantic foreign places.'

'It isn't like that,' said Stella drearily. 'When I married Johnnie — you never knew Johnnie, did you — I thought what fun it would be. Being married, I mean. I thought we'd live at Mallow, or somewhere near it in Sussex or Kent, and that everything would be lovely. I actually thought that I should "live happily ever after" just like they do in fairy stories!'

She gave a short laugh, startling in its bitterness, and getting up from the bed walked over to the window and stood with her forehead pressed against a pane, looking down at the narrow, darkening street and speaking in an undertone, almost as if she had forgotten Miranda's presence and was talking to herself.

'It didn't work out that way. Perhaps it never does. We had to go to India. He ... *I hated it!* The dirt, the dust, the flies, the dark, secret faces. The horrible heat and that awful club life. And I was ill; always ill.' She shivered so violently that her teeth chattered.

'It was heaven to come home again. To see green fields and cool grey skies—— Oh, the awfulness of that brassy sunlight! But then the war came and he had to go back there without me. And I never saw him again. When he — when the telegram came I thought I should never be happy again. But you can't go on being unhappy for ever. That's the merciful thing about it. And after the war I met Robert.'

Her voice rose again suddenly, and she turned to face Miranda, her pretty mouth working and her slim fingers clenching and unclenching against the suave lines of the grey travelling dress.

'But it was only the same thing all over again. They sent him to Egypt, and they wouldn't let me go with him. They said I hadn't enough "points". *Points!* As if love and marriage were things on a ration card! Later the families were all sent away anyway, but that didn't make it any better for me. And when he did get back, the regiment was in Germany so we get sent to Berlin! This, believe it or not, is a "Home posting". *Home!* And now to be told that it will be Malaya next. I can't *bear* it!'

Stella turned away to stare desperately down into the street once more.

'Stella, darling,' Miranda spoke soothingly as though addressing a fractious child, 'you're feeling tired and nervy, and I don't blame you. It's all this wretched packing and moving. But it isn't as bad as all that, you know. There won't be flies and heat and oriental faces in Berlin, and Robert says your house is one of the nicest ones. And you are sure to be allowed to go to Malaya with him.'

'You don't understand,' repeated Stella tonelessly. 'No one really understands. I don't want to live in Germany. I've dreaded the idea. When I was six I had a German governess and I loathed her. And mother insisted on sending me to a finishing school in Brussels, and I hated that too: every minute of it. I don't want to go to Malaya. I'm like that girl in one of Nancy Mitford's books who hated "abroad". *I* hate "abroad" too. I want to live in England. In my own home, with my own things around me. Not this awful endless packing and moving and separation, and living in soulless army-furnished quarters.'

'In that case,' said Miranda briskly, 'I can't see why you don't stay at home.'

'And be separated from Robert? I couldn't bear it! That's the awful part of it. I swore I'd never marry another soldier. But I couldn't help it. You don't mean to fall in love with people. You just do, and then it's too late and you find yourself being pulled in two between loving someone and hating the untidy, nomadic life you will have to live if you want to be with them. Oh well——! I suppose I shall just go on living the sort of life I don't like, in places I loathe, until I'm an old hag and Robert retires with a tummy and a pension! Never marry a soldier, Miranda.'

'Moral, never marry anyone,' said Miranda, hugging her. 'It sounds much safer and far more comfortable to remain a resolute spinster — like me!'

Stella gave a dreary little laugh and turned away from the window: 'What a mess I must look! I'm sorry, 'Randa. I've been behaving like a hysterical lunatic. I suppose it's seeing it all start again; and being older this time, and — oh forget it darling! I'm tired and I feel as if we'd been travelling for weeks instead of less than two days.' She turned on both washbasin taps and peered disconsolately at herself in the inadequate square of looking-glass above them. 'Do you suppose if I slosh my face with cold water it will do any good? I can't go down to the dining-room looking like this.'

'Would you like to have your supper sent up here?' suggested Miranda.

'No. I must go down. Robert has asked that Control

Commission man to have dinner with us. You know — the elderly man we met on the train. Brigadier something or other.'

'Brindley,' supplied Miranda.

'That's it. I don't think the poor man realized that he'd have to eat his meal with Lottie and Mademoiselle as well, or he'd probably have refused. He doesn't look the type who likes children. Those gossipy old bachelors seldom do. What time is this train supposed to leave for Berlin?'

'Well there's an extremely military notice downstairs which says it "departs 22.55 hrs", but I haven't taken time off to work that one out yet. You'd think they'd run a through-train from the Hook, wouldn't you? — instead of throwing us all off and dumping us in a hostel for hours on end.'

'Russians,' said Stella splashing her face with cold water.

'What do you mean, "Russians"?'

'Apparently they won't let us run trains through their zone except by night. I suppose they're afraid we'd hang out of the carriage windows clicking our Kodaks. Do I look any better?'

'You look marvellous,' said Miranda lightly, and turned quickly away, thinking, with a sudden sense of shock, that Stella looked more than middle-aged; she looked old.

Stella Carrell, who had then been Stella Radley and was now Stella Melville, had been a grown woman of twenty-seven when Miranda, a leggy and frightened six-year-old, had first seen her. Then, and for many years afterwards, she had seemed old to Miranda. It was only during the last two or three years that Miranda had begun to think of Stella as an attractive woman in her thirties, and to admire her looks and copy her taste in clothes and hats. Stella had seemed to grow younger as Miranda grew older, for there was a curious touch of immaturity about her character and outlook that somehow made Miranda feel protective and as though she were the elder of the two. Yet now, in the space of a few minutes, although the spoilt child had been apparent in her recent outburst, she had suddenly seemed to age ten years in appearance.

Looking back, Miranda could not remember ever having seen Stella look anything but immaculately neat and beautifully dressed. There was a term for Stella that the glossier women's magazines were inordinately fond of, although Miranda had always considered it more suitable for horses: Stella was 'well-groomed'. Now, however, her blond hair hung about her face in damp disorder and Miranda noticed for the first time that its yellow fairness was touched with silver and that without benefit of powder and rouge her skin appeared faded and almost sallow, with a network of fine lines and spreading crowsfeet marking it about the eyes and mouth.

Miranda was suddenly reminded of the roses in the garden at Mallow: one day so beautiful in their velvety perfection, and the next, overblown and fading. Stella was like the roses, she thought; and like them, she would fade quickly. Her looks were not of the kind that will outlast youth, and soon there would be nothing left of that bright prettiness, and little to show that it had ever existed.

Seized by a disturbing thought Miranda turned quickly to stare at her own face in the looking-glass. It gazed reassuringly back at her with eyes the colour of a winter sky: wide of cheekbone, pointed of chin, framed in curling dark hair and set on a long slender throat the colour of warm ivory. A face startlingly like Thompson's portrait of Charlotte Brontë, that in Charlotte's day had been dismissed as 'plain' but which, allied to a slimmer-than-slim figure, had earned Miranda Brand a very comfortable income during the past two years as a fashion model.

I shall wear well, decided Miranda dispassionately. When I am seventy, people will say: 'Who is that distinguished-looking old lady?'

She laughed suddenly: being young enough to enjoy picturing herself in old age without believing in its possibility.

'What are you giggling about?' demanded Stella, completing her make-up with an expert hand before the mirror above the wash-

21

basin. She looked, once more, serene and poised, and as completely out of place in the dull setting of the hostel bedroom as an expensive orchid worn on the ample bosom of an elderly German *hausfrau*.

'Nothing,' said Miranda hastily. 'If you're ready let's go down and see if this caravanserai can produce some drinkable sherry.'

2

The dining-room of the Families' Hostel was large, long and high-ceilinged, and smelt strongly of past meals, floor polish and over-heated radiators. Miranda, seated at one of the larger tables between her cousin Robert Melville and a retired brigadier in the Control Commission, looked about it with interest.

The room was overfull of empty tables, but either the travellers who had been on the boat-train tended to huddle together, or else the German waiters, anxious to economize in time and labour, had shepherded them to conveniently adjacent ones.

The Melvilles' table was between one occupied by a Colonel and Mrs Leslie, and another shared by two of Robert's brother officers and their wives — Major and Mrs Marson and Lieutenant and Mrs Page.

Beyond the Leslies sat Mrs Wilkin and her five children. Mrs Wilkin, a small and sparrow-like woman on her way out to join her husband, a sergeant whose unit was stationed in Berlin, looked anxious and exhausted: and with good reason, since her offspring, who had been noisy and unmanageable for the past twenty-four hours, were now completely out of hand. The eldest Wilkin, addressed by his mother as 'Wally', was throwing bread. A demon-child, thought Miranda with a grin. Wally, intercepting the grin, paused in his bread-throwing and returned it. It split his plain, freckled face in an engaging though gap-toothed manner, and temporarily dispelled his striking resemblance to the Don Camillo imp. Conscious of an audience he threw an even larger piece of bread, and Miranda's gaze moved hurriedly on.

None of the other tables was occupied, and noting the fact, she felt childishly disappointed. And unreasonably annoyed with herself for feeling so. She had hoped to see someone else in that dining-room. Someone she had seen for the first time only the day before. But he was not there.

Miranda turned her attention to the soup, but as the meal progressed she became aware once more of that odd, indefinable prickling of apprehension. She wondered if perhaps she, like Stella, was overtired? Perhaps everyone in that echoing, ugly room with its depressing sea of empty tables was equally tired, and it was the accumulative effect of their weariness and taut nerves that created this inexplicable feeling of unease? Could tiredness, too, be the explanation of Mrs Leslie's odd behaviour? Miranda crumbled her bread and looked thoughtfully at the occupants of the table on her immediate left.

Colonel Leslie commanded one of the British regiments on duty in Berlin, and he and his wife Norah were returning there from three weeks' leave in England. Norah Leslie might well have stood for a model of the 'Army wife', for she was typed just as surely as though she had a placard about her neck proclaiming her status and occupation. One knew instinctively that she referred to her husband's regiment as 'My regiment', to the regimental wives as 'My wives', did her duty as to Welfare, and all that concerned the good of the battalion, played an excellent game of bridge, an adequate game of tennis and golf, read all the bestsellers, and was sincerely convinced that there was only one regiment in the British Army that counted.

The Melvilles' party had shared a carriage with the Leslies from London to Harwich, and it appeared that Norah Leslie had been a near neighbour of Robert's during their childhood and adolescence. But although Colonel Leslie had made polite conversation, Mrs Leslie had been curt to the point of rudeness. When, at Harwich, they had found the Harwich-to-Hook boat to be crowded and Stella, Miranda, Mademoiselle and seven-year-old Charlotte had been directed to a six-berth cabin, the other two occupants of which were Mrs Leslie and Elsa Marson, wife of

24

Major Harry Marson of Robert's regiment, Mrs Leslie had complained to the stewardess. She insisted that there had been a mistake, since her husband had expressly asked that a two-berth cabin should be reserved for them. The stewardess had been patient but unhelpful. She said that the boat was very full, and intimated that Mrs Leslie would have to make the best of it. Mrs Leslie had announced her intention of complaining to the authorities, taken several pills as a precautionary measure against sea-sickness, and retired to her bunk.

She was gracious to Miranda next morning as they waited in the Customs shed at the Hook, and inquired as to her reasons for coming to Germany. 'Oh, you're only coming for a holiday? A month? But what a very *odd* place to choose for a holiday! Now before the war——! But frankly, there's nothing worth looking at nowadays. Unless you are interested in mangled ruins, and even then, once you've seen the wreck of the Reichstag and a mass of rubble where the Chancellery and Hitler's bunker used to be, you've seen everything. Are the Melvilles relations of yours, or just friends? ... You are Robert's cousin? I used to know Robert very well. His family lived almost next door to us for a great many years. I hadn't met his wife before. I didn't realize——' But at that point Robert and Stella had joined them, and Mrs Leslie had turned abruptly on her heel and walked away.

Robert had looked slightly surprised, and Stella hurt; she was unused to rudeness, and for a moment her blue eyes had widened and her mouth turned down at the corners like a snubbed child's. Miranda had felt both angry and curious: angry on her cousin's behalf, and curious to know what was behind Mrs Leslie's odd behaviour. Whatever the reason, it was patently clear that neither Robert nor Stella was aware of it.

Yes, mused Miranda, observing Mrs Leslie with a desultory interest from her place at the table in the Families' Hostel: there *is* something there. I wonder what? Norah Leslie was looking at her husband, but Miranda was sure in her own mind that her attention was not concentrated upon what he was saying, but on

25

the conversation at the Melvilles' table, and she was trying to decide why she should be so sure of this, when Mrs Leslie turned her head. It was not possible to tell whether she looked at Robert's squarely turned back, or his wife's face as she sat opposite him listening to Brigadier Brindley's views on growing sweetpeas. But the look itself did not require any interpretation. It is never possible to mistake naked hate.

Miranda turned away quickly; uncomfortable and more than a little startled. But no one else seemed to have noticed that smouldering stare. Brigadier Brindley had abandoned sweetpeas in favour of the ballet, and Robert and the elderly Swiss governess, Mademoiselle Marie Beljame, were occupied with Charlotte — Robert in answering his daughter's questions and Mademoiselle Beljame in fussily supervising her table-manners.

Charlotte, renamed 'Lottie-the-Devil-Cat' by Miranda, was a remarkably plain child who appeared to have inherited nothing of Robert's charm and outstanding good looks. Her mother, Robert's first wife, had been a beauty; but she had died giving birth to this plain little girl, and a year later Robert had married Stella Radley. Robert was younger than Stella by several years, though until now Miranda had never found it noticeable. But tonight, sitting in that unkindly lighted dining-room, it was suddenly apparent. Perhaps Stella's recent tears had something to do with it; or perhaps it was the contrast between Stella's carefully made-up face and the fresh, glowing prettiness of the girl who sat so near to her at the next table . . .

Sally Page had married a junior officer in Robert's regiment when she was barely eighteen, and despite four years of matrimony she still looked and behaved like a charming and giddy teenager. Andy and she had been stationed in Fayid during the two and a half years that Robert had been in the Suez Canal Zone, and now they too were rejoining the regiment.

If Stella looked like a florist's rose, thought Miranda, Sally Page looked like a wild rose: sweet and fresh, heartbreakingly young and essentially English. And from behind Stella's shoulder she was

26

smiling now at Stella's husband. It was a revealing smile, as revealing as Mrs Leslie's look had been; and Miranda, observing it, was aware of a swift little jab of anxiety. No; perhaps it had not been such a good idea after all, this holiday in Berlin ...

'Number twenty-eight, did you say?' said Brigadier Brindley. 'Why, of course I know the house. And I can assure you that you will find it most comfortable. Quite one of the pleasantest houses in Charlottenburg. You have been fortunate.'

'That's what Robert says,' said Stella. 'But you know what army husbands are like. They tend to overdo the selling angle just to cheer you up.'

'Well, in this instance he is perfectly correct. A charming house, and quite undamaged. Interesting too: though only by association.'

'How do you mean?' Robert leant forward and joined in the conversation: 'Did it belong to some spectacular Nazi?'

'No, but it belonged to the mother of Herr Ridder — Willi Ridder. And I suppose one could almost call him a spectacular character. Or if not spectacular, at least mysterious and intriguing.'

'Do tell us,' begged Stella. 'I adore being mystified and intrigued.'

The Brigadier had a reputation as a raconteur, and was not at all averse to holding forth to an interested audience. He cleared his throat and took a small sip of wine.

'Willi Ridder,' began Brigadier Brindley, 'was a prominent member of the Nazi Secret Service. He was not one of those who took the spotlight at the front of the stage, but rather one of the puppet-masters who stayed in the background and pulled the strings. As far as outward appearances were concerned, he was merely a wealthy Berliner in high favour with the Nazi hierarchy.'

'And he lived in our house? It sounds as if it ought to be very Park Laneish,' said Stella.

'No, it was only his mother who lived in your house. He and his wife lived in another house not so very far from yours, which is a ruin now: it stopped a stray bomb fairly early in the war, I believe. In spite of his wealth he lived comparatively simply. No large staff, just a married couple who lived in; one of them the cook-housekeeper and the other a sort of valet-cum-major-domo. There were the usual "dailies", I suppose, and reliable extra help who were called in only when required, for special occasions.'

The Brigadier paused as though he had made a point, and took another sip of Niersteiner, and Robert said; 'I don't suppose big shots in any Secret Service like having a lot of hangers-on around the house. Two dyed-in-the-wool trusties are probably preferable to a platoon of doubtfuls, even if it does mean that the soup is sometimes lukewarm and there is the odd spot of dust on the drawing-room chimneypiece.'

'Quite,' agreed the Brigadier. 'But in the light of after-events I am inclined to put a less obvious and more sinister interpretation upon it. In my opinion it was part of a plan.'

'What plan?' said Stella. 'How exciting you make it sound! Did you know this man Ridder?'

'I did,' said the Brigadier impressively. 'I met Herr Ridder in 1937 when he was over in England visiting the Gore-Houstons. Lady Gore-Houston was a cousin of mine, and she was, unfortunately — like some others I could name — inclined to be somewhat pro-facist in those days. In the following year I happened to be in Berlin for a short spell, and Herr Ridder invited me to stay with him. I spent only one night in his house, but my memory of that visit is most distinct — probably because I have thought of it so often since then ...

'In the ordinary course of events I do not suppose I should have had occasion to recall it, and so the details would, in time, inevitably have become blurred in my mind. But owing to what happened afterwards I have frequently thought back over that brief visit with great interest.'

'What *did* happen?' begged Miranda, still young enough to wish to leap to the point of a story, and impatient of frills.

'All in good time, my dear,' said Brigadier Brindley, who disliked being hurried towards his dénouement and preferred to extract the full flavour of suspense from his story. He refreshed himself with another sip of wine before continuing.

'Perhaps you will remember — those of us who are not too young,' (here he made a courtly little bow in the direction of Miranda) 'that in the late spring of 1940 Germany made a savage and unprovoked attack upon Holland. Well, at that time there happened to be, in Rotterdam, a fortune in cut diamonds ready for transhipment to Britain and the United States. The Nazis were aware of this and their capture was an important part of the surprise attack. They knew exactly where they were, and they dropped special paratroops to surround the house. Only one of the men who was concerned in that operation knew what they were after, and that man was Herr Ridder, who was entrusted with the task of taking over the diamonds and bringing them back to Berlin. The plan worked admirably, and Ridder took possession of several million pounds worth of diamonds.'

Brigadier Brindley, well aware that conversation at the two neighbouring tables had ceased and their occupants were openly listening, paused to help himself with some deliberation to stewed fruit and custard.

'Oh, do go on,' urged Stella. 'What happened then? That isn't all, is it?'

'By no means!' said the Brigadier, accepting the sugar bowl handed to him by an interested German waiter: 'No, that is not all. *Danke.*'

A well-aimed bit of bread landed with a thump on the table, narrowly missing Brigadier Brindley's glass, and the Brigadier closed his eyes briefly and shuddered.

'May I eat my pudding at Wally's table?' asked Charlotte.

'Mais non!' said Mademoiselle firmly.

'Then I shan't eat my pudding,' said Charlotte, equally firmly: 'Why can't I? Wally's mother wouldn't mind. Daddy, can I eat my pudding at Wally's table?'

'You heard what Mademoiselle said, Lottie.'

'But she doesn't like Wally. She says he's a nasty, rude, rough boy. But I like him. Why can't I go? *I* shan't let him throw bread.'

'Oh, let her go,' said Stella impatiently, 'and then perhaps that child will stop heaving crusts. Don't let's have a scene. All right, darling, you can go and ask Mrs Wilkin if she'd mind your sitting at her table. But do behave nicely. No, there's no need for you to go too, Mademoiselle.' She turned back to Brigadier Brindley: 'Do go on. You were telling us about how Herr Ridder got the diamonds.'

'Ah, yes. The diamonds. Well, of course we knew — that is, our Intelligence Service knew — that the diamonds had fallen into German hands. And from our point of view that, so to speak, was that. We did not learn the end of the story — if indeed it can be said to have ended, which I doubt — until the war was over. It was only then, through the medium of captured documents and a certain amount of interested evidence, that we learned the rest of the story.'

The Brigadier paused and looked impressively about his audience, which now included all the occupants of the two adjacent tables.

'Willi Ridder, supposedly carrying the diamonds, returned to Berlin. He was flown in by night, and landed at Tempelhof airfield. His arrival was, purposely, as unobtrusive as possible. There he was met by his personal car and driven to his house. And neither he nor his wife was ever seen again.'

'You mean they were — liquidated, or purged, or whatever they called it?' asked Miranda. 'Because they knew about the diamonds?'

'No, they simply disappeared.'

'But what about the diamonds?'

'Those disappeared too.'

'You mean they skipped with the lot?' asked Robert.

The Brigadier gave him a reproving look, cleared his throat

again, and said: 'Possibly no one will ever know whether Herr Ridder and his wife had planned it carefully beforehand, or whether the fact that he suddenly found himself in possession of this fantastic fortune proved too much for him. But after reading some of the files on the case I am inclined to think that it was all planned. Ridder knew that Holland was to be attacked, and that he was to be sent in person to take over the diamonds. Then, you see, there was the new garage that was in the process of being built at the end of his garden ...'

The Brigadier paused expectantly, and Miranda did not disappoint him: 'What on earth had a new garage got to do with it?' she demanded, puzzled.

'Ah, what indeed! It was to be built of stone and brick, and large enough to take two cars. Stone needs mortar, and mortar needs quicklime. There was a pit of quicklime behind the garage so that the mortar could be mixed on the spot, and the building had been completed all except the roof. When Herr Ridder failed to report next day, a search was made of the house. There was no one in it, and no diamonds either. Later, the wreckage of the car and the body of the chauffeur were found in a town near the Dutch border. And later still the bodies of the cook and the valet were found buried in quicklime at the back of the unfinished garage in the Ridders' garden.'

There was silence for a moment, and Stella shuddered audibly.

'Did no one ever find out what had happened to the Ridders?' asked Robert.

'No. They could only guess. Their guess — and mine — is that Ridder and his wife murdered their two servants and used their passports and papers to conceal their own identity. The names of Herr and Frau Schumacher would have meant little to anyone; but far too many people in the S.S. knew Herr and Frau Ridder. The driver of the car was a picked S.S. man, but he would have thought nothing of being told to drive his employer and wife to some place outside Berlin. He would not have known about the diamonds — only a very few people knew. He obeyed Herr Ridder's orders, while at the same time sending a detailed report of all Herr Ridder's movements to his chief in the S.S. The Ridders presumably shot him on a lonely stretch of road, and drove as far as they dared towards the Dutch frontier, leaving the car and the corpse in a town that was being bombed at the time. After that they ceased to be Herr and Frau Ridder and became Karl and Greta Schumacher, refugees.'

'But what do you suppose they meant to do?' demanded Robert. 'Where are they supposed to have gone? They couldn't have expected to get away. Why, I mean to say, the place must have been *crawling* with panzer divisions and all the rest of it at that time.'

'The supposition is that the diamonds never left Holland. That Herr Ridder managed to conceal them in some safe hiding-place and returned with an empty bag to Berlin. His intention being to go back and collect them, after which he and his wife would escape in the guise of refugees to England or Spain; and from there to America, which was not at that time in the war. With a fortune of such magnitude in their hands it must have seemed worth taking very great risks. And in the chaos of those days there were many people who escaped out of Europe. All the same, it should have been a fairly simple matter to trace them; and it is certain that the S.S. had no doubts as to their ability to do so.'

'And yet they got away.'

'They got away. And from that day to this they have never been heard of again; although ever since the war ended not only the German police but the police and Intelligence Services of four continents have been looking for them. They had a young child — a daughter I believe — who vanished too; though there was a story that the Ridders had sent her to relatives in Cologne some months before, and that she and her aunt had subsequently been killed with a great many other people when an air-raid shelter they were in received a direct hit. That may well have been true. Herr Ridder's mother was taken to a concentration camp and died there, but Willi and his wife and the diamonds apparently vanished into thin air.'

'Has nobody ever found a clue? Or heard even a rumour?' asked Stella.

'Yes, there was a clue. And though nothing ever came of it, I myself have always thought it provides the most intriguing part of the story. The unexpected and fantastic twist!' The Brigadier's voice was all at once less pedantic and almost eager, and it was obvious that the tale held a peculiar and recurrent fascination for him.

'In May 1940 a little band of refugees were landed in England from a small fishing boat. Among them was a child.'

'You mean you think it may have been the Ridders' child?'

'Oh no. This was an English child. Her parents had been in Belgium when the German attack came, and they had both been killed. None of the other refugees appeared to know anything about her and they had all imagined her to be French, for until an Englishwoman at the Centre spoke to her in English, and she replied in that language, she had only spoken French. She was sent with a batch of sick refugees — England was full of refugees in those days — to some hospital or home in Sussex, until she could be identified. She was carrying a large doll from which she refused to be parted.'

The silence about the table changed in an instant, and became curiously intent and charged with something far more than interest in an unusual story. But if the Brigadier noticed it he evidently put it down to his powers of narration.

'Some time later she broke the doll, and a kindly doctor offered to see if he could mend it for her. It was then discovered that the hollow body of the doll was stuffed with jewels and over five thousand pounds in high-denomination British and American banknotes. The child had no idea how they came to be there and could offer no explanation for their presence. She insisted that the doll had been given her for Christmas, and that nobody had touched it but herself. The jewels were later identified as being the property of Frau Ilse Ridder.'

There was a long, long silence.

Brigadier Brindley beamed complacently upon his audience, pleased at the sensation his dénouement had created. Robert was looking thunderstruck, Miranda's face had paled and she and Stella were staring at him literally open-mouthed.

'*Well, I'm damned!*' said Robert with explosive violence.

Stella's face flushed a vivid pink and she stuttered a little when she spoke.

'B–But – but — Oh, it can't be true! This is the most incredible thing I ever heard!'

'My dear lady,' said the Brigadier a little stiffly, 'I assure you . . .'

'Oh, of course he hasn't made it up!' interrupted Miranda, her face pale and her eyes enormous. 'It's just a staggering coincidence. It's fantastic!'

'I am afraid I do not quite understand,' began the Brigadier, patently bewildered.

'No, of course you don't!' said Stella. 'How could you? It's just that your story has knocked all the wind out of us. You see it really is the queerest possible coincidence. That hospital you mentioned — the one in Sussex — well, it wasn't a proper hospital. It was only being used as a sort of nursing home during the war. It was my house — Mallow — and I was nursing there. And Miranda was the little girl with the doll!'

'Well, I'm damned!' said Brigadier Brindley, echoing Robert's words with equal fervour. He pulled out a handkerchief, and mopping his forehead looked a little wildly round the table. 'You are not by any chance pulling my leg?' he inquired suspiciously.

'No, I promise you we're not! It's quite true. Isn't it, Robert? Ask Miranda! She must remember it.'

'Of course I do,' said Miranda unsteadily. 'I dropped Wilhelmina — that was the doll — on the paving stones of the terrace, and her head came off. It had always been a bit wobbly I think. I was bathed in tears and despair, and a nice young doctor said he would mend her for me. He started in to see how she worked and before we knew where we were the place was a mass of diamonds and emeralds and banknotes. No wonder she was so heavy!'

Miranda shivered and made a little grimace, as though the memory was an unpleasant one.

'*Amazing!*' The Brigadier's voice was almost devout as he realized that he now had a story with which he could hold the attention of fellow diners for years to come.

'Wasn't it? I hadn't an *idea* how they got there, and I still haven't. To tell you the truth, I don't really remember much about what happened between the time the bombing started and arriving at Mallow. I don't think I wanted to remember it. But I do remember that they confiscated all Wilhelmina's stuffing, and I howled the roof off. I didn't mind about the banknotes, but the jewels sparkled, and I naturally thought that as they had come out of my doll I should be allowed to keep them. In the end they gave me a cheesy little chain bracelet to keep me quiet. It wasn't even gold or silver. Just a lot of thin links in some white metal, with a little Egyptian charm, an ankh, dangling from it. I lost the bracelet years ago, but I still have the charm. And what's more, I'm wearing it now! How's that for proof?'

Miranda held out her left hand with a flourish. About her wrist she wore a gold charm bracelet jingling with an assortment of miniature nonsense in the form of lucky coins, signs of the Zodiac, replicas of windmills, sailing boats and ship's lanterns, and among them, slightly larger than the rest, was a small ankh — the ancient Egyptian life-sign that appears again and again on the walls of tombs and temples in the Land of the Pharaohs, and can best be described as a loop standing on a capital T. It was fastened to the bracelet by a link attached to the top of the loop, and was made of some steel-grey metal that had been engraved on the flat surface with Egyptian hieroglyphics, and on the edge by deep parallel lines.

'I've worn it for years,' said Miranda. 'Stella gave me this bracelet for my tenth birthday, and I've added something to it almost every year. The ankh was the first thing to go on it, because at the time it was the only charm I possessed.'

35

'Really? This is most interesting,' said Brigadier Brindley. 'Extraordinarily interesting. Incredible! Might I have a look at that trinket?'

'Of course. Wait a minute and I'll undo the catch. It's a bit stiff. I've often meant to jettison that charm because it doesn't really go with the others, but now I shall cherish it as my prize piece.'

She struggled with the stiff clasp of the bracelet and having managed to remove it, handed it across the table to the Brigadier, who examined the ankh with absorbed interest and seemed disappointed.

'I'm afraid it's not very exciting,' apologized Miranda. 'It hasn't even got a date or a name or initials or anything on it. I remember a lot of men came and peered at it once, and one of them said it was modern and the signs on it were only for decoration, because they didn't make sense, but that it was made from some alloy that might be worth looking into. He tried to bend it, I remember. But it wouldn't bend, and because I thought he'd break it, I began to howl dismally, and one of the other men said, "Oh, let the kid have it!" and gave it back to me.'

The bracelet was passed around the table. 'It is very interesting, is it not?' said Mademoiselle, peering at it doubtfully before returning it to its owner.

'It's like a sort of fairy story, isn't it?' said Miranda pocketing the bracelet in preference to wrestling further with the clasp. 'A rather creepy one by the Brothers Grimm. I never did like their stories, anyway.'

'It is certainly a very remarkable coincidence,' said Brigadier Brindley. 'A most romantic story.'

'It is even more romantic than you think!' said Miranda with a laugh. 'In fact if it hadn't been for me, we should none of us be sitting here now. You see, I stayed at Stella's house while the authorities were trying to trace my next-of-kin, who turned out to be mother's brother, General Melville. Uncle David rushed over to see me, but he was just off to the battle, and as Aunt Frances was dead and their son — that's Robert here — was fighting

36

somewhere in the Middle East, he was in a bit of a flap as to what to do about me, and he simply jumped at Stella's noble offer to keep me for the duration. I never saw him again, because he got killed about a year later, but when the war was over Robert turned up to collect the family burden, and stayed and married Stella instead. And Stella and Robert asked me if I'd like to spend a month with them in Berlin — and so here we all are!'

'And there you have the end of your story,' said Stella.

Brigadier Brindley turned and looked at her, smiling. 'The end of *your* story, my dear Mrs Melville. But not the end of the story I have just told you. It is only another small piece of that story.'

'I see what you mean, sir,' said Robert. 'Your story won't end until the Ridders are discovered.'

'Perhaps they will never be discovered,' said Brigadier Brindley. 'And if so, no one will ever know the end. Perhaps they are dead — blown up by some bomb among the ruins of some broken city. I think it is very likely.'

'Why, sir?'

'Because if they were not dead, one of them at least should have been easy to trace. Frau Ilse had a deformity that was not a common one. The second and third fingers of her left hand were joined together. She had never attempted to have them operated on and was, curiously enough, rather proud of the fact, for she wore a specially made ring on the double finger. It was this ring that was largely responsible for establishing the ownership of the jewels found in — er — Wilhelmina.'

'But surely she could have had an operation performed?' said Robert. 'That sort of thing is not so unusual, after all. I've known of a case myself, a child who ...'

'Ah, a child,' interrupted the Brigadier with a tolerant smile. 'If it is done in childhood it does not leave quite so noticeable a scar. But to perform such an operation on a grown woman would be a more difficult matter, since it would undoubtedly leave scars that would be impossible to disguise. And that is why I feel sure that Frau Ilse, at least, is dead. A physical defect or peculiarity is like an illuminated sign: it attracts attention. And not only that. Once seen it is not forgotten. It sticks in the memory of the observer when all else has faded to a blur. One seldom fails to notice, or remember, a freak of nature.'

Miranda saw Mademoiselle's spine stiffen and her sallow face flush a painful shade of puce. The governess was one of those distressing persons who appear to be perpetually taking offence, and on this occasion she had obviously taken the Brigadier's words as a personal affront, since she herself possessed a noticeable physical peculiarity in that her eyes were of different colour — the left being blue and the right a grey that verged on hazel. A deviation from the normal that afforded Lottie and her young friends endless amusement. Mademoiselle had suffered a good deal from their uninhibited questions and comments, and Miranda, suspecting as much, smiled consolingly at her across the table. But Mademoiselle refused to be comforted. Her mouth narrowed into an offended line and she returned Miranda's smile with a frosty stare, and turned to Stella.

'If you will excuse, Madame, I would go now to find me some hot milk for the thermos. The little Charlotte will sleep better in the train if she drink the cup of hot milk when she is ready for bed.' She rose from the table and rustled away, wounded feelings in every line of her back.

Miranda suppressed her smile and turned again to Brigadier Brindley: 'What was she like?'

'Frau Ridder? Not a very remarkable woman in any way. Youngish, dark hair and eyes. Medium height, medium size, passably good-looking, but dressed in excruciatingly bad taste. I remember thinking that she must be colourblind. She favoured very bright colours. That peculiar and cruel shade of blue satin that sets one's teeth on edge.'

'And what about him? Herr Willi?'

'The same. A rather average Teutonic type. Blond and ordinary, except for a pair of very pale blue eyes that somehow gave you the impression that they could bore holes through the side of a battleship. A deceptive sort of chap. The kind who would always choose to be the power behind the throne rather than the man who sits on it.'

Stella said: 'Well, I've never been so thrilled in my life! I shall be able to dine out on this for the rest of my days. Robert, tell the waiter we'll have our coffee in the hall, will you, darling? Coming, Miranda?'

3

The train rocked and swayed to the clattering rhythm of the iron wheels, but Stella did not hear them for she was already asleep. She had borrowed two capsules of sleeping powders from Brigadier Brindley, who apparently never travelled without them, and these, combined with fatigue and the emotions of the earlier evening, had sent her into deep and dreamless sleep barely a minute or so after her head had touched the pillow. She had taken the upper berth, and the dim glow of the small reading-light at the head of Robert's berth below faintly illuminated her face and the blond waves of hair that were as neatly pinned for the night as though she had been in her own bedroom at Mallow.

Robert stood looking at her for a moment, swaying to the swing of the train. In that dim light she appeared strangely young and exhausted. Poor Stel', thought Robert, how she does hate it! But there was nothing he could do about it. He could not, as Stella wished, leave the Army. It was the only profession he knew and he had few illusions as to his abilities. If I'm lucky, thought Robert dispassionately, I may be able to retire as substantive lieutenant-colonel — but only if I'm lucky. That's about as far as I shall get. But if I chucked the Army now and tried for a civil job, I should probably end up as an office boy or a tout for vacuum cleaners. Stella doesn't understand. I'd retire tomorrow and try and farm the place myself, if we had the money. But we haven't, and that's all there is to it. It's a pity she hates this sort of life; it's not a bad one really, but I suppose you have to have some sort of vocation or a military background to enable you to follow the drum and like it.

He yawned tiredly and sat down on the edge of his berth to remove his slippers. He had not realized that the Pages would be on the same train. A bit awkward, their being in Berlin. He would have to be careful. Sally was a sweet creature, but ... Robert wriggled in between the sheets and switched off the light——

Fancy meeting old Brindley again! He hadn't seen him for over eight years — or was it nine? Not since before his father had been killed on the Anzio beaches. Queer story that. It had given Miranda a bit of a jolt. A fortune in diamonds, lost and perhaps still unclaimed. He could do with a handful of diamonds himself ... and who couldn't?

In the compartment next door Mademoiselle Beljame lifted a woollen dressing-gown of Edwardian design from an aged Gladstone bag, moving quietly so as not to wake Lottie who lay in the shadows of the upper berth. A flannel nightdress followed, and a pair of hand-knitted slippers. Mademoiselle laid them out upon the berth and half filled the small washbasin with warm water. The water sloshed to and fro with the movement of the train and made a soft, slapping sound that provided a counterpoint to the squeaks and rattles of the train. Mademoiselle peered at her watch and then held it to her ear to make sure that it was still going; it was late then! She placed the watch carefully on a little shelf over the basin and, catching sight of herself in the mirror above it, leant forward and peered intently at her reflection. It was time she gave herself another application of the dye. She lifted a bony finger and touched the centre parting of her severely dressed hair. Tomorrow, or the next day, she must see to it.

Before the war, thought Mademoiselle, you were a young woman. Yet now you are an old one. Old and ugly.

She drew a long, quivering breath, and began to undress. It was well that she had been able to procure hot milk for the child. And what luck that the elderly Englishman should have offered her a sleeping powder, for to sleep well on trains was not always possible. But tonight, thanks to the Brigadier, a sound night's sleep could be guaranteed.

'Well here we are, almost back in Berlin!'

Harry Marson yawned and pulled the blankets up about his chin: 'I shall be quite glad to get back to some central heating again. That house of Uncle Ted's is hellishly draughty — though I must admit that his port more than makes up for it!'

Major Marson ruminated for a moment or two, but his wife remained silent, and presently he spoke again.

'What did you make of that old bird's story this evening? Queer, wasn't it? I remember hearing about that chap Ridder when I was staying with Uncle Bill in Berlin before the war. I may even have met him. Odd coincidence about the Melvilles' kid cousin, wasn't it? If you read that in a book you'd say "too far-fetched". Except that when one comes to think of it, the Brigadier has probably told that story to so many people that the odds against his eventually telling it to another army chap like Robert are not so high as you'd think.'

There was still no sound from the lower berth.

'A fortune in diamonds!' mused Harry Marson. 'No wonder the blighter decided to stick to them. Any man of sense would probably have felt like doing the same. I wish to God I could get my hands on a fortune! In fact just now I'd settle for a thousand quid, cash down. How the hell we're going to—— Are you asleep, Elsa?'

But Elsa Marson was not asleep. She lay quite still, staring into the darkness and wishing with all her heart that the train was taking her anywhere but to Berlin. If only she need not have come back! If only Harry had allowed her to stay behind in England. But he would not hear of it: 'Not go back to Berlin? Don't be silly, darling! No housework, no servant troubles, no rationing; lovely house and loving husband. What more could you want? Besides I can't do without you — and anyway I can't afford to keep you at home.'

So here she was, with the train rushing remorselessly through the night and every mile bringing her nearer and nearer to the ruined, fear-haunted, faction-torn capital of Germany.

Elsa Marson, whose soft speaking voice with its slight broken accent so plainly proclaimed her foreign birth, turned on her pillow and wept for the safety of humdrum English towns with as passionate a longing as Stella had wept for Mallow: though her reasons for doing so were not entirely similar.

Odd seeing George Brindley again after all these years, thought Colonel Leslie. Wonder if he recognized me? Probably not. It's been a longish time. Just the same talkative ass. Sleeping pills! It used to be quinine. Never knew such a man for dosing himself. I wonder ... He climbed cautiously up into the upper berth.

Norah Leslie removed her hat, and taking off her gloves, frowned at the sight of their blackened palms and fingers. Continental trains were so dirty, and British ones almost worse. Perhaps if she gave them a quick wash now they would be dry before morning? The carriage was very hot and she could hang them near the pipes. She removed her coat and skirt and pressed the taps of the small fitted basin, wondering if her sons, left behind in England, would be asleep. Yes of course they would be. Hours ago! It must be very late ...

Her thoughts veered off at a tangent: Robert — Robert and that woman! Why had it got to be Robert? Why didn't men see through women like that? Selfish, spoilt, grabbing, dog-in-the-manger women. The kind who would always try and eat their cake and have it, and who so often succeeded in doing both.

Mrs Leslie reached for the soap and began to wash her gloves, scrubbing savagely at the inoffensive fabric.

Sally and Andy Page were quarrelling. They quarrelled too often these days and about too many trivial things. They were young, and had yet to learn that the strength of the matrimonial tie is not best proved by subjecting it to constant strain.

'All right then! You don't care a damn about him, and he's just

43

a charming chap who dances like a dream! But is that any reason why you should look at him as though you were some frightful bobbysoxer goggling at the latest American crooner?'

'I did nothing of the sort!'

'Oh yes, you did! Everybody must have noticed it. It was quite blatant. You used to do it in Fayid, and now here you go again. One look at that glamorous profile, and you go weak at the knees.'

'The trouble with you,' said Sally furiously, 'is that you're small-minded and riddled with jealousy and inferiority complexes! Just because someone is better looking and better mannered and senior to you, you're jealous of him, and I'm not allowed to be even polite to him. If he were uglier and more junior, you wouldn't give a damn! I ought never to have married you. What do I get out of it? I pinch and scrape and save and wear old clothes and never have any fun, and when anyone under sixty speaks to me there's a vulgar, selfish, jealous scene!'

'Sally, you *know* that's not true!'

'It is! *It is!* You are jealous — and you're selfish too. You only think of yourself. You wouldn't let me have a fur coat, but you bought yourself that camera! You sit around and scowl and gloom, and when I talk to Bob Melville, who is amusing and interesting, you resent it and accuse me of behaving like a drooling bobbysoxer!'

'Sally, that isn't fair. You know it's not. You knew before you married me that we'd be very hard up. But you wanted us to get married at once . . .'

'That's right! Blame it on to me. And I suppose *you* didn't want to marry me at all?'

'Darling, *don't!* You know I did. Desperately badly. Only I knew what it would let you in for. I can't buy you fur coats: and as for the camera, you know quite well that I swopped it with John Ellery for two quid and that set of hunting prints you liked. We shan't always be as broke as this, darling. And you do have fun, whatever you say. We never seem to stop going to parties. Or giving them — in fact that's what keeps us permanently in the red!

44

That, and the fact that you spend a small fortune on Chanel scent and Lizzie Arden make-up, and always having your hair done by the most expensive hairdresser you can find, even though you know quite well that it's "coals to Newcastle" and that you'd look every bit as good if you used no make-up at all and just left your face and your hair alone. No wonder we're always——'

'Oh, never mind,' said Sally drearily. 'Don't let's talk about it any more. We shall only start talking about bills again, and I can't bear it. I wish I had those diamonds that Brigadier was talking about. Millions! — just think of it! It isn't fair. I wonder who's got them now?'

But Andy did not answer.

Amazing! thought Brigadier Brindley drowsily. Quite extraordinary! Chance in a thousand ... He was asleep.

4

... *clickety-clack, clickety-clack, clickety-clack*. The train rushed on through the night towards Berlin, and Miranda began to put words to the monotonous song of the wheels as an alternative to counting sheep. It was long past midnight, but she could not sleep.

'I want to go home ... I want to go home ... I want to go home.' That would be Stella. Poor Stella! It must be cruel to have to live a life you hated in order to be with the man you loved. Well you can't have it both ways, thought Miranda. But why not? Millions of people did. Stella was just unlucky.

'Shan't go to bed! Shan't go to bed! Shan't go to bed!' 'Lottie-the-Devil-Cat'.

'Cela suffit! Cela suffit! Cela suffit!' Mademoiselle. A repellent woman, thought Miranda. Bony, greying and bespectacled: apparently suffering from a perpetual cold and given to nibbling caraway seeds like some desiccated Victorian spinster. It was difficult to realize that anyone like Mademoiselle had ever been young and lighthearted, yet traces of feminine vanity evidently lingered even in Mademoiselle's flinty bosom, for despite the fact that her scanty hair was obviously grey she persisted in secretly doctoring it with the contents of a small sticky bottle of dye; although the resulting jetty blackness, especially after a fresh application, added to rather than detracted from her years. She had been in Lille when the German Army had swept through France, and had been unable to return to her native Switzerland. Later, under suspicion of being involved with the Underground Movement, she had been sent to a concentration camp in which she had spent the greater part of the war. Mademoiselle was

fond of enlarging on her sufferings during that time, but although one could not help feeling sorry for her, it was impossible to like her.

Miranda yawned, wriggled, jerked irritably at her blankets, and wished fervently that she had accepted Brigadier Brindley's offer of a sleeping pill. She had refused them, watching with inward scorn as the Brigadier swallowed two with his coffee, and thinking that he was just the sort of man whom one would expect to carry about little boxes and bottles of capsules. 'Never travel without 'em!' said the Brigadier: 'Can't sleep in a train. I found that out years ago, so when I can't avoid travelling by night I take a couple of these. Works like magic. Like to try one? No after-effects I assure you. Excellent stuff.'

Mademoiselle, who had an incurable passion for pills in any form, had accepted one, and Stella had taken two, saying that she would try anything if only it would give her a decent night's sleep after the torture of the Harwich crossing. She had broken the small capsules in half, and stirring the powdered contents into her coffee, drunk it there and then. Miranda envied them their forethought.

There were not many passengers travelling to Berlin that night, and the train being half empty, Miranda and Brigadier Brindley had each been allotted a two-berth compartment to themselves. The Brigadier was next door to Miranda, and, she thought crossly, undoubtedly sleeping like a log. Somewhere down the corridor 'Lottie-the-Devil-Cat', soothed by hot milk, would be asleep and probably snoring (Lottie suffered from adenoids), while Stella and Mademoiselle, thanks to the Brigadier's pills, would also be sleeping soundly. Only she, Miranda, was awake ...

The narrow compartment was close and stuffy and she wondered if she would do better on the upper berth, but a vague recollection that hot air rises caused her to abandon the idea. She threw off her blankets instead, and after a few moments discovered that it was, after all, colder than she had thought, and pulled them back again. She shut her eyes and tried to will herself to go to sleep, but it was no use, and she opened them again and lay staring into the darkness.

A latch clicked somewhere near at hand and a faint thread of light showed under the locked door that lay between the two compartments. So much for the efficacy of the Brigadier's sleeping pills! thought Miranda.

The light vanished, and Miranda yawned and presently decided that she was thirsty. She would have a drink of water and read a book.

Almost on the heels of the thought she remembered that she had not got a book: she had lent it to Stella, and Sally Page had borrowed her only magazine during the afternoon and had failed to return it. Worse still, she had no drinking water, having upset the carafe while cleaning her teeth.

'Damn!' said Miranda, speaking aloud into the darkness.

She thought she heard someone pass down the corridor, and on a sudden impulse wriggled down to the other end of her berth, and groping for the handle of the door, turned it and pulled the door open. If the elderly and kindly faced sleeping-car attendant was patrolling the corridor to see if all was well with the passengers, he could probably get her a glass of water — or better still, a hot drink.

Miranda thrust her feet into her bedroom slippers and reached for her dressing-gown and having tied the sash round her slim waist, stepped out into the corridor and closed the door behind her. The attendant — if it had been him — had vanished, and the corridor stretched emptily away on either hand, bounded on the one side by a long line of closed doors and on the other by a blank wall of black window-blinds.

It was colder out here than it had been in her compartment. The train rocked and jiggled to the click and clatter of the flying wheels, but the corridor seemed uncannily silent, and for a fleeting moment Miranda had the disturbing fancy that behind every closed door there was someone who stood quite still, holding their breath to listen.

She shivered suddenly, and pulling the warm velvet folds of her dressing-gown closer about her throat, marched briskly off in search of the attendant.

The *Dienstraum*, the small cabin occupied by the sleeping-car attendant, was empty, and the lavatory beyond it boasted no drinking water. Miranda gave it up and decided to return to her own compartment: there was sure to be a bell there and it was stupid of her not to have thought of that before. Nevertheless she lingered by the open door of the attendant's brightly lit room, half hoping that he might return, and seized by an inexplicable reluctance to return down that long, cold, empty stretch of corridor.

What *is* the matter with me tonight? thought Miranda impatiently. Why do I keep imagining things? She would never have suspected herself of being a person subject to nerves or delusions, or even especially receptive to atmosphere; but even here, in a deserted corridor of the Berlin train, with a dozen people sleeping peacefully near at hand and twenty or thirty British troops not two coaches distant, she was conscious of a queer tremor of uneasiness: a prickling of the scalp as though unseen eyes were watching her, and a nervous desire to look over her shoulder.

Succumbing to that impulse, Miranda glanced quickly over her shoulder and started violently. But it was only the reflection of her own face in a looking-glass in the attendant's compartment that had startled her, and not someone standing behind her. Feeling exceedingly foolish and more than a little cross, and with her heart still beating uncomfortably fast, Miranda turned and walked rapidly back along the corridor.

The door of her compartment was ajar, and she pushed it quickly open and went in. It seemed very dark in there after the comparative brightness outside, and she groped for the electric light switch, but could not find it. Well, it did not matter, for she had lost all desire for a drink and could get back to bed quite easily in the dark.

The train rocked round a curve and Miranda's foot slipped

suddenly, and she stumbled and flung out a hand to feel for the edge of her berth.

But the berth appeared to be further from the door than she had imagined, and moving forward, she hit herself sharply against something hard and unyielding. Catching at the edge of it she discovered with surprise that it was one of the fitted basins with which each of the compartments was provided. But surely the basin had been on the opposite side of the carriage? Miranda took another cautious step and found herself touching a smooth wooden surface. Her berth seemed to have vanished.

And then suddenly she realized what had happened. She was in the wrong compartment!

The sleeping compartments on the Berlin train were in pairs, with a communicating door between each pair which could be opened if parents and children were travelling in adjoining compartments. The positions of berths and basins and light switches were reversed in each compartment, and Miranda, suppressing a strong desire to giggle, realized that she had invaded the bachelor sanctum of Brigadier Brindley.

Thank heaven for those sleeping tablets! thought Miranda fervently. At least she had not awakened him.

The door into the corridor was still ajar, and her eyes becoming accustomed to the darkness she could make out the Brigadier, lying imposingly upon his back with one arm hanging over the edge of the bunk and sleeping like the proverbial log. Miranda tiptoed to the door, and once in the corridor, closed it cautiously behind her.

A moment later she was back in her own compartment, sitting on the edge of her berth with the lights turned on and giggling helplessly.

What an idiotic thing to have done! How *could* she have been so stupid? How Stella would laugh!

All at once, and for the first time that night, Miranda felt relaxed and sleepy. She yawned largely and untied the sash of her dressing-gown. There was a wet smear on the velvet folds; she must have splashed some water on it from the basin in the next cabin. What a bore! thought Miranda, frowning. It was a new dressing-gown and its purchase had been an unwarrantable extravagance on her part. She brushed her hand over it. But it was not water ...

Miranda sat very still, staring down at the stain on her palm.

The carriage rocked and swayed in time to the clattering cadence of the wheels, and the harsh light of the ceiling bulbs threw a black, swaying shadow across the lower berth.

'It's the dye,' said a voice in Miranda's brain. 'It's only the dye from the velvet.'

But no dye was so richly red. So sticky ...

There was blood on the ruby-red folds of the dressing-gown. A wet, red patch of blood just above the level of her knee. Her stunned gaze moved slowly downwards towards the floor and her eyes widened incredulously, for there were marks upon the carriage floor that had not been there before. The dark, neat, damp prints of a shoe.

Miranda reached down with unsteady hands and pulling off her slippers sat staring at them in horrified unbelief. Both narrow leather soles were as wet and red as though they had walked through a pool of blood——

She dropped them onto the floor and stood up. There was only one possible explanation. The blood must have come from the Brigadier's compartment, and that meant the Brigadier had had a haemorrhage or broken a blood vessel. He might be bleeding to death! She must go to his help at once — surely there must be a doctor on the train?

Miranda jerked open the door of her compartment and stood once more in the cold, empty corridor. There were more marks on the floor of the corridor. The dark prints of her slippers, leading out of the door of the Brigadier's compartment.

This time she knew where to feel for the electric light switch, and it clicked under her hasty fingers.

The light seemed unnaturally bright and the clatter of the train wheels no more than a muted murmur like the sound of a sea shell

51

held to the ear. The whole scene seemed to have taken on something of the detailed, lunatic quality of a Dali painting.

The train rocked and jolted and Miranda caught at the edge of
the door to steady herself; staring, not at the silent figure on the
narrow berth, but at the bright pool of blood upon the floor and
the evilly stained knife that lay beyond it, half in and half out of
the swaying shadow of Brigadier Brindley's overcoat.

She must fetch someone ... Robert ... Which was Robert's
compartment? She could not remember. The attendant — surely
the attendant would be back by now?

Miranda turned and fled wildly down the deserted corridor.

A man appeared at the end of the corridor: a slight young man
wearing a heavy military overcoat and walking quickly towards
her, and she had run into him and was clutching at him before she
could stop herself. It was the man who had returned her bag to
her at Harwich after she had walked out of the Customs shed,
leaving it behind on the counter among the jumbled piles of hand
luggage.

'Oh, it's you! *Do* something — quickly! He's dead!'

It seemed to Miranda that she had shouted the words aloud in
the silent corridor, but to the man who steadied her with his arms
against the sway of the train her voice was no more than a gasping
whisper.

He put up his hands and caught her by her shoulders, his fingers
gripping them painfully through the soft velvet, and stared down
into her white, terrified face: 'What is it? Who's dead?'

'The Brigadier—— Oh, do come! Someone's killed him!'

The man did not speak, but for a moment his fingers bit into
her shoulders. And then he had released them and caught her by
the arm and jerked her round, and they were running down the
corridor. He checked abruptly at the sight of the footprints outside
the Brigadier's compartment, and pulled her to one side, his gaze
moving swiftly from the prints to her bare feet, but he made no
comment and pushed open the door.

Brigadier Brindley was lying as Miranda had left him: on his back and inclining slightly towards his right side, at the outer edge of the berth. His right arm hung down over the edge, the slack fingers touching the floor, and the blankets had been drawn back neatly as far as his waist.

The Brigadier had apparently worn dentures, and without them his face looked older and thinner. The breast of his lilac silk pyjamas was disfigured by a spreading stain, and blood from the wound in his chest had run down inside the sleeve on his right arm to form a pool on the floor.

The stranger stood quite still just inside the door of the small compartment. He appeared to have forgotten Miranda. He did not touch the body of the Brigadier or make any move to pick up the oddly shaped knife that lay on the floor, but his eyes, which were a queer pale grey that seemed to reflect the light like a cat's, were wide and bright and alight with some emotion that Miranda could not understand. They ranged slowly about the small, brightly lit compartment, noting, calculating, summing up and storing away detail after detail. Once he reached out and touched the dead man's cheek, but otherwise he did not move.

Miranda began to shiver, and her teeth chattered. It was a very small sound among the myriad noises of the train, but he must have heard it for he turned, and taking her by the arm went out into the corridor, closing the door quietly behind him.

Miranda spoke in a jerky whisper: 'Aren't you going to do anything? Get a doctor or – or something? He might not be dead.'

'He's dead all right. There's nothing anyone can do for him. Which is your compartment?'

'This one.' Miranda laid her hand on the adjoining door and saw a sudden flare of astonishment in the intent eyes.

'Who has the other berth in there?' The words were still spoken in an undertone, but this time they were clipped and hard.

'Nobody.' Miranda was shivering again and she found it difficult to speak. She saw her companion's eyes go once again from her feet to the prints on the floor of the corridor, and suddenly realized what he must be thinking: 'Those are mine,' she said unsteadily. 'But I didn't do it. I found him like that.'

The man looked at her oddly but made no comment, and pushing open the door of her compartment, he propelled her gently inside and said: 'Stay in there and don't move out of it until I get back.' He paused for a moment in the narrow doorway and glanced quickly about the small compartment as though assuring himself that there was no third person concealed there, and then without looking at her he closed the door softly and was gone.

Miranda sat down on the edge of her berth, her feet dangling just clear of the floor and jerking to the movements of the train and her hands locked tightly together in her lap.

A short time ago she had thought the compartment overheated. But now she was very cold, and she remembered that it was the first day of March. Outside the darkened windows the night air would be cold and sharp and tinged with frost, and that same cold air was seeping now through a hundred crevices into the warm atmosphere of the train, bringing with it a smell of wet earth and engine smoke.

It was very late. Soon they would reach Helmstedt, and after that the train would enter the Russian zone, where no window-blind might be drawn back, and guards would patrol the corridors. Miranda was seized with a sudden and passionate longing to be back in England; dear, safe, matter-of-fact England, where there were no Russian zones, sullen ex-Nazis or bullying 'People's Police', and trains did not keep closely drawn blinds over their windows by night or permit their passengers to be murdered in their sleep.

'. . . I want to go home . . . I want to go home . . . I want to go home,' chattered the wheels. But this time it was for her they spoke, and not Stella.

Because she had gone into the Brigadier's compartment would they think that she had killed him? It had been such a stupid thing to do. Would it sound like a story that she had made up . . . a very thin story? 'I am so sorry, but I walked in by mistake——'

54

She wondered who that man was, and why he was going to Berlin? He appeared to be a person who knew what he was doing, and did it without fuss; an inordinately quiet-looking man. He had been on the boat, and on their train from the Hook. He had sat facing her, two tables away, in the dining-car, and she had thought that there was something about his face that was vaguely familiar. Once he had looked up, and encountering her speculative gaze, had smiled. Miranda had smiled warmly back at him; and had then been astounded and enraged to discover that she was blushing . . .

There were footsteps in the corridor outside and subdued sounds of movement in the next compartment. People came and went, but always quietly, and the cold minutes seemed to stretch into hours. Then at last the handle turned and the man of the corridor was standing in the doorway.

He came in and closed the door behind him and stood looking down at her.

'Now, Miss Brand — that is your name isn't it? — do you mind answering a few questions?'

His voice was quiet and impersonal, and his face, thought Miranda, looked like the windows of the train — as though it had a blind drawn down over it.

'What were you doing in the next compartment?'

Miranda shivered.

'You're frozen!' His voice was suddenly kind and no longer impersonal and he reached up and pulled down the folded blankets from the upper berth, and wrapping one warmly about her unresisting shoulders, lifted her feet up onto the berth and tucked the second one about them.

'They'll dirty the blankets,' said Miranda childishly.

'What will?'

'My feet. They must be very dirty, because I took off my slippers. You see there was blood all over them and I . . .' Her voice trailed away uncertainly.

He stooped and picked up the discarded slippers, and after examining them, dropped them back onto the floor.

'Do you mind if I sit down?' He took her permission for granted and seated himself at the far end of the berth, moving her feet over to make room; his head a bare inch from the low ceiling formed by the berth above them.

'Suppose you tell me all about it. What were you doing in there?' He jerked his head towards the locked door between the two compartments: 'Did you go in that way?'

'No. I went in by the door in the corridor. You see I couldn't sleep and I was thirsty, but I'd spilt my drinking water, and ...' Miranda was suddenly aware that there was more than a touch of hysteria in her voice, and she bit her lip and stopped.

'Go on.'

'I'm sorry. I seem to be behaving very badly. It's – it's the shock I suppose.'

'Don't let that worry you.' He smiled unexpectedly, as he had done once before on the train from the Hook. It was an extraordinarily pleasant smile that altered his face completely.

'Alec Guinness!' said Miranda abruptly. 'I knew you reminded me of someone!'

'Good God,' said the man absently, and Miranda flushed hotly, conscious that she had been gauche and schoolgirlish.

'As a matter of fact,' he said mildly, 'my name is Lang. Simon Lang. You were saying that you couldn't go to sleep ...'

Miranda took a deep breath and steadying her voice with an effort, told him exactly what she had done from the moment that she left her compartment in search of the sleeping-car attendant.

When she had finished Simon Lang said: 'Are you quite sure that's all? You don't remember anything else? No sounds from the next compartment or anyone moving in the corridor for instance?'

Miranda's eyes widened suddenly and she caught her breath in a little gasp: 'Yes. There was something else. I heard a door being opened and then I heard someone moving about in there. I thought it was funny — "funny peculiar", I mean.'

'What was peculiar about it?'

'Oh, nothing really, except that he had taken sleeping pills.'

'What's that?' Simon Lang's quiet voice had a sudden edge to it. 'How did you know that?'

'Because I saw him take them. We all did. He had dinner with us at the Families' Hostel in whatever the name of that place was, and he took them with his coffee. He said he couldn't sleep in trains unless he did. Mademoiselle and Stella took some too.'

'You say you all saw him take the pills. Who do you mean by "all"?'

'Well, all of us. That is, Robert and Stella — I mean Major and Mrs Melville, and the governess — Mademoiselle Beljame — and Lottie, Charlotte — she's only seven. But everyone else was having coffee in the hall too, and people were wandering in and out of that little office-cum-reception-desk thing in the hall, paying their bills and so on. I should think almost everyone must have seen him. He gave us a long lecture on sleeping tablets; apparently he had tried every known brand.'

'Let's have some names, please. Who else would you say was actually in the hall at the time?'

'Why? What does it matter?' Miranda was suddenly angry and completely exhausted. She had slept little during the crossing from Harwich and not at all during the past day. It was long past midnight, she had been subjected to a violent and horrible shock and she was very tired. So tired that she wanted to lean her head back against the wall behind her and sleep . . . and sleep . . .

Simon Lang said: 'I think we shall find that it matters rather a lot. Whoever killed the man in there must have known that he had taken a sleeping draught and was unlikely to wake. You can't just stab blindly at people in the dark. Or if you do, the chances are about a hundred to one against your hitting them in a vital spot. This was a quick stab straight to the heart, and whoever delivered it must have either turned on one of the lights or carried a torch. And known that it was safe to do so.'

'There was a light,' said Miranda tiredly. 'Mine was off, so I could see it at the edge of the door. It wasn't on for more than half a minute.'

'When was that?'

'I don't know. But only a few minutes before I went out in the corridor. I remember thinking "so much for the Brigadier's sleeping pills". And then I heard someone in the corridor and I thought it must be the sleeping-car attendant, so I got up and went out. But there wasn't anyone there ...'

'This person you heard in the corridor — which way did they go?'

Miranda wrinkled her brow, and then shook her head. 'I can't remember. I don't think I knew at the time. It was such a soft sound; more an impression than anything else. Perhaps there wasn't anyone there after all.'

'Unfortunately we know only too well that there was,' said Simon Lang grimly. 'Now about the people who were in the hall of that hostel, please — and then you can go to sleep. Who else would you say was there at the time that the Brigadier took those sleeping pills?'

Miranda pondered the question. She tried to tick them off on her fingers as she spoke, and their faces seemed to float in front of her. Sally Page with her wild-rose face and her pretty shallow laugh, smiling that revealing smile at Robert. Andy Page, with his red hair and angry blue eyes. Elsa Marson, black-haired, dark-eyed, with her unmistakably foreign voice. Harry Marson, red-faced, cheerful, pugnacious and Anglo-Irish. Colonel Leslie, thin, tall and grey-haired, with an expression of dreamy boredom and a clipped military moustache. Mrs Leslie — dark hair streaked with grey, brightly coloured tweeds, Welfare and 'My wives' — who had looked at her, Miranda, with such hate ... No, not at her ... at someone else, surely? Who? She could not remember——

Who else? Mrs Wilkin, a bedraggled hedge-sparrow coping with a brood of unruly fledgelings. Wally, with his plain, freckled, pugnosed face and his endearing grin. A German waiter — several German waiters. And then there was Brigadier Brindley. Of course: he had been there too. But why had he forgotten to put back his teeth? He looked so very odd without them. Odd and old and pathetic ...

Another face floated in front of her and blotted out the jumble of different faces. A strange face, and yet somehow familiar. It was someone she did not recognize, and yet felt that she had known all her life.

'It's time you got some sleep,' said the unknown face.

'That's a very sensible suggestion,' murmured Miranda. 'Goodnight, Guinness.' She smiled drowsily at it, and was instantly asleep.

5

Miranda awoke to find the train at a standstill and cold grey daylight filtering into the carriage around the edges of the window-blind.

For a moment, between sleeping and waking, she thought that she was in her own bedroom and wondered why her bed seemed so narrow? Then almost in the same instant she remembered. She was in Germany — probably by now in Berlin — and on the other side of a door in her compartment lay the body of a murdered man.

Miranda's mind jerked away desperately from the memory of Brigadier Brindley as she had last seen him. She did not want to think of it. The thought of blood and that slack-mouthed dead face brought back too many things — forgotten and shadowy pictures of other dead faces; the sight and smell of death, and the horror and fear of that long-ago time when a small girl had been lost and alone in the terrible storm of war.

Pushing those memories resolutely back into a locked room of her mind from which they were threatening to escape, she sat up abruptly, knocked her head against the reading-light above her pillow, and pulling back the bedclothes was surprised to find that underneath them she was not only still wearing her dressing-gown, but was swathed in a cocoon of blankets.

That man — what was his name? — Simon Lang, must have pulled the bedclothes over her and subsequently tucked her in. Who was he? What was he? What had he been doing in the corridor so late last night and by what right had he questioned her? Why hadn't she refused to answer those questions and ordered him out of her compartment? She should have rung for the attendant to fetch Robert. Instead of which she had sat meekly on her berth for hours on end waiting until a complete stranger should decide to come back and question her; and then, to make matters worse, she had made a gauche and personal remark about his appearance.

Miranda flushed hotly at the recollection and wriggled herself free of the enveloping blankets. He had probably thought that she was a gushing film-fan attempting to compliment him by comparing him to a popular actor, and had not realized that what had prompted her remark was less a matter of personal resemblance than the fact that it had suddenly occurred to her that he possessed an actor's face. A face that was in itself unremarkable, yet capable of altering completely to each change of its owner's mood; becoming a blank mask, or assuming a dozen different characteristics at will.

She bundled the blankets to one end of the berth and pulled aside the edge of the window-blind. It was daylight outside, and the train was standing at a station. There were several men who appeared to be policemen on the platform; one of whom stood with his back to the train, immediately outside her window.

Someone tapped on the door, and as it opened to admit Stella, Miranda saw that the blinds were no longer drawn over the corridor windows, and that beyond them a grey morning sky dripped a thin drizzle of rain onto railway tracks and gaunt buildings.

'You're awake,' said Stella. 'We were told to let you sleep for a bit. 'Randa, what a ghastly thing to happen! You found him, didn't you? Hurry and get your clothes on. They want to see us. No, don't pull up the blind. The platform is cordoned off and crawling with policemen. I'll turn the light on. Here's a cup of tea for you. It's not very hot, I'm afraid.'

She turned on the light, and closing the door behind her, sat on the edge of the berth and continued to talk while Miranda swallowed the lukewarm tea, washed in cold water and dressed in a hurry.

Stella looked both excited and resentful, and her voice had an injured edge to it as she explained that their section of the train had been shunted into a side platform on arrival at Charlottenburg station, and that no one had as yet been allowed off it — although all the passengers from the other coaches had left. A police guard had been placed on it, and hot tea and sandwiches produced by a uniformed member of the W.V.S. But they had already been stuck there for over two hours while police and special service officers had, according to Stella, swarmed all over the train taking photographs and hunting for clues and fingerprints.

'And they've taken all our luggage off,' complained Stella indignantly. 'They wouldn't let us keep a thing. They just came and took everything, and said that we'd find it all ready for us when we left. A man called Lang seems to have arranged it all. He was on our train from the Hook and he seems to be something to do with police or intelligence or M.I.5. He told Robert what had happened and explained that since you'd been kept up pretty late over all this, you might as well be allowed to sleep. He says that we shall all have to answer a few questions and then they'll let us go. It's only a matter of routine, or something silly. He let Robert and Colonel Leslie talk to some people who had come down to meet us. Oh, and he said to tell you to leave all your things in the carriage. He'll see that you get them back.'

'So I should hope!' said Miranda crisply. 'Switch off the light, will you, Stella.' She pulled up the blind and let in the wet daylight. 'Have I got to leave my bag as well? It's got my passport and all my papers and things in it.'

'No. We're allowed to keep those. But I gather they'll want to have a look at them too before they let us leave.'

'Well, I think it's a lot of nonsense,' said Miranda unreasonably. 'I suppose it's just that officious Guinness creature throwing his weight about!'

'Who?' inquired Stella, puzzled.

Miranda flushed and bit her lip. 'That man Lang. Why on earth can't he just let us go off to our own houses and answer questions later on?'

'But don't you understand?' said Stella impatiently. 'They think one of *us* did it!'

'Don't be silly,' begged Miranda, shivering. 'Of course they can't. It was obviously some thief who got into the carriage at one of those stations we stopped at during the night. It *must* have been.'

'They say it couldn't have been. I don't know why, but they seem to be quite sure. They say it must have been someone in this coach.'

Stella gave a little shudder that was half disgust and half unwilling excitement, and Miranda, looking at her, realized suddenly that none of this was real to her. It was merely some fantastic story in which she did not believe and had no part. She might resent the temporary inconvenience that it caused her, but her resentment was to a certain extent offset by interest in what was, to say the least of it, an unusual situation.

But then Stella, thought Miranda, had not seen the dead face of Brigadier Brindley, or that hideous, sprawling stain across his breast and on the carriage floor.

Miranda shivered again and turned away to touch up her mouth with lipstick, annoyed to find in the process that her hand was not entirely steady, and that the face that looked back at her from the square of mirror was unnaturally pale in the cold light: the grey eyes with their lovely tilting lashes wide and frightened. She pulled the collar of her soft squirrel coat close about her throat and said: 'I'm ready. What do we do now? Just wait here until someone comes to put the handcuffs on us?'

Stella said: 'Darling, you *are* upset! I'm so sorry. What a pig I am: I forgot how utterly hellish it must be for you. I ought to have been distracting your attention instead of talking about this sordid mess. Leave all this clutter and come and sit in our carriage. I daresay the police are very neat packers.'

'What about the children?' asked Miranda, closing the door

behind her. 'Lottie and the Wilkin kids? It's a bit tough on them being kept hanging about like this with no breakfast.'

'Oh they're all right. A charming W.V.S. girl turned up and took them all off to have a meal in some refreshment room or other. I don't envy her the job; the Wilkin gang are a bit of a handful. Mademoiselle is madly upset because she wasn't allowed to go with Lottie. She's soaking herself with smelling salts and muttering in French. What a trial foreigners are! Robert darling, here's Miranda, and we're both famished. When do you suppose they're going to let us off this beastly train?'

Robert, who had been staring out of the window with his hands in his pockets, swung round and smiled at Miranda, and she thought fleetingly, and for perhaps the hundredth time, how astonishingly good-looking he was. It was what most people thought when they looked at Robert, and some of them added as a mental note 'too good-looking'.

'Hullo, 'Randa. I hear you had a pretty hectic night?' He put his arm about her slim shoulders and gave her a friendly hug. 'What exactly happened? Why didn't you call me?'

'I meant to,' admitted Miranda, sitting down tiredly on the edge of the lower berth, 'but I couldn't remember which compartment you two were in. How much longer are we going to stay here, Robert?' She did not wish to discuss the happenings of the past night and hoped that the question might sidetrack him.

'Not much longer, I imagine,' said Robert, turning back to the window again. 'They appear to be taking the Brigadier away at last: can't think why they didn't do it earlier.'

Stella went to stand beside him and their bodies shut out the view of the grey platform so that Miranda did not see the stretcher-bearers carry a blanket-covered burden past the window.

A few minutes later a military policeman walked along the corridor and told them they were to leave the train, and Stella slipped into a silver-grey musquash coat and picked up her handbag: 'Ready, Miranda?'

They left the compartment and were ushered, with the other

passengers of the coach, along endless yards of wet platform under the curious gaze of the police guard and a sprinkling of unidentified bystanders, down a flight of steps, along a chill, vaulted passageway and, eventually, into a hastily cleared waiting-room where several officials and three British officers in uniform were grouped about a table. Suitcases, hatboxes, and other pieces of hand luggage that had accompanied the passengers on the sleeping coach, were neatly arranged against the wall.

'Isn't it thrilling?' whispered Sally Page, catching at Miranda's arm. Her blue eyes were wide and excited and she looked impossibly fresh and dewy — in marked contrast to the majority of her fellow-passengers, who appeared jaded and travel-worn: the men unshaven and the women weary.

Mrs Leslie, huddled inside a shapeless coat of purple tweed and wearing a muffler and fur gloves, was looking cold and cross and managing to convey without words that in her opinion the wife of a commanding officer of a regiment should be entitled to more consideration. She said acidly, for the benefit of anyone who might be listening: 'I can see no reason why we should be kept here. It's not as if I had even seen the man before.'

Colonel Leslie was looking bored and resigned, Major Marson amused and Andy Page sulky, while Elsa Marson and Mrs Wilkin were talking earnestly together in undertones; discussing, incongruously enough, the respective merits of gas and electric cooking stoves. Mademoiselle, wearing an expression of the deepest suspicion, had ostentatiously taken up a position by her own and Charlotte's luggage as though she feared that at any moment it might once again be reft from her.

There was no sign of Lottie or the young Wilkins, but Simon Lang was there, standing with his back to the window; his slight figure dark against the grey daylight and his bland, actor's face entirely expressionless. His eyes seemed to be focused on nothing in particular and he appeared to be relaxed and almost lethargic. He did not look at Miranda, or indeed appear in the least interested in the proceedings, but she had an uncomfortable conviction

65

that he missed no word or gesture or fleeting expression from anyone in that room, and that he was in fact about as relaxed as a steel spring.

The proceedings were mercifully brief. Each passenger in turn produced a passport or identity card, gave the address to which they were going, and, in the case of the women, handed over their handbags for a cursory inspection. Sally Page's, Mrs Leslie's and Stella's each contained a cigarette lighter, and these were taken away and put into envelopes marked with the owner's name. Robert, Andy Page and Colonel Leslie also handed over lighters, which were treated in the same manner and added to a row of six torches that lay on the table and had evidently been removed from the passengers' luggage.

A small snapshot had fallen unnoticed from among the jumbled contents of Sally Page's bag, and Miranda, seeing it, stooped and picked it up: 'Here, Sally, you've dropped this.' She held it out, and Sally turned, and glancing at it, snatched it from her hand and crumpled it swiftly in her own.

'Oh ... thank you.' Her cheeks were scarlet, and Miranda was seized with a sudden and uncomfortable suspicion as to who had been the subject of the snapshot. She looked thoughtfully across the room to where Robert stood talking in an undertone to one of the British officers, and as though he felt her gaze, Robert looked up at that moment, and catching her eye grinned at her. Miranda flushed guiltily, ashamed of her suspicions, and Simon Lang saw the flush and misinterpreted it.

The last handbag was returned to its owner and the passengers were informed that they could now remove their luggage, with the exception of the torches and the lighters which would be returned as soon as possible. There were cars outside to take them to their several destinations.

A middle-aged man wearing a dark blue uniform with the crown and star of a lieutenant-colonel apologized charmingly for any inconvenience they might have suffered and thanked them for their patience and co-operation. Mrs Wilkin was led away to collect her offspring, and Mademoiselle hurried off in search of Charlotte, clutching a piece of luggage in each black-gloved hand and refusing all offers of assistance. Only Miranda was still luggageless.

'When do I get my things?' she inquired of the affable gentleman in the blue uniform. 'I was told to leave everything in my carriage and I've left two suitcases and a hatbox in there.'

'Well — er—— It's Miss Brand isn't it? I am sure your luggage will be along soon. If you would not mind waiting——' The affable gentleman looked suddenly less affable, and Simon Lang abandoned the contemplation of his shoes and spoke for the first time.

'I'll send them along to the hostel. There's no need to wait for them. I expect you could all do with some breakfast.'

He looked directly at Miranda, but voice and look were as blankly impersonal as though he were addressing someone he had never seen before.

'I'll wait,' said Miranda flatly. She was both annoyed and frightened. Why had they kept all her hand luggage? Why was Simon Lang behaving as though she were some complete stranger?

'I wouldn't advise it,' said Simon Lang softly. 'We are a little busy just now and it might mean waiting an hour or so. You shall have them as soon as possible.'

Miranda wanted to cry out to him: 'You mean when you have looked for bloodstains! But you know there are bloodstains — you saw them last night! I showed them to you myself. Why do you have to look again?' She choked back the words with an effort that made her hands tremble, and turning blindly away, caught at Robert's arm, and clinging to it, walked quickly out of the room.

Stella, following, said: 'Darling, don't look so upset! I'm sure they'll let you have your stuff soon, and if there's anything you need in the meantime I can probably lend it to you.'

'He's a suspicious, soft-spoken, officious little man!' said Miranda furiously; unaccountably near to tears.

Robert said: 'Who? Lang? I think he's rather a decent type. He

67

went quite a bit out of his way to be helpful this morning. Why have you got your knife into him, Miranda?'

'I haven't. I mean . . . is this the car?'

'Yes. Get in. This is a Volkswagen. The Families' Hostel, please, Corporal.'

Stella said: 'What about Lottie and Mademoiselle? We can't all fit into that.'

'I've sent 'em on ahead with the Leslies. Colonel Leslie very decently offered to drop them at the hostel. The Pages are going there too, so Andy will keep an eye on them.'

Robert bundled them into a small khaki-green beetle of a car driven by a corporal in battledress, and they drove away from Charlottenburg station in the thin, drizzling rain.

Looking back on it, Miranda could never remember much of her first sight of Berlin. She had stared out with unseeing eyes at grey buildings and grey rain. At blocks of shops and houses, interspersed with open spaces where only a rubble of bricks and stone and blackened, twisted steel remained to show where other houses had once stood. At unfamiliar notices that said *Fleischerei, Friseur, Bäckerei, Eisengeschäft* . . .

Robert, who had been in Berlin for several months before he had returned to fetch Stella and Charlotte, pointed out various places of interest as they passed.

'That's the Rundfunk, Stella; the Soviet-controlled wireless station, the one the Russians still keep in our zone. It's a bit of a mystery still. Looks as dead as a morgue, doesn't it? You never seem to see anyone going in or coming out of it, and I've never met anyone who has even seen a face at one of the windows. But I suppose there must be a collection of comrades circulating around somewhere inside it. That? . . . That's a circus that's doing a season here. Very good one. I went with a party one night. We must take Lottie, she'd love it. That's the Funkturm. Sort of Eiffel Tower effect. You can go up it in a lift and have a look at Berlin from the top, or eat in the restaurant in that bulgy bit halfway

68

up — if you can afford it. It's supposed to be the highest building with the highest prices in Berlin; one of those places where they soak you ten bob for a cup of tea and fifteen-and-six for a biscuit to go with it. That's the Naafi building, where you'll do a good bit of your shopping; this used to be called Adolf Hitler Platz, but it's now called the Reichskanzler Platz. Here we are; out you get. Down that paved path and the door's straight ahead of you. Run, or you'll get wet.'

Robert had decided that it was better for them to spend the first night at the Families' Hostel, so that Stella need not bother with meals and housekeeping while taking over the new house, which they would move into on the following day.

The hostel was a large, tall building where they were taken up in a lift and then down a long passage, vaguely reminiscent of a hospital, to two rooms on the third floor. There were sounds of splashing from an adjoining bathroom, and Lottie's voice and Mademoiselle's singing *'Malbrouck s'en va t'en guerre'*.

The Melvilles' luggage was carried into the larger bedroom, the smaller one being already strewn with toys and redolent of caraway seeds. Stella went off to talk to Lottie, and Robert turned to the German who had carried up the suitcases: 'Where is this lady going? We need another room. A single room for the *fräulein*.'

The man nodded cheerfully. *'Ja, ja*. The *fräulein* will come with me, please.'

He led Miranda back down the passage, and after several turnings ushered her into a small room that looked down upon an open concrete space and the ruined shell of a bombed building, and departed.

Miranda pushed open the window and stood looking out at the grey sky and the falling rain, and down at the ruined walls.

So this was Berlin! It had sounded so exciting. 'Where are you going for a holiday this year, Miranda?' 'I'm going to Berlin!' *'Berlin?* My dear, what fun! Bring us back some lovely cut-glass and don't get arrested by the Russians!'

Well, she was here; and she wished passionately that she was

69

back again in the tiny flat near Sloane Street. Oh, how right Stella had been! Travelling in foreign countries was all very well when things went smoothly, but when everything went crazily awry, as they had last night, it was an additional horror that one was in a strange land and surrounded by unfamiliar things and people. She had not felt like this — frightened and unsure and lost — since she was a small girl wandering through terrible, ruined streets and crying for parents whom she was never to see again.

It was not only the sight of a murdered man that had brought those days back, dragging them out of that dark attic in her mind into which her conscious and subconscious mind had thrust them. She should never have come here, to this shattered city where the very language in the streets tugged at shadowy memories that were better forgotten.

6

Robert had left for the barracks, and Stella, Mademoiselle and Lottie had all gone off to see the new house. There had not been room for Miranda in the Volkswagen.

'Are you sure you don't mind being abandoned like this?' Stella had inquired anxiously. 'I'd leave Mademoiselle and Lottie instead, but I know Lottie would only rampage up and down the passages with that awful Wally, and Mademoiselle may as well start making herself useful in the new house.'

'No, of course I don't mind,' said Miranda untruthfully. 'In fact I'd far rather stay quietly here and have a hot bath.'

But she did mind. She did not want to be left alone in this large, strange, impersonal building with its rabbit-warren of passages and stairways that smelt faintly of disinfectant, hot pipes and stale cooking, and its windows that looked out upon grey rain and grey, bomb-scarred buildings.

Her own luggage had still not arrived, but the Melvilles had left a cake of soap and a bath towel in the bathroom adjoining their rooms, and Miranda lay and soaked until the water cooled, and then dressed slowly. But there was still an hour and a half to fill in before the others would return for lunch.

She combed back her dark, shining waves of hair, pinning them so that they curled above her ears, and wondered if the Pages were still in the hostel — only to remember that Andy too had left for the barracks and Sally had announced her intention of taking over her new flat, which was less than five minutes' walk away. And neither the Leslies nor the Marsons would be at the hostel, for they had driven direct to their own homes.

71

Miranda decided to go down to the lounge and see if there were any papers or magazines she could read.

She did not use the lift, but walked down by the stairs, and turning left at the first landing found that she had lost her way. There was no lounge or dining-room here: only a narrow hall with bedrooms leading off it. She paused, at a loss. Should she have turned to the right, or was she on the wrong floor? As she hesitated, she heard the lift come up from below and stop at the landing that she had just left. There was a subdued clash of metal as the doors slid back, and someone began to talk swiftly and urgently in German.

Once, long ago, Miranda had spoken German with a child's fluency; but she had forgotten it, with much else, and the conversation on the landing, even if she could have heard it clearly, meant nothing to her. But the voice that spoke in an undertone barely above a whisper held an unmistakable ring of desperation that was oddly disturbing.

It was a woman speaking; a woman not far from tears, who was answered by another; a sullen voice this time, clearer and harsher. 'Not so loud!' begged the first voice, unexpectedly in English. There were footsteps on the stairs above the landing and Miranda heard one of the women gasp in alarm, and realizing that she herself would seem to be eavesdropping she turned and walked around the corner and back onto the landing.

A dark-haired woman, hatless and wearing a wet raincoat, was standing with her back to Miranda, and a second woman was entering the lift. The steel gates clashed together and the lift sank out of sight as the woman in the raincoat turned on her heel, and brushing past Miranda disappeared round the corner into the passage.

Miranda stood on the narrow landing and frowned into the darkness of the empty lift-shaft, thinking that she must have been mistaken. She had only caught a brief glimpse of the back of the woman who had entered the lift, but the colour and cut of the coat had been familiar, for Mrs Marson had worn a similar one during

72

the journey to Berlin. But Mrs Marson spoke no German. She had said as much on the platform at Bad Oeynhausen, when there had been some difficulty over a porter, and Stella, whose German was halting and rusty from disuse, had had to act as interpreter.

The woman on the landing had spoken fluent German, so obviously it could not have been Mrs Marson; there were probably plenty of women in Berlin who wore dark red coats with black *passementerie* on the collar and cuffs, and small black hats. All the same, it was odd and unsettling, and of a piece with the strange, uneasy atmosphere of the past forty-eight hours. But it was not to be the only unexpected incident of that morning.

As Miranda reached the turn of the stairs leading down to the next floor, a man coming from the direction of the dining-room and the lounge passed quickly along the landing below her and vanished down the staircase leading to the ground floor. It was Robert. Then it must be later than she thought, and Stella would be back!

Miranda reached the lower landing and turned to her left, and this time she was on the right floor for the lounge lay before her. But the hands of the clock stated that it was barely fifteen minutes to twelve, and standing alone in the middle of the lounge, facing the door, was Sally Page.

'Oh!' said Sally Page on a half gasp. 'Oh—— Hullo, Miranda.' Her flower face flushed pinkly.

'Hullo,' said Miranda, surprised. 'I thought you were taking over your flat?'

'I am — I mean I was. But it all seemed such a muddle that I thought I'd wait until Andy could give me a hand. There's a corporal there now checking lists, and the carpets are old and dirty and hideous and none of the curtains seem to match——' Sally's voice was a little breathless and she appeared to be talking for the sake of filling an awkward silence — 'so I just gave it up and thought I'd come back here and see if I could get a cup of coffee or something. But as there doesn't seem to be anyone about, I think I'd better run back. Perhaps I shouldn't have walked out on them.'

Miranda did not attempt to dissuade her, and with a childish toss of her head and a heightened colour, Sally walked quickly out of the room.

Miranda looked after her thoughtfully. Surely Robert couldn't be such a fool as to ...? There you go again! she accused herself. Imagining things. Making mountains out of molehills like some gossiping old spinster. What if Sally *has* got a schoolgirl crush on Robert? A good many far more mature women had experienced something of the same emotion when looking at him, and those same women probably cherished a sentimental admiration for some glittering and unobtainable hero of the screen, which in no way impaired their affection for their own far less spectacular husbands!

As for Robert, he had probably had some perfectly legitimate reason for making a brief return to the hostel, and there was no need to suppose that he had been keeping a sentimental assignation with Sally.

Miranda picked up a dog-eared copy of a women's magazine and determinedly embarked on a story that turned out, maddeningly, to be the first instalment of a full-length novel.

Mademoiselle and Lottie returned at lunchtime with a message from Stella to say that she was having lunch with the Marsons, whose house was near hers, and would probably return for tea. And a few minutes later Robert rang up to say that he was lunching at the Mess; adding that they would be moving into the house next morning.

Miranda's luggage was delivered at the hostel after lunch and carried up to her room with the assistance of Mademoiselle and Lottie. Mademoiselle's offer to stay and help unpack being refused, she swept Lottie off to rest, and Miranda was left alone.

Whoever had examined the contents of her suitcases had repacked them with incredible neatness but a complete disregard for the cut of feminine clothes. Even her rolled underwear had been folded into small squares the size of a man's handkerchief.

Miranda removed only what she would need for the night and left the suitcases on the floor.

The thin drizzle of the morning had turned to a steady rain that drummed on the window ledge and spattered up against the panes. But except for the sound of the rain, the room and the rambling building and the wet afternoon seemed very quiet.

A hinge creaked faintly in the silence, and reflected in the dressing-table mirror Miranda saw the door behind her opening very softly, an inch at a time, as though a draught swung it slowly inwards.

Something moved in the widening gap — a face. A hideous, idiot face of white and scarlet blotches with a wide grinning mouth. And for a brief moment Miranda's heart seemed to jerk in her breast and her breath stopped. The next moment she had swung round and leapt at the door.

The head dodged back and its owner fled down the passage with Miranda in pursuit.

The small figure darted round the turn of the passage, and Miranda, rounding it a split second later, crashed full tilt into someone coming from the opposite direction; and for the second time in less than twelve hours found herself in the arms of Simon Lang.

'Oh!' gasped Miranda furiously, tears of fright and rage in her voice: 'Now look what you've done! I'd have caught that little horror if it hadn't been for you!'

'What little horror? The small boy who just streaked past me?'

'Wally Wilkin! I'd like to murder that child!'

Her voice broke on a sob; and then a sudden realization of what she had said, and to whom she had said it, struck her like a slap in the face, and she jerked herself away from Simon Lang's supporting arm, her white face flushing scarlet. 'And that doesn't mean I murdered the Brigadier last night, so you needn't look at me like that!' she said, her voice unnaturally high and unsteady.

'Take it easy,' advised Simon Lang mildly. 'What's the matter? You seem a bit upset.'

75

'So would you be if that sort of thing came peering round a corner at you!' She gestured to where a brightly coloured cardboard mask, cut from the carton of a well-known brand of breakfast cereal, lay on the floor.

Simon Lang's lips twitched and Miranda said tremulously: 'You needn't laugh! It scared me.'

'I can see it did. And I'm not laughing. You're feeling pretty jumpy, aren't you? Is it that business of last night, or is it something else?'

'I don't know.' Miranda's anger had suddenly evaporated and she felt tired and bewildered. 'Partly last night, I suppose. But it's not only that. I just wish I'd never come to Berlin. I thought it was going to be such fun, but it's been hateful instead. Hateful and frightening. What are you doing here?' she finished abruptly.

'I wanted to talk to you. Has your luggage arrived all right?'

'Yes, thank you. Is that all you wanted to talk about?'

'No. Do you mind if we go along to the lounge? There isn't anyone there just now, and I think it would be more comfortable than standing talking in the passage — and more in keeping with the conventions than using your bedroom.'

The lounge looked gloomy and inhospitable in the grey light of the wet afternoon. There was no one else there and the whole hostel appeared to be empty and deserted.

Simon Lang selected two armchairs farthest from the door and offered Miranda a cigarette. He lit it for her and she looked up from leaning down to the lighted match and met his eyes. The flame was reflected in them, turning them to an odd shade of amber and there was a curious look in them very like surprise.

Miranda sat back in her chair and said uncertainly: 'Why do you want to see me? Who are you?'

'The Officer Commanding 89 Section Berlin, if that means anything to you; and in the regretted absence of the D.A.P.M. Security and Intelligence Branch, who is at present incarcerated in an isolation ward with mumps, this murder is my pigeon.'

'Oh,' said Miranda, and was silent for a moment. 'What do you want to talk about?'

'About you,' said Simon Lang amiably: 'I'd like you to tell me again just exactly what happened last night. Try and remember everything, however trivial it may seem.'

Miranda thought for a moment. 'I couldn't go to sleep,' she began . . .

She told the story as accurately as she could, trying to relive it exactly as it had happened, and Simon Lang listened without interruption, and when she had finished, said: 'You say that you felt nervous and on edge the first time that you went out into the corridor, and as though you wanted to look over your shoulder. Any particular reason why you should have felt like that? Are you sure that you hadn't heard or seen something that had frightened you?'

'Quite sure. There wasn't anything to be frightened of. Not then. That's what made it all so silly. Anyway, it wasn't just on the train. I'd been feeling a bit Aunt Hettyish all day.'

'A bit *who*?'

Miranda flushed. 'I'm sorry. It's a sort of family catchword of the Carrells — that's Stella's — Mrs Melville's — family. They've got an aunt who detests cats, and she's always saying: *"I have a feeling in my bones that there is a cat somewhere about!"'*

'I see. And you had a feeling in your bones that there was something wrong somewhere. Is that it?'

'Well . . . not quite,' said Miranda, moving restlessly in her chair. 'It's a little difficult to explain. I just felt a bit scared and on edge and — oh, I can't describe it. It isn't a thing you can pin down!'

'All right,' said Simon equably, 'leave it for the moment. Can you tell me instead if there was any particular moment at which you began to feel — *um* — Aunt Hettyish?'

Miranda considered the question. 'I don't think so,' she said at last. 'I felt in terrific form when I went off to meet Stella and Robert at Liverpool Street station. We had tea at the Station Hotel and it was quite a party. It was only later on that there seemed to be a sort of queer feeling about things.'

'When you arrived at the Hook? Or while you were still in England?'

Miranda wrinkled her brows: 'In England, I think. I'm not quite sure. Why? Is it important?'

'Perhaps it isn't. It merely struck me as an interesting point that, according to your own story, you should have felt scared and uneasy before you had any reason to be so, and that possibly you may have seen or noticed something — perhaps without knowing it — that would account for it. Was there anything at all, at any time, that struck you as unusual?'

'No,' said Miranda flatly. She had no intention of telling him of those two looks, so utterly different from each other, that she had surprised on the faces of Sally Page and Mrs Leslie on the previous evening. 'I expect it's only Germany. Coming back here, I mean. You see I used to live in Germany when I was a child. My father had a job here, and when the war came we moved over into Belgium. Then Belgium was attacked, and my parents were killed and I got over to England somehow with a batch of refugees. I thought I'd forgotten about it — or very nearly. But coming back here seems to have stirred it all up again. And then of course there was that impossible coincidence of the Brigadier's story.'

'What story was that?' Simon Lang's voice was deceptively casual, but his eyes, which appeared to be able to change colour — or did they reflect colour? — were suddenly bright and intent.

Miranda repeated the story that the Brigadier had told on the previous evening — abridging considerably — and her own connection with it.

Simon Lang did not appear unduly interested. He wanted to know when Miranda had met the Brigadier and if she had ever, at any time, known him or seen him before? He asked a great many questions in that quiet, casual voice, some of which appeared to have little point. How had they been seated at the dinner table? Who had been sitting at the next tables, and would they have been near enough to overhear what was said? At what time had they moved into the hall? What had they done there and who had been standing where? When had they gone back to the station and in what order? What exactly happened when they boarded the train? Had there been much visiting between the various compartments before or after the train started?

Miranda answered his questions to the best of her ability, and when there appeared to be no more, asked one of her own: 'Why do you want to know all this? Is it — was it one of us?'

Simon Lang did not pretend to misunderstand her.

'Yes.' The monosyllable was curt and uncompromising.

'How can you possibly know? There were so many people on that train. Dozens of others!' Once again there was a thin edge of panic to Miranda's voice.

'It's quite simple,' said Simon Lang softly. 'He was killed with a knife that had been taken off the reception desk at the hostel at Bad Oeynhausen. It belonged to the manager who used it as a paperknife and for sharpening pencils, and it was on his desk during the earlier part of the evening, because one of the staff remembers using it to cut a piece of string. Someone must have picked it up between then and the time that the passengers left for the train. And it could only have been one of the people who had used the Families' Hostel. Which rules out everyone except the people you have mentioned.'

'But – but one of the Germans — a waiter at the hostel — one of the staff could have taken it.'

'None of them were on the train.'

'But they could have given it to someone! The attendant ...'

'The attendant was with a sick man in the next coach at the time the murder was committed; and five people can prove it.'

Miranda said: 'How do you know when it was committed?' Her voice had wavered a little for she could not believe — she would not — that one of the people who had sat near her at supper only last night could be capable of that savage act.

'Blood,' said Simon Lang. The single, softly spoken word

sounded horribly loud in the quiet room. 'It clots and dries very quickly. You had brushed against it; there was a wet stain on your dressing-gown and your slippers were soaked with it. When I reached the carriage it was still wet, but it was beginning to coagulate and the body was warm. Brigadier Brindley cannot have been killed more than ten to fifteen minutes at the most before you entered his compartment. Possibly less. If the murderer had only had the sense to leave the weapon in the wound instead of pulling it out, we should probably not have discovered the murder until the attendant went round calling people in the morning; and by that time it might have been a little more difficult to fix the time of death. As it was the murderer pulled out the knife, which would have served to plug the wound, and the resulting rush of blood was the cause of your discovering it. I imagine that the first idea was to get rid of a weapon that could be traced, and then the difficulty of carrying it away without getting smeared with blood resulted in its being dropped on the floor and left.'

'It can't be true!' said Miranda. 'There must be some other explanation. I've talked to these people. They are all three perfectly nice and very ordinary people.'

'Three?' Simon Lang's expressive eyebrows lifted slightly.

Miranda said quickly: 'If you think Robert could possibly murder anyone it shows that you don't know the first thing about him. Well I do. I've known him for years, so I know he couldn't conceivably do it.'

'Calm down, my child,' said Simon equably. 'No one is casting doubts upon your cousin. Although I imagine that given sufficient incentive, more people are capable of murder than one would suppose. In fact some of the world's most notorious killers have been mild little people whom their families and friends were convinced "wouldn't hurt a fly".'

'You've forgotten Stella,' interrupted Miranda scornfully. 'If Robert had left the compartment during the night, Stella would have heard him.'

'But Mrs Melville had taken sleeping powders,' said Simon

Lang gently. 'Quite a few people saw her take them, including yourself. It might have given him just the opportunity he needed.'

'You can't believe that!' said Miranda. 'You *can't*!'

'Oh, don't worry. I wasn't advancing it as my opinion. At the moment I'm keeping an open mind. No, I was merely interested in your arithmetic. Why "three"? I make it eleven. Or a round dozen, if we are to include the young dead-ender you were pursuing down the passage earlier on.'

'You mean you think a woman . . . ? It *couldn't* be!'

'Why not?' There was a distinct glint of mockery in his eyes. 'Don't tell me you think women are frail flowers incapable of violence? We have it on record that *"The female of the species is more deadly than the male!"* My dear, anyone could have done the job — in the circumstances.'

'What do you mean? In what circumstances?'

'Brigadier Brindley had taken two capsules of a particularly effective sleeping powder, and we can take it the murderer was aware of the fact. The weapon was exceedingly sharp and had a double edge and a point like a needle. Whoever used it walked calmly into the Brigadier's compartment, either turned on the small reading-light over the top berth or used a torch or a cigarette lighter, drew down the blankets to make things easier, and stabbed the knife home to the hilt. Given those advantages — a doped man and a knife of that type — a child could have done it. And I mean that quite literally. Even young Wally could have done the job; granted he had the nerve and some elementary knowledge of anatomy. However I think we can safely count him out, which leaves us with eleven suspects. Two Marsons, two Melvilles, two Pages, two Leslies, Mademoiselle Beljame, Mrs Wilkin — and Miss Miranda Brand.'

' "And the last shall be first," ' quoted Miranda flippantly, an angry sparkle in her eyes. 'Is that what you mean?'

'Not necessarily,' returned Simon Lang without heat. 'I told you that I'm keeping an open mind. So far, I will admit, you are our most promising suspect. Whoever killed Brigadier Brindley either wore gloves or wrapped the handle of the knife in a handkerchief, and we haven't found anything among the luggage that shows signs of having had bloodstains on it. But the chances are that whoever killed him got some blood on him — or her. On their hands if nowhere else.'

'But – but *I* had blood on my hands,' whispered Miranda: 'I rubbed my hand over the mark on my dressing-gown ... That was how I – I saw what it was.'

'I know,' said Simon Lang quietly.

He reached out and took both her cold hands in his and held them for a moment in a warm clasp that was curiously comforting: 'Don't let it worry you. You'll be quite safe as long as you stick to the truth.'

'I've told you the truth,' said Miranda shakily.

'I believe you have. With reservations——! He released her hands and smiled a little crookedly. 'Anyway, you would appear to have no motive. Not that that is much help in the present instance, since the same seems to apply to all of you. What we need are a few really reliable alibis.'

'*I'm* the only one who needs an alibi,' said Miranda with an uncertain laugh. 'Everyone else has got one, because they were all sleeping two to a compartment. That's an alibi in itself.'

'Not always. Husbands and wives are odd in that way. They will alibi each other for any number of reasons, ranging from devotion to a desire not to be involved, in any way whatever, with anything as socially damning as murder.'

Miranda said: 'Well, you can cut Stella off your list, for one.'

'Why?'

'You told me a minute ago that Robert hasn't an alibi because he knew that Stella had taken the same amount of dope as the Brigadier and was therefore out like a light. And you can't have it both ways.'

'But I can,' Simon Lang assured her, 'I can merely look at it from another angle. Suppose Mrs Melville merely pretended to take the pills? It's perfectly possible.'

'Why should she do anything so silly?'

'To fake an alibi perhaps? It would be quite a good one and very difficult to disprove.'

'And I suppose Mademoiselle was also faking up an alibi?' said Miranda coldly.

'Not such a good one,' said Simon, unruffled. 'She only took one capsule.'

'Or pretended to take one!'

'Or pretended to take one,' agreed Simon. 'So you see we still have eleven suspects and not one watertight alibi among them.'

'That's where you're wrong,' declared Miranda. 'Stella has one, and I'll tell you why. She *did* take those sleeping pills and I can prove it. She hates swallowing pills. She always powders them up first. She didn't swallow the capsules; she broke them open and stirred the stuff into her coffee and drank it. And we all saw her do it. So unless you think that the Brigadier deliberately palmed off two fake capsules on her, and she knew it, and knew that she was taking something that wouldn't make her sleep, you've lost one suspect.'

'Are you telling me the truth, the whole truth and nothing but the truth?' inquired Simon Lang seriously.

'I don't have to say that until you've got me in the witness-box,' retorted Miranda bitterly. 'And I'm not there yet. Yes, of *course* I'm telling you the truth! Ask Mademoiselle if you don't believe me. Ask Robert. Ask Lottie! Telephone Bad Oeynhausen and ask the waiter who served the coffee!'

'All right, all right, all right,' said Simon Lang pacifically. 'The point is taken. And disabuse yourself of the idea that I am trying to pin the crime on some innocent person merely for the sake of collecting a victim.'

Miranda's tense attitude relaxed and she sank back in her chair and gave a shaky laugh.

'That's better,' approved Simon.

There were voices in the hall beyond the lounge, and he glanced at his wristwatch and stood up.

'Well, that's about all for the moment. I'm afraid you'll probably be asked to go over the same ground again during the next few days, so I shall be seeing you. Thank you for bearing with me so well.'

He smiled down at her. A slow smile that broke up the planes of his face and transformed him into an entirely different and very likeable person.

The next moment the lounge was full of people and Simon Lang had gone.

Miranda went out onto the landing where she found Lottie and Wally Wilkin playing in the lift.

Wally turned to fly at the sight of her, but this time Miranda was too quick for him.

'Listen to me, you young menace,' said Miranda, retaining a firm grip upon the writhing child. 'If I ever catch you creeping into other people's rooms wearing paper masks again, I'll – I'll bastinado you!'

Wally's eel-like struggles ceased and an unexpected look of interest came over his freckled face: ''Ow could you do that? Mum's got 'er marriage lines: I seen 'em.'

'What on earth——?' began Miranda, puzzled; then the sudden realization that he had confused the word with one more familiar to him betrayed her into a laugh.

'You ought not to know the meaning of words like that!' she said with attempted severity. '*Bastinado*, you precocious little imp. It's a Chinese torture!' Miranda put a slim forefinger to each temple, drew her lovely eyes up into an oriental slant and pulled her curving mouth into a grimace that would have done credit to any cereal package.

'*Coo!*' said Wally, a wealth of admiration in the tone. 'D'you know any more Chinese tortures?'

'Lots!' said Miranda mendaciously. 'So just you watch your

step, young Wally, or you'll find yourself on the receiving end of them one of these days!'

Wally favoured her with a wide and gap-toothed grin. *'Garn!'* he said, 'yer too soft-'earted!'

Miranda tweaked his nose and released him: 'And now get out of that lift, both of you, or you'll have the manager after you. What are you doing down here anyway, Lottie? Waiting for your mother to come back?'

'She's back,' said Charlotte. 'She came back a long time ago. Hours 'n hours.'

'Oh. Well I'd better go and find her.'

Stella was in her bedroom. And looking remarkably pretty, thought Miranda, for a woman who had travelled non-stop for over forty-eight hours, been interviewed by the police over a murder case, and worked hard taking over a new house and a foreign staff in a strange city. She had lost all trace of weariness, and her manner was almost feverishly gay. A brilliant colour burned in her cheeks and her eyes were over-bright.

'Hullo, Miranda darling. *What* a day! I hear you've been spending the afternoon being third-degreed by the police? They were around asking endless questions half the morning. They had a session with Mademoiselle too, and another with Lottie. Let's get Robert to take us out on the town tonight. We may as well eat, drink and be merry while we have the chance, just in case they throw us all into jail tomorrow——

'Mademoiselle had a *crise de nerfs*. She said that they were all picking on her because she was a poor, defenceless foreigner, and they would send her to the guillotine — innocent as she was — solely in order to save the head of a guilty Englishman! And Lottie said it wouldn't be the guillotine because we don't chop people's heads off in England, we hang them (how *do* they learn these things?) and Mademoiselle rushed wildly out of the room in a cloud of smelling salts . . .

'The cook can't speak any English, and Robert's batman is in hospital with jaundice and won't be out for another week. Where is Robert, by the way? I haven't seen him all day. Harry Marson brought me back. Let's send for a bottle of champagne, 'Randa: I feel we should do *something* to celebrate our first, gay, glorious day in Berlin!'

Her laugh held a note of hysteria, and Miranda said: 'What you need is a cup of tea and some aspirin. We'll try the champagne later. Let's see what happens if we press a bell. Or do you suppose they only serve tea in the lounge?'

It was well after six o'clock before Miranda returned to her own room.

Sally Page had suggested that they should all go over to the Officers' Club for dinner, and Stella had enthusiastically seconded the idea and gone upstairs to change and say good-night to Lottie.

Miranda turned on her bedroom light and drew the curtains over the rain-spattered windows.

The room looked much the same as when she had left it earlier that afternoon in pursuit of Wally Wilkin, but for one difference: someone had visited it in her absence. Someone who had searched through her suitcases and had not had time to repack the contents neatly, but replaced them in a haphazard manner so that shoes, stockings, underwear and toilet articles were inextricably mingled. The drawers of the dressing-table had been opened, and in the cupboard her squirrel coat hung crookedly on its hanger. Even the bed was rumpled, as though someone had searched under the pillows and the mattress and then hurriedly drawn the coverlet straight above the disarranged bedding.

So *that's* why he wanted me to go down to the lounge! thought Miranda. So that some of his ham-handed underlings could go through my things again. Why, when they've done it once already? What did they think they might have missed? Something that I might have had on me? A handkerchief or gloves with stains on it?

Another thought slid into her mind like a thin sliver of ice. The searching of her room meant something else. Simon Lang had not

86

believed her. He had been kind and friendly and had made her feel that he was on her side. But he was on no one's side; unless it was the dead man's.

Once again she seemed to hear his voice saying: 'Whoever killed him must have got some blood on them — on their hands at least.' But there was only one person who had had blood on their hands: Miranda Brand.

'Circumstantial evidence'. Why had she suddenly thought of that phrase? What exactly did it mean?

Miranda turned slowly away from the disordered suitcases and began to take off her coat and skirt with stiff, unsteady fingers. And as she dressed for the Club, and all through the evening that followed, a mocking little rhyme seemed to beat in her brain with the same monotonous cadence as the train wheels on the previous night: *Miranda Brand had blood on her hand ... Miranda Brand had blood on her hand ... Miranda Brand ...*

7

The sky was a clear spring blue full of small white clouds, and the sun was shining as Robert drove the car down Bundes Allee, and turned left into the long sweep of the Herr Strasse.

On either side there were widely spaced houses standing back from the road; some of them set among pine trees and the pale green of new spring leaves, and others — a good many others — only ruined shells standing among a wilderness of stunted bushes, weeds and tangled briars.

'Not bombs — Russians,' said Robert in answer to a query from Miranda. 'They burnt them. "Houses of the bloated enemy capitalists" and all that sort of thing. Or so I am told.'

He turned the car off the Herr Strasse, and after crossing one or two parallel and smaller streets, pulled up in a quiet, tree-lined road before a red-roofed house flanked by budding lilacs and approached by a short flagged path.

'Here we are: bundle out. I'm late. See you at lunch.' He kissed Stella, released the brake and went on his way to the barracks which lay some half-dozen miles distant.

The house, though sparsely furnished, was comfortable and not without charm. A white painted staircase led up from a wide hall to a narrow landing that ran round three sides of the stairwell and gave access to four bedrooms. A large drawing-room and a smaller dining-room looked out on half an acre of garden that lay at the back of the house and consisted mainly of a lawn surrounded by a hedge and more lilac bushes and ending in a high reed fence. There were two pine trees in the garden, a few cherry trees and some sad, sandy-looking flowerbeds. A single almond tree provided a gay splash of colour and the cherry trees were already in bloom.

A shallow alcove off the hall held a telephone, and to the right an archway and a short passage led to the kitchen quarters and the back staircase. There was a small study for Robert and a smaller cloakroom.

'The cellars are about the largest part of the house,' said Stella. 'A ghastly waste of space, as there's nothing down there but a boiler and piles of coke and coal. But thank heavens we have two bathrooms! This is your room, and Robert and I are in here and Lottie next door to you. Mademoiselle's in there. There's another bathroom and two servants' rooms in the attic, but only the house-maid sleeps in; she seems a nice woman and mercifully can speak quite good English. My German is pretty rusty. When you've gone, I'll turn your room into a schoolroom-cum-playroom for Lottie, but until then she'll have to use that little room downstairs. Robert will never really use it.'

A woman wearing a starched white apron passed along the landing carrying a pile of clean linen, and Miranda caught at Stella's arm:

'Who's that?'

'That's Friedel.'

'Madam?' The woman turned, thinking she had been addressed.

'*Es ist nichts, Friedel,*' Stella waved a hand in dismissal. 'What is it, 'Randa?'

'I've seen that woman before. She was at the hostel yesterday.'

'Was she? Probably collecting her papers or a reference or something. She used to work there once. Now I'm going to leave you to your unpacking while I go down to wrestle with the cook. What's the *Deutsch* for "braised"?'

Stella ran down the stairs to the hall, but Miranda stood gazing into space. There was no reason why Stella's explanation of the woman Friedel's presence in the hostel should not be the right one. It seemed obvious enough. And yet standing there in a square of bright spring sunlight in Stella's house, Miranda had a swift and fleeting impression that she was looking at part of a pattern.

It was as though everything that had happened since she had left Liverpool Street station less than three days ago was all part of the same pattern, and that if she could only stand back from it, and see it from far enough away, she would be able to see a shape and a meaning. But she could not do so, because she herself was part of it. A small, coloured thread caught up in the machinery and woven in and out, willy-nilly, with other threads of other colours ...

I'm being Aunt Hettyish again, thought Miranda ruefully. I'm worse than Aunt Hetty! At least when she had a feeling that there was a cat about, there always was, while I keep peopling the place with imaginary cats. I must need a dose or a tonic or something.

Towards twelve o'clock a Mrs Lawrence arrived to call, and Friedel produced coffee and cakes in the drawing-room.

Mrs Lawrence, the wife of Robert's commanding officer, was a tall woman with auburn hair and an energetic personality. She was, Miranda surmised, more interested in the murder than in Stella's possible domestic problems, for having accepted their assurances that they were in no immediate need of assistance, she turned to the more interesting subject of Brigadier Brindley's death.

According to Mrs Lawrence, the B.B.C. had mentioned the murder in a news broadcast, a London daily had headlined it, and several German newspapers had already printed columns on the subject. But both Stella and Miranda had made their accounts as colourless as possible. Stella because she had slept throughout the entire proceedings, and Miranda because she had been too closely and unpleasantly involved to relish discussing the matter.

Mrs Lawrence was thrilled and sympathetic, but a little disappointed. She gave it as her opinion that the police would undoubtedly discover that the poor man had committed suicide after all, urged them once more to call upon her if they needed anything, mentioned that there was a Wives' Meeting at her house on Monday at three o'clock which she hoped Stella would attend, refused the offer of a glass of sherry, and left.

During the afternoon two members of the Public Safety Branch

90

called at the house, and once more Stella, Miranda and Mademoiselle were interviewed in turn. The two men were friendly and pleasant and managed to give their visit the atmosphere of an informal call rather than that of a police inquiry, so that even Mademoiselle thawed and remarked after their departure that they were *'très gentils, très comme il faut'*!

The remainder of the day passed quietly enough except for one small, disturbing incident that occurred in the late afternoon. Stella, who was lining her dressing-table drawers with paper, looked up from the task to ask Miranda if she would telephone Robert and remind him to bring back ration cards for them. There was a telephone extension on the bedside table, and Miranda, who had been lying on Stella's bed reading a new copy of *Vogue*, reached out and idly lifted the receiver.

Someone was talking on the other end of the line: a quick, low voice speaking in German. The girl at the exchange, thought Miranda, turning a page of the magazine and waiting for the voice to ask what number she wanted.

The voice changed suddenly to a mixture of German and English.

'Speak then in English! *Es wäre mir sehr angenehm?* I must meet with you this night. If you come not I come myself upstairs to your house, and that will make trouble for you! . . . *Nein, danke!* . . . *wie du willst* . . . By the third house then, where the light is not . . . *Das ist gut!* . . .'

Miranda broke firmly into the conversation: 'Exchange?'

There was an indescribable gasp at the other end of the line, followed by a sudden click as a receiver was replaced. And then silence.

'Exchange!' repeated Miranda impatiently.

Stella looked up from cutting lengths of paper and said: 'Don't be silly, darling. It's a dial phone.'

'But someone was speaking in German.'

'I expect you got a crossed line or something. Robert's number is at the top of that pad.'

Miranda reached out, and turning the telephone to face her, dialled a number; but with no result.

'It's not working. I can't get a sound out of it.'

'What an idiot I am!' said Stella, dropping the scissors and standing up. 'This is only an extension of course, and it won't work unless you switch it up here from the hall. Don't bother. I'll run down and put in a call from the one downstairs.'

She left the room and Miranda sat looking thoughtfully at the telephone . . .

The downstairs telephone. Of course, that was it. She had been listening to the conversation of some person in the house. And that person could only be the woman Friedel, for the cook spoke no English.

Who had Friedel been talking to in that half-whispered, threatening voice?

Robert returned about six o'clock bringing Major Marson with him. The Marsons lived in the same road, their house being separated from the Melvilles' by that of Colonel and Mrs Leslie, who were next door.

Robert mixed gin and vermouth and he and Harry became immersed in regimental shop.

Harry Marson's usually high spirits seemed to have temporarily deserted him. He looked tired and morose, and his comments appeared to be mainly confined to criticism of the Army. Presently Stella smothered a yawn with nicely calculated effect, and the conversation became more general.

Harry, who before the war had spent three weeks' leave in Berlin with an uncle in the British Embassy and knew the city reasonably well, described it in the days of its Nazi glory when the flags had flown and panzer divisions and steel-helmeted, goose-stepping ranks had paraded down the great stretch of the Kaiserdamm.

The house that Brigadier Brindley had talked of, from which Herr Ridder and his wife had disappeared, was, said Harry, less than half a mile away. It was only a burnt-out shell now, but the unfinished garage still stood. He had driven past it only that day and had stopped out of curiosity to look through the rusted iron gateway. 'Tell you what — I'll take you round on Sunday,' offered Harry. 'That is, if you're interested.'

He, too, it appeared, had been interrogated by the S.I.B. on the subject of the murder, as had Elsa, Colonel and Mrs Leslie, the Pages and Mrs Wilkin. Elsa Marson had apparently not taken the inquiries in good part. She had wept and been what Harry described as 'a bit upset'. In other words, had behaved on the same lines as Mademoiselle, thought Miranda. Stella caught her eye and pantomimed *foreigners!* and Miranda's attempt to turn a fit of the giggles into a cough was not entirely successful.

Next morning Robert had rung up from the office to say that he could get three seats for a bus tour of Berlin on the following day, and would they like to go? It would, he said, take the best part of four hours, as the buses toured the British, American and Russian sectors of the city. Shortly afterwards, Mrs Leslie made an unexpected appearance and offered — somewhat surprisingly in view of her attitude during the journey from England — to take Miranda to see the shops. An offer that Miranda accepted with alacrity, since Stella, who was far more interested in overseeing the hanging of her newly unpacked curtains, plainly did not need her help.

Norah Leslie drove up the Herr Strasse, circled the Reichskanzler Platz and proceeded by way of Masuren Allee and Kant Strasse, to the Kurfürstendamm, the luxury shopping street of Berlin.

She parked the car not far from the fantastic ruin of the Kaiser Wilhelm memorial church, and Miranda stood in the clear spring sunlight and looked up at the broken towers and the vivid colours of the mosaics that could be glimpsed through the shattered walls, and marvelled that a ruin could look so beautiful. Before war and bombs had blasted it, it could not have been a particularly impressive building, but now, lifting against the pale sky out of a surge of shops, cinemas, hotels, apartments and the clatter of trams and traffic, there was something strangely ancient and oriental about its shattered silhouette; as though it were some beautiful, lost ruin from Angkor Wat — instead of the wreckage of a late-nineteenth-century Christian church.

Mrs Leslie touched her arm, and Miranda turned away and followed her through a maze of traffic and hurrying pedestrians, across the busy street. But it soon began to dawn on her that there had been an ulterior motive in Mrs Leslie's offer to take her to see the shops, although she certainly fulfilled the letter of her promise. Together they gazed at china shops and antique shops, admired hats, dresses, shoes and glass, and wandered through the crowded aisles of the KaDeWe, a hive-like multiple store. But this window-shopping was only a background and an opportunity for talk, and the talk was almost entirely on the subject of the Melvilles . . .

Mrs Leslie, it seemed, had known Robert for many years. They had played together as children, and the families had only lost touch when Robert's father had sold his house on his wife's death in 1935. Norah had been in India then, newly married. But it was obvious that she did not wish to talk of herself: it was the Melvilles who interested her, and Miranda was as yet too young and inex-perienced to be able to parry her questions with much skill. Besides, the questions themselves appeared to be harmless enough, and no more than one might have expected from someone who had once known the family well and took an interest in their affairs. Yet Miranda felt vaguely uncomfortable. There was some-thing behind Mrs Leslie's questions. A hint of animosity? An undertone of spite? Miranda could not quite place it, but she gained the impression that Norah Leslie would not have been displeased to hear that Robert and Stella were unhappy, and their marriage a failure.

She was especially curious about Stella: her character, her interests, her clothes. She had heard of Stella, but had never met her until Robert had introduced them at Liverpool Street station. 'She's very pretty,' said Mrs Leslie in a brittle voice. 'You would hardly know that she was older than Robert. Somehow I had not expected her to look so — soft. I had imagined something harder. But appearances are very deceptive, aren't they? Of course women have a sort of instinct about these things, but men only go by appearances.'

She stopped to look at a window containing an exquisite display of modern porcelain, and added in a bright, conversational voice: 'She killed Johnnie, of course.'

'What?' Miranda checked, unable to believe that she had heard aright, and a stout German *hausfrau*, hurrying along the pavement behind her, cannoned into her and muttered crossly under her breath before continuing on her way. But Miranda had not even noticed. She was looking at Mrs Leslie with eyes that were bright with anger, and she said the first thing that came into her head. 'So you knew him well enough to call him by his Christian name, did you? Then why did you pretend that you had never met him before?'

Mrs Leslie turned to stare at her. 'What *are* you talking about?'

'Brigadier Brindley. You've just accused Stella of killing him.'

'Brigadier Brindley? You must be mad! I said she'd killed Johnnie Radley, her first husband. And it's quite true.'

'I don't think you know what you're talking about,' said Miranda icily. 'Stella's first husband was killed in Libya in 1941. He got a posthumous V.C. I've read the citation. I think it is you who must be mad!'

Mrs Leslie gave a short mirthless laugh.

'It's odd how women like that can always get people to stick up for them. And people like Johnnie — and Robert — to marry them ...'

Her voice cracked a little on the last word, as though she was suddenly near tears, and all at once Miranda was sorry for her. There was some tragedy in Norah Leslie's past; a tragedy that was still real and alive and unforgotten. Perhaps she had once loved Robert, or Johnnie Radley, or both, and had lost them in turn to this unknown Stella?

Miranda thrust her hand impulsively through the older

woman's arm and said quickly: 'You don't really know Stella at all. How could you, when you only met her for the first time about three days ago? She's a darling. Really she is; wait until you know her better, and then you'll see for yourself.'

Mrs Leslie smiled. It was a smile that did not quite reach her eyes, but her voice had lost its hard, brittle tone when she spoke: 'I'm sorry. I should not have said that. You are her cousin and her guest. It was unpardonable of me to discuss her with you. I don't know why I—— Oh well, shall we forget it? There's a shop near here where they sell all sorts of odds and ends of china and glass. Let's go in and poke about.'

The Melvilles were not mentioned again and the remainder of the morning passed pleasantly enough. Mrs Leslie dropped Miranda back at the house a little before one o'clock, and actually accepted an invitation to come in for a drink.

Stella was in the drawing-room arranging sprays of cherry blossom in a green celadon vase. She had hung her own cream brocade curtains in place of the somewhat uninspired cretonne ones supplied by the Army, her own pictures were on the walls, and the room already looked individual, elegant and essentially Stella's. She dispensed sherry and admired the tiny china roses that Miranda had bought at a junk shop, and Mrs Leslie, possibly in an effort to atone for her outburst in the Kurfürstendamm, was friendly and pleasant until Robert arrived home, when she rose abruptly, and with something of a return of her former manner said she had no idea it was so late, and left.

'You know, she's really quite a nice woman,' said Stella. 'I thought she was utterly beastly when we first met her.'

'Oh, Norah's all right,' said Robert easily. 'I wonder why she married old Leslie? Nice chap, but a bit of a bore. Funny, I always had an idea that she'd married a foreigner. But perhaps that was Sue, her kid sister. I wonder what happened to Sue? I must ask Norah.'

8

The two buses, both full of sightseers and provided with English-speaking guides, left for their tour of Berlin from the Naafi building in the Reichskanzler Platz, and rolled off down the magnificent sweep of the Kaiserdamm towards the Charlottenburg Gate and the Victory Column.

The guides began to point out places of interest. The Opera House. The heap of rubble that had been the Technical University, from the battered steps of which Hitler had stood to review his bombastic military parades. The Charlottenburg Gate ...

Miranda looked out at the shattered ruins and began to wish that she had not come. It was interesting no doubt, but also appalling. The magnificent work of men's hands — the colleges built to increase knowledge and the boastful monuments to commemorate past glories, the golden-winged Victory atop a towering column whose decoration consisted of the gilded barrels of guns captured in the Franco-Prussian war — all pockmarked and disfigured by man-made weapons of destruction, or blasted into senseless heaps of rubble.

The stupidity of it all! The waste and horror of man's inhumanity to man.

She gazed at the scowling statues of Moltke and Bismarck and Roon, joint architects of this ruin, and, a few hundred yards away, at the new Russian war memorial — a signpost pointing the way to more and greater destruction — and she shivered in the airless warmth of the overheated bus.

Above the Brandenburg Gate flew a great red flag, flapping out against the sky. 'We are now entering the Russian sector,' said the guide: 'To the left you will see the ruins of the Reichstag that the Nazis burnt as an excuse for a purge of the Communists.'

The palace of Marshal Blücher; the French Embassy; the Adlon Hotel — more ruins. Mile upon mile of ruins. The skeletons and skulls and bones of houses. The evil birds let loose on Rotterdam and Coventry, London and the Loire, Malta and Crete, and a thousand towns and hamlets of Europe, coming home to roost . . .

It will take years and years to clear all this away and build it up again, thought Miranda with horror.

'Well, they asked for it, and they certainly got it!' commented a stout lady in a puce coat and a magenta hat who was sitting next to Miranda: 'Serve 'em right, I says. But it's a proper mess, ain't it. Seems a pity some'ow.' She sighed gustily and relapsed into silence.

Marx–Engels Platz. A noticeable absence of pictures of Stalin. Lenin Allee and the headquarters of the People's Police. Stalin Allee and the First Socialist Road — the New Utopia and the New Hope personified by a long canyon of newly built and half-built apartment houses; block upon block of 'Workers' flats', identical, yellow-tiled, ugly. The Unter den Linden, that once-gay thoroughfare, now a drab street where the famous linden trees were smashed and stunted and the few pedestrians wore sullen and unsmiling faces. The Waterloo Memorial, ironic reminder of the days when the great-grandfathers of the *Luftwaffe* and the S.S. had been the admired allies of Britain.

The buses drew up outside a pair of ornamental park gates and the guide said: 'We are now at the Soviet Garden of Remembrance. It is the burial place of many hundreds of their soldiers. We may dismount here and enter the park. It is requested that you do not light cigarettes or make jokes in the sanctuary, and gentlemen who enter must remove their hats.'

Stella and Robert, who had been sitting together just behind Miranda, waited for her by the door.

'You're looking very seductive, Miranda,' commented Robert, tucking her hand under his arm. 'Isn't she, Stella? Who would have believed that such a hideously plain kid could grow up into such a delectable eyeful? When I left for Egypt she was a scruffy schoolgirl with a perpetual sniff and a gym tunic; and now look at her!'

'She looks marvellous,' agreed Stella, taking her other arm and giving it a little squeeze.

'You look pretty good yourself, darling. But far too expensive for this sort of party,' said Miranda. 'With so many red-hot comrades surging around, you look almost offensively capitalist.'

Stella laughed. 'Then it only goes to show how deceptive appearances can be!'

Her words brought back an echo of Mrs Leslie's conversation of the previous day, and Miranda frowned at the memory, and turned to look at her. She has changed, she thought; but could not be sure in what way or even why she should think so. Perhaps it was something to do with the way in which Stella looked at Robert. It was, thought Miranda, a new look and one that she had only noticed during the last few days: a strange compound of anxiety and strain; a look at once protective and possessive.

Had Sally Page been the cause?

Sally was there now, walking buoyantly on the other side of Robert and chattering in her clear, high voice; her inexpensive teenage clothes making Stella's tiny grey-feathered hat and silvery-grey fur coat appear sophisticated and expensive and mature.

Miranda looked up at Robert and was conscious of a sudden pang of anger and resentment. It wasn't fair, she thought. Robert would continue to look outrageously handsome when Stella was old and grey-haired and Sally middle-aged and faded. When Robert was sixty there would still be women who would sigh when they looked at him. His hair would be grey at the temples but they would think it added to his attractions, for the clean, beautiful planes of his face would still be there and his grey eyes would still crinkle at the corners when he smiled — as he was smiling now at Sally Page.

Robert was a darling. Good-tempered, indolent, charming and

99

entirely lacking in vanity, and Miranda had a deep affection for him. Nevertheless she was suddenly sorry for Stella.

Turning a corner, they stopped in involuntary admiration at the sight before them. They had been walking along a wide path between neatly kept flowerbeds towards a large statue of a dejected and drooping woman — 'Mother Russia mourning for her children,' murmured the guide behind them — that stood at a convergence of paths and faced a long, wide, stone-paved causeway that ended in a short flight of stone steps. Flanking the steps on either side rose a wall of polished red marble that had once formed the floors of Hitler's Chancellery, but had now been fashioned into the shape of two vast, stylized red flags, half lowered in salute to the dead.

Below each flag, and at the top of the steps, was a statue of a kneeling Russian soldier, his bared head bent in homage — statues, steps and the towering expanse of red marble dwarfing the stream of sightseers to pigmy proportions.

Robert gave a low expressive whistle, and Andy Page said, *'Crippen!'*

The expression might have been inappropriate, but the tribute was none the less sincere.

From the top of those steps they looked down upon a sunken garden with stone-paved paths that skirted grassed lawns, each lawn bearing an immense iron laurel-wreath and flanked by large blocks of stone sculptured in low relief with scenes depicting Soviet soldiers in battle, Soviet citizens being bombed by German planes and Soviet troops liberating cities. At the end of each block were inscriptions in Russian, evidently extracts of speeches by Stalin, and at the far end of the sunken garden stood a tall, grassy mound.

A steep flight of stone steps led up the face of the mound to the sanctuary; a small, circular building on its summit that was topped, and entirely thrown out of proportion, by a gigantic bronze statue of a Russian soldier, sword in hand, holding a 'liberated' child and crushing a huge broken swastika under one booted foot.

'They certainly do things in a big way,' said Andy Page, busy with a camera. 'How long do you suppose this will stand?'

'Until about five minutes after the Russians move out of East Germany, whenever that is,' said Robert. 'A pity, because it would make a magnificent ruin. Something that future ages would run tourist trips to see — like Karnak and Luxor and the Acropolis. Let's go and take a look inside that sanctuary arrangement.'

They moved down the steps towards the sunken gardens, and Miranda released Stella's arm and fell back. She did not in the least want to join the slow-moving queue of people who were filing up that steep stairway towards the tiny building on top of the mound. It gave her an unpleasant claustrophobic feeling even to look at it, for the small sanctuary seemed a wholly inadequate pedestal for the colossal bronze figure it supported, and strongly suggested that it might collapse at any moment under the strain of the weight above it.

Miranda preferred to remain outside in the sunshine and the cold spring wind.

She walked slowly round the sunken garden, looking at the bas reliefs, and presently turned into a shaded path between shrubs and flowerbeds that led away from that part of the garden.

The path was deserted except for a solitary woman wearing a small black hat and a dark red coat trimmed with black *passementerie*. And this time there was no mistaking Elsa Marson.

There was no reason why Mrs Marson should not be there. She had obviously travelled in the other bus, which accounted for the fact that Miranda had not noticed her before. But why was she behaving so oddly?

She stood at the junction of two intersecting paths and peered furtively down them, first on one side and then on the other; quivering anxiety in every line of her body and turn of her head; and when footsteps sounded from the path to her right, she shrank back, stiff and tense, until they died away again.

An entirely natural and unmentionable reason for her display of agitation occurred to Miranda, and stifling a laugh she moved

101

discreetly back round the angle of the path where a cluster of bushes and young trees provided a thin screen of leaves between herself and Mrs Marson. If anyone approached them from this direction she could at least cough loudly to warn her!

But she had been wrong about Elsa Marson.

Quick, light footsteps crunched the gravel of one of the paths, and a man wearing a shabby raincoat and a dark, peaked German cap appeared beside her.

Miranda saw him look swiftly over his shoulder to the right and left as Mrs Marson had done: a frightened, furtive look. It seemed impossible that he should have failed to see Miranda when she herself could see him so clearly through the thin screen of leaves, but he obviously did not do so, and there was that in his face, and in Elsa Marson's white-faced fear, that kept her from moving.

The man spoke quickly, but in so low a tone that she could not make out what he said or even in what language he had spoken. She saw Elsa Marson's stiff lips move in reply, and once again the man threw a swift, hunted look around him. Then drawing a small packet from under his coat, he handed it to Mrs Marson, and turning on his heel walked quickly away.

Elsa Marson opened her capacious handbag and stowed the packet away with trembling fingers. Even at this distance Miranda could see that her hands were shaking uncontrollably. She managed to shut the clasp, and then with another hunted look up and down the paths, she turned and hurried away in the opposite direction to which the unknown man had gone.

Miranda remained where she was, staring down the deserted path. What *had* Elsa Marson been up to? Stories of the notorious Berlin black market flashed across her brain: was that why she had looked so frightened? Had Harry Marson accompanied his wife on the conducted tour, and if so, where was he?

A bank of cloud had come over the sun and the day was suddenly cold and drab. Miranda shivered.

'Bird's nesting?' inquired a gentle voice behind her. Miranda started violently and whipped round.

'Captain Lang!'

'Simon, to you.'

'What are you doing here?'

'Oh, just seeing the sights you know.'

'And keeping an eye on your suspects at the same time, I suppose!' said Miranda angrily.

'That, of course — among other things.' He met her indignant gaze with a bland look that held a trace of amusement; though whether the amusement was directed against her or himself she could not be sure.

She said abruptly: 'Why did you go in for a job like this? Being a policeman. Did you have to?'

'Frankly, because I like it. For an unspectacular type with a morbid taste for drama and the seamy side of life, it offers a pleasurable escape from monotony. Or were you merely inquiring as to whether I have an adequate private income? It's all right. I have.'

Miranda turned and began to walk rapidly away down the path, Simon Lang beside her.

'What are we training for?' he inquired after a moment. 'The quarter mile, or London-to-Brighton?'

Miranda's sense of the ridiculous overcame her temper, and she laughed.

'That's better,' approved Simon. 'Now suppose we walk gently back to the bus at a normal pace.' He glanced at his wristwatch and said: 'We've got about five minutes more here.'

'How did you get here?' demanded Miranda.

'The same way as you did. As a matter of fact, in the same bus.'

'But I didn't see you!'

'Why should you? I'm a very unobtrusive sort of chap,' said Simon Lang regretfully.

'Only when it suits you!' retorted Miranda tartly. And stopped suddenly to turn to look at him: 'Why is it,' she demanded, puzzled, 'that I always seem to quarrel with you?'

Simon Lang looked slightly surprised. 'Do you? I can't remember quarrelling with you.'

'Oh, *you* don't quarrel,' said Miranda impatiently. 'I can't imagine you quarrelling with anyone. You're too – too——'

'Dull?' offered Simon Lang.

'I was going to say "lazy". Or too detached.'

'Let's just say that I have a nice, peaceable disposition.' He took her arm and turned her into a long, gravelled path that ran parallel with the paved way that led up to the red marble flags: 'You only try to quarrel with me because you feel on the defensive. There's no need for you to be you know. I'm not your enemy.'

'Then why do you behave like one?' said Miranda with a quiver in her voice. 'If you don't suspect me, why don't you tell me things straight out?'

'What sort of things?' asked Simon gently.

'Things like why you had my room searched, and why you have followed me here and——'

'What's that?' Simon's voice was suddenly sharp and he stopped dead and pulled Miranda round to face him: 'When was your room searched?'

'While you were so conveniently interviewing me in the lounge of the hostel, I imagine,' said Miranda bitterly. 'Or are you going to pretend that you didn't know anything about it? Surely your underlings don't do anything like that without orders, or a search-warrant or something?'

'Wednesday afternoon ...' murmured Simon Lang. He was looking directly at Miranda but his eyes appeared curiously blank and opaque as though they did not see her but were looking inwards at some picture in his mind.

A knot of East Berliners in the drab clothes and shabby rain-coats that seemed to be almost a uniform of the sector passed by and stared at them curiously, but Simon did not move.

'What is it?' asked Miranda uncertainly.

His eyes seemed to focus her again and his fingers tightened about her arm. 'I don't know. That's the devil of it. Listen to me,

Miranda, if anything like that ever happens again — or anything odd or unusual — will you tell me at once? I mean that. This isn't just a social gesture of the "let me know if there's anything I can do to help" variety. This is important.'

He did not wait for an answer, but releasing her arm, took a small flat leather-bound notebook out of his pocket, and having scribbled something on a leaf of it in pencil, ripped the page out and gave it to her: 'That's my personal telephone number. If I'm not there myself there will always be someone who is and who can contact me.'

He glanced at his watch again and said: 'If we don't get a move on, we shall find that the bus has got tired of waiting for us and we're stranded behind the Iron Curtain. In fact here, I think, is a search party.'

Sally Page ran towards them, waving. 'Where on earth have you been?' she panted. 'We're all waiting for you and the driver is fuming. We thought you'd been kidnapped by the Kremlin or something. Do hurry!'

The remainder of the tour was uneventful. They did not again leave the bus, but were driven through the American sector, past the Tempelhof airfield where something like a huge, curving, three-fingered hand groped helplessly at the impersonal sky, and was, the guide explained, a memorial to the Airlift: an 'abstract' in concrete, symbolizing the three air corridors by which West Berlin had been fed and fuelled during the Russian blockade of the Allied sector.

More ruins; a honeycomb of roofless, ruined walls like a modern stage setting for hell.

The Kurfürstendamm; the Haffensee Brücke; the tall, steel trellis work of the Funkturm. The Reichskanzler Platz once more, and the parked cars waiting to take the sightseers to their homes in the swiftly gathering dusk.

9

It was raining again next morning, and Robert drove his family
to morning service at St George's in a steady downpour.

Stella huddled the collar of her fur coat about her ears, its
delicate silver-grey exactly matching the heavy rain outside the car
windows. She looked cold and tired, and the eye-veil of her smart
little hat failed to disguise the dark shadows of sleeplessness under
her blue eyes.

Mademoiselle, lean and taciturn in black, also appeared to
be in poor spirits. She had discovered, with considerable annoy-
ance, that the Wilkins lived in a small house less than a quarter
of a mile from the Melvilles, and Wally, exploring the neighbour-
hood, had been caught by Mademoiselle on the previous afternoon plastering Charlotte's face with coal dust in the Melvilles'
boiler-room. Mademoiselle had pursued him, armed with one
of the boiler-room pokers, but Wally had been too quick for
her.

The three houses now occupied by the Melvilles, Leslies and
Marsons had previously been lived in by three families whose
children had been inseparable friends, and gaps in the hedges and
the wire that separated each garden from the next had been made
for their convenience, so that they could go from one garden to
the next without running out into the road. These gaps still remained open, and Wally had darted through the one in the
Melvilles' hedge and escaped across the Leslies' lawn and by way
of the Marsons' garden into the no-man's-land beyond.

Mademoiselle had been forced to abandon the pursuit, and had
not been appeased by Charlotte's assertion that she had *asked*

106

Wally to make her face black, as how could she be Eliza crossing the ice with a white face?

Despite the rain there was a large congregation, and Miranda, glancing surreptitiously around her during the singing of the psalm, saw that they were all there — Simon Lang's eleven suspects. We ought to get up a cricket team, thought Miranda wryly: 'Suspects versus the Rest'.

She did not realize that Simon was also present until the service ended and the congregation were streaming out of the church. She had not seen him out of uniform before and thought how different and unfamiliar he looked in a dark suit.

I suppose he's keeping an eye on us, even in church! she thought bitterly; and then remembered what Simon had said of her only the day before. She was being on the defensive again.

Stella stopped to speak to him while Robert went to fetch the car, and Miranda said sweetly: 'I didn't recognize you without your uniform.'

'I practise being a plain-clothes man on Sundays,' explained Simon Lang, straightfaced. He turned back to Stella, and Miranda walked quickly over to the car, feeling both snubbed and childish.

The rain had stopped and there were patches of blue sky overhead, and a rainbow drew a gleaming arc over the distant skeleton tower of the Funkturm. The air held a fresh, clean smell as of newly mixed mortar — that characteristic smell of Berlin on a wet day, that has its origin in rain falling on mile after mile of rubble.

They did not go straight back to the house, but drove instead to the Lawrences: Mrs Lawrence having buttonholed Robert and asked them to come in after the service for drinks.

Colonel Lawrence, in contrast to his wife, was small, thin and vague, and looked more like the popular idea of an atom scientist than the commanding officer of a regiment. He obviously did not know who Miranda was, or catch her name, but he smiled kindly, pressed a glass into her hand and made a few observations on the weather before drifting off to meet more of his wife's guests.

'What did you think of old Snoozy?' inquired Robert, exchang-

107

ing Miranda's pink gin — a form of drink that she detested — for a tomato juice. 'The Colonel. He always behaves like that on social occasions, but don't let it fool you. It's protective colouring. He loathes large gatherings, unless they are strictly in the way of business.'

'Like Simon,' said Miranda thoughtfully.

'Like who? Oh, you mean Lang? I shouldn't have thought he hated large gatherings.'

Miranda flushed. 'I didn't mean that. I meant what you said about protective colouring. He seems to have quite a lot of that.'

Robert looked interested. 'I think I see what you mean. You don't notice him unless he wants you to.'

'That's it,' approved Miranda. She slipped her hand through his arm and smiled at him. 'Oh Robert, you are such a comfortable person! I don't have to explain things to you.'

Robert grinned affectionately at her. 'Probably something to do with blood being thicker than water,' he suggested. 'Are you by any chance getting interested in young Simon Stylites?'

'He's interested in me!' said Miranda bitterly. 'And not in the way you mean, either!'

'You mean you think he suspects you of having bumped off the Brigadier? Don't you believe it! If he's given you that impression you can take it from me that he's after something quite different. That young man has not acquired a reputation as the best poker player in the combined British, French and American sectors for nothing. You should hear "Lootenant" Decker on the subject. Hank Decker says it's plumb against all the laws of nature that a limey should be able to clean out a bunch of boys who cut their teeth on poker chips and could say "I'll raise you" before they could say "Da-da"!'

Miranda did not smile. She was silent for a moment, and then she said abruptly: 'Robert, who do *you* think did it?'

Robert did not answer her. He was looking past Miranda to someone behind her, and she saw his mouth tighten queerly as

Sally Page's clear voice cut through the babble of talk and the clink of glasses.

'I'm so sorry we're late, but Andy had to go down to the office about something.'

Robert's eyes came back to Miranda. 'I'm sorry — what did you say?'

Miranda repeated the question.

'Stuck a knife into the Brigadier, you mean? God knows! Some nasty little ex-Nazi I suppose. I'd stop worrying about it if I were you 'Randa.'

'But Simon Lang says it could only have been one of the people who went to the Families' Hostel in Bad Oeynhausen; because of the knife. And that means us — those of us who dined there I mean.'

'Oh yes, I heard that too. But I don't believe it means a thing. Look at that bunch of kids for instance. Any one of them might have walked off with the paperknife — you know what a fascination knives have for children — and then got bored with it and dropped it on the platform or in the corridor or the loo. Forget it sweetie!'

He smiled down at her anxious face and covered the hand on his arm with one of his own in a brief and comforting pressure.

Miranda grinned at him affectionately, and looking away, encountered Simon Lang's coolly observant gaze.

She had not realized he was here and the discovery came as something of a shock. He was standing at the far side of the room near the door that led into the hall, and he did not make any attempt to disguise the fact that he had been watching her. His face was unsmiling and his eyes, across the width of the room, were very bright. He looked, thought Miranda, as though a new and interesting idea had suddenly occurred to him.

She tried to stare calmly back at him, but could not do it; and after a moment her gaze wavered and turned aside. Her hand tightened convulsively on Robert's sleeve and Robert said: 'I can't think why we should be having such a gloomy conversation at a

Sunday morning beer party. Let's talk about something cheerful
... Hullo, Norah!'

Miranda released his arm and turned to see Mrs Leslie, wearing
a distressingly sensible tweed suit, standing beside her.

'We saw you in church,' said Robert. 'Is your husband here?'

'Yes. He's gone into a huddle with your C.O. and one or two
others in the dining-room. They appear to be talking shop as
usual. Good-morning, Miranda.'

Mrs Leslie smiled at Miranda and sat down on the arm of a
chair. 'Do you think you could get me a glass of sherry, Robert?'
I do so dislike beer before luncheon.'

Robert departed in the direction of the dining-room, and Mrs
Leslie turned to Miranda.

'Well, what do you think of Berlin? I hear you went on a
conducted tour yesterday.'

'Interesting, but very depressing,' said Miranda. 'It looks as if
it would take a hundred years to clear up the mess. It must have
been a beautiful city once.'

'It wasn't. Imposing perhaps — bits of it — but not beautiful.
And you're wrong when you say it will take a hundred years to
restore it. You don't know the Germans! Frankly, they terrify me.'

'Terrify you? Why? Do you think they'll go Nazi again?'

'Oh, I'm not worrying about their politics. It's their industry
that frightens me. Haven't you noticed it yet? My dear, in our last
army house at home we had to have the place painted and a few
odd jobs done. It took over a month; and a large proportion of
that time was spent making and drinking tea. It took three full
days to put a gate up, and a fourth morning to come back and fetch
the tools that had been left behind because it was a nuisance
carrying tools in a bus during the rush hour!'

'At least you weren't paying for it yourself,' said Miranda with
a laugh.

'My dear girl,' said Norah Leslie tartly, 'you miss the point.
Someone was paying for it. And it was pretty slipshod work at that,
let me tell you! I could have done most of it myself single-handed

in half the time and for a quarter of the money. Our country is still too intent upon its tea-breaks and its next pay rise to buckle to. But not the Germans! Have you watched them build a house out here? I have and it scares me. No tea-breaks or "go slow", or a good workman being forbidden by his union to lay more bricks than a mediocre one. No five-day week either! They are willing and eager to work flat out. I watch a gang of German workmen spitting on their hands, and I get a cold feeling in the pit of my stomach. These people are finding their feet again and bursting with confidence. They know where they are going, and just exactly how soon they'll get there. And that's going to be too soon for a lot of us! Oh, thank you, Robert!'

'I seem to have slopped it about a bit,' apologized Robert.

Mrs Leslie removed her gloves and accepted the glass gingerly.

'It's nice to see you again, Norah,' said Robert leaning on the back of the chair: 'I thought I'd see something of you in Fayid, but you went home to take a child to school or some-thing, and I never saw you at all; except once in the middle distance. Amazing really how families who live next door to each other for years can lose touch completely as soon as one of them moves away. The war had a lot to do with it I suppose.'

'Partly that; and of course I was abroad a great deal,' said Mrs Leslie. 'I heard news of you from time to time, and I saw the announcement of your marriage in the *Telegraph* of course.'

'That's where women have the advantage of us,' said Robert with a laugh. 'Not many men read the Births, Marriages and Deaths columns — or not until they reach the age when it's only the last of those that interests them! When were you married, Norah?'

'I married Edward in 1948,' said Mrs Leslie.

'Good Lord! You're a mere bride! I imagined you'd been married for years.'

'My first husband was killed in the war. You and I, Robert, have both married twice.'

'Oh!... Oh — er — yes,' said Robert. He appeared momentarily disconcerted. 'That reminds me,' he said after a perceptible pause, 'where's Lottie, 'Randa? I hope she's not creating mayhem somewhere?'

'She's in the garden with the Lawrence children. They're being policed by Mademoiselle,' said Miranda.

'Thank God for that!'

Mrs Leslie laughed. 'The penalties of fatherhood catching up on you, Robert?'

'You're telling me!' said Robert. 'By the way, how are your parents, Norah? And Sue?'

There was an infinitesimal pause before Mrs Leslie answered. Then: 'They're dead,' she said flatly.

She stood up abruptly and handed him her empty glass, and Robert said: 'I'm sorry, Norah.'

'You needn't be,' said Mrs Leslie. She nodded at Miranda, retrieved the gloves that had fallen off her lap onto the chair, and walked quickly away across the crowded room.

'That was obviously an unfortunate question,' said Robert slowly. 'But how the hell is one to know? Oh, well——' He shrugged his shoulders and turned away, and a little later Miranda saw him talking to Sally Page. He was looking young and gay and insufferably handsome, and once again, as in the Soviet Garden of Remembrance, Miranda was conscious of a sudden pang of irritation and anxiety.

She was for the moment alone and could allow her attention to wander, and it was perhaps because of this that she became aware that from different parts of the room three other people were also watching Robert. Stella with a little anxious frown on her white forehead, Andy Page with a sullen scowl, and Norah Leslie with a curiously speculative look. And that from the open doorway that led into the dining-room Colonel Leslie was watching his wife; his expression a mirror-image of her own.

With a confused idea that she should do something about it, Miranda edged her way through the chattering guests towards

Stella, but just before she reached her an unknown man claimed her attention and Miranda turned instead to Andy Page.

Andy Page was a slim young man who looked as though he should have been an artist or a writer, or a newspaper correspondent. Almost anything but a soldier. A stray lock of hair was perpetually falling over his forehead, giving his thin features something of the look of a young stage genius, and even when in uniform there clung about him a vaguely Bohemian air.

But Andy Page was anything but a genius. He was in fact a fairly ordinary and rather likeable young man of no more than average intelligence, and people were apt to wonder why such an outstandingly pretty creature as Sally Barclay had ever married him: forgetting that he was probably the first man she had had a chance to fall in love with; Sally being barely seventeen when she met him, and having married him, in the teeth of parental opposition, three days after her eighteenth birthday.

'Hullo, Andy,' said Miranda gaily. 'What did you think of the conducted tour yesterday? Do you think you got any good photographs?'

Andy turned quickly. He would really be quite good-looking if he didn't look so sulky, thought Miranda — and smiled at him.

Miranda's long lashes tilted charmingly when she smiled, and the ghost of a dimple accented the lovely curve of a mouth that Rossetti might have painted. Her shining hair curled about an absurd little hat that was no more than a triangle of topaz velvet that matched her deceptively simple woollen frock and brought a glint of sherry-coloured light into her grey eyes. Andy Page was only human. His scowl vanished and he smiled back at her.

'I hope so. It's quite a good camera. A bit elderly, of course, but I can't afford a better one just now. You know, Miranda, if I thought I could get away with it I'd go into the black-market racket in a big way, if only to get my hands on some of those new German cameras. They're marvels! Do you know what I'd like to do?'

His face was suddenly animated and his eyes bright, and for a moment he looked as young, or younger, than Sally: 'I'd like to chuck the Army and take up photography. The sort of thing Beaton and Schiavone and Olins do. It fascinates me! I buy up all the fashion magazines I can get my hands on just to gloat over those photographs. I saw some Italian ones the other day — outdoor ones of cottons, taken in Rome, in a wind. All movement and light. Terrific!'

He sighed, and the enthusiasm drained out of his face and his voice went flat again: 'Oh, what's the use? I shall never do it.'

He looked Miranda up and down and said abruptly: 'Your clothes always make everyone else's look too fussy. Even that bundle of junk you wear on your wrist looks all right on you, though I detest jangling charm bracelets on most women.'

Miranda laughed. 'Thank you, Andy. I expect it's because I can afford so few clothes that I have to choose really plain ones that not only look good, but wear well.'

'I wish you'd tell Sally that,' said Andy moodily. 'God knows I can't afford to give her a decent dress-allowance, but she will buy things that look all right the first time she wears them and pretty dreadful ever after.'

'When you are as pretty as Sally it doesn't matter what you wear,' said Miranda firmly. 'If she wore a sugar sack she'd look lovely in it, and you know it!'

'Sugar sacks are about what she'll be reduced to at the present rate,' said Andy bitterly. 'That is if——' He stopped suddenly in mid-sentence and flushed, and Miranda, in a praiseworthy attempt to change the conversation, asked after the new flat. But the topic was not a success. Andy replied morosely that it was sordid and uncomfortable, but that he supposed that they would just have to pig it there for a year.

Miranda was saved the necessity of commenting upon this gloomy statement by the appearance of Stella. Mademoiselle and Lottie, said Stella, were already in the car, and Robert was waiting to drive them home. Miranda gave Andy what she hoped was an encouraging smile, and departed.

*

114

Rain fell again during the afternoon, but towards evening the sky cleared and sunlight glittered on the wet rooftops.

'Who's for a walk?' asked Robert. 'We could all do with some fresh air after stuffing indoors the entire day. Lottie and Mademoiselle can come too.'

They set off down the road, choosing the direction at random and taking any turning that seemed promising, and some five minutes later met the Leslies, who turned and walked with them along the clean-washed streets that glistened with rain.

Early cherry blossom and deep pink almond frothed among the wet spring leaves in the late evening sunlight, and at first, in contrast to most of Berlin, the roads down which they went seemed to be singularly untouched by war. But presently between the neat houses with their white-painted gates and green gardens there appeared gaping, weed-grown spaces where other houses had once stood and where only ruined walls and fallen rubble now remained.

'What's that?' inquired Miranda, pointing to a long, low hill just visible above the distant treetops. 'Were there houses on there once?'

Colonel Leslie, to whom the question had been addressed, shook his head. 'It is houses.'

'I mean the hill over there.'

'So do I. It wasn't there before the war. It has been made from the rubble of bombed houses. Every day lorry-loads of rubble are brought from the ruins and dumped there. And that is the second hill! The first one already has grass and greenstuff growing on it. In winter the Berliners ski on them, and there will come a time when people will have forgotten how they came to be there and accept them as natural features of the landscape.'

'How gruesome!' said Stella.

'Why? The London that we know is built on the ruins of many earlier Londons.'

'"Cities and Thrones and Powers stand in Time's eye almost as long as flowers——"' quoted Miranda under her breath.

' "—which daily die".' Colonel Leslie finished the quotation for her. 'Yes, one must not take the close view of these things, but try to look at them with the eye of history.'

'But that's so cold-blooded,' protested Stella.

'One should be cold-blooded,' said Colonel Leslie. 'Hot-blooded people are responsible for two-thirds of the world's tragedies. An action done in hot blood is merely violent and frequently messy. Those performed in cold blood are at least calculated, and probably, in the long run, necessary.'

'I'm no good at arguing,' said Stella, 'so I'm not going to try. Lottie, darling, don't walk through all the puddles, there's an angel-chick. Isn't that the Marsons, Robert?'

They had turned into a quiet street overshadowed by trees. Along one side ran a high wall with the tops of trees showing above it, while on the other was the gutted ruin of a house standing in what must once have been a large and well-kept garden bounded by a shoulder-high wall and a tangle of laurels. Gazing in at the ruin through a rusty wrought-iron gate were Harry and Elsa Marson.

Harry Marson turned and waved as they approached: 'Hullo, have you come to see the cross that marks the spot where the accident occurred? Elsa wanted to see it too.'

'What accident?' inquired Miranda.

'*The* accident, of course. Do you mean to say you didn't know? This is it. Herr Whatisname's house. The character who bumped off his domestic staff and decamped with a Rockefeller's ransom in Dutch diamonds.'

'Is it really? What a thrill! Let's go in and have a look.'

They pushed open the rusty gate and walked up a sunken, weed-grown path to where a short flight of steps led up to the gaping space where a front door had once been. The button of the doorbell was still there, a white china circle incongruously bright and unbroken against the blackened stone.

The bomb that had hit the house had caused less damage than the fire that had followed, and the greater part of the building was still standing. 'No. Don't go in!' warned Colonel Leslie sharply, pulling Miranda back. 'It isn't safe to go exploring this sort of ruin. Everything might cave in at any moment. That's why most of these bomb-damaged buildings carry warning notices — like that one ...' He pointed with his walking-stick at a weather-worn notice-board, half-hidden by weeds, near the foot of the steps.

Sun had blistered and faded the once-bright letters, and wind, rain and snow had combined to make them barely legible. But it was till possible to read the red-printed warning *ACHTUNG!* that headed it, and, further down, another favourite and all-too-familiar word *Verboten*. Though exactly what was forbidden was by now in doubt.

'Not that it matters,' concluded the Colonel, commenting on that fact, 'because no one who's been in this country for longer than half an hour could fail to realize what those two words mean. And in this case it's sound advice — "Keep out!" '

'Yes, *do* let's!' agreed Stella with a shudder. 'Besides, it's getting late. Mademoiselle, will you start back with Lottie? Come on, 'Randa.'

She tugged at Miranda's arm, and as they went back down the steps to the path, the others following, Harry Marson suggested a visit to the garage.

Weeds had grown up about it and weather and rain had left their mark on the walls that the builders had left unfinished before the fall of France. 'But you can still see where the lime pit was,' said Harry Marson, poking about interestedly among the weeds and rubble.

No one else appeared to share his enthusiasm. They stood in silence, looking at the discoloured walls and the tangle of weeds.

The sun had been moving swiftly down the sky and now, as they stood in the deserted garden, it dipped behind the long hill of rubble that rose behind the far trees, and left the weed-grown garden and the shell of the ruined house to the cold spring twilight.

'I wonder if they'll ever come back?' mused Harry Marson. 'The Ridders, I mean.'

'To haunt it?' said Stella with a shiver.

'Oh Lord, no! I mean, if they're still alive. They say that murderers always return to the scene of their crime. It has some fatal attraction that draws them back like a trout on a long cast. For all we know they may be here now, in Berlin. Perhaps they walk down this road and peer furtively over the wall in the dusk and picture it all happening again.'

His voice had dropped to a half-whisper and, involuntarily, Miranda looked quickly over her shoulder, as though she thought that someone might even now be peering through the rusty gates.

And there was someone — a shadowy figure, barely distinguishable in the deepening twilight, standing just within the gateway and half-hidden by the straggling laurels.

The next moment it had gone; so swiftly and noiselessly that Miranda wondered for a moment if there had really been anyone there, or if some trick of the fading light had made her imagine it.

'Harry, stop! I do not like it!' said Elsa Marson with sudden violence. 'Let us go away now. This is not a good place.'

'Yes, let's!' said Stella fervently. 'I couldn't agree with you more. Come on, or it will be dark before we get home.'

She took Robert's arm and they turned and walked away across the silent garden and out into the quiet road.

10

'Did I tell you that I'm having tea with Mrs Lawrence this after-noon?' asked Stella, helping herself to cheese: 'It seems she's having several of the wives over. Some sort of committee meeting of Welfare, I gather. And we shall be cook-less this evening because Frau Herbach wants to leave early today. I told her we'd have hot soup with a cold supper and she can leave it ready. Friedel can deal with that. It's your half-day isn't it, Mademoiselle? What are you going to do?'

'I shall go me to the British Centre,' said Mademoiselle. 'One tells me that they have the books there and many lectures.'

'How nice,' said Stella absently. 'All right, Lottie darling, I'm sure Mademoiselle won't mind your getting down if you've finished. Now don't be a nuisance this afternoon, there's a sweetie, because Mademoiselle and I are both going to be out.'

Stella left the house shortly before three o'clock: 'I have to be there at three,' she explained, 'but I shan't be back late — unless I get arrested for bad driving! Robert left me the car, but as I've never had to drive on the right-hand side of the road before I shall proceed at a slow crawl. If you don't hear of me before eight o'clock you'd better ring up the police and tell them that they've got another body on their hands!'

She went out of the front door, banging it behind her, and Miranda, reminded of something, plunged her hand into the pocket of her grey suit. Yes, it was still there; the small square of paper on which Simon Lang had written down his telephone number in the Soviet Garden of Remembrance. Miranda smoothed it out and stared at it for a moment, frowning, and then crumpling it into a small pellet tossed it into the waste-paper basket with the air of one who is mentally saying 'So there!'

The drawing-room door opened behind her and Norah Leslie walked into the hall.

'On, there you are! I hope you don't mind me walking in on you like this, but it's so much shorter to come through the gap in the hedge. I came over to ask if you'd have supper with us this evening. We're having a few of our subalterns in, and I want some pretty young things to entertain them. Sally Page is coming because Andy has to dine in some Mess, and I've got the General's niece. Now don't say you won't come! I'm sure the Melvilles would like an evening to themselves.'

Miranda laughed. 'I expect they would. Thank you. I'd love to come.'

'Good. Then that's fixed. See you at about a quarter to eight. Short frock.'

Mrs Leslie turned and left by the way that she had come, through the open french window in the drawing-room, and Miranda was about to settle down with a book when she was once more interrupted; this time by the ringing of a bell. She put down her book, wondering idly if it was the telephone or the front door, and hoping that Friedel had heard it, when she heard Mademoiselle come out of the cloakroom and lift the receiver.

' *'ullo? Oui!* . . . Ah, Major Melville! . . . Madame is not here. She takes the tea with Madame Lawrence . . . Law-rence. The wife of Monsieur le Colonel . . . That I know not. M'selle Brand is here . . . *Oui* . . . *Merci.*'

The receiver was replaced and Mademoiselle appeared in the drawing-room, gloved and hatted and clasping a tightly rolled umbrella.

'It is Monsieur le Major,' she announced. 'He reports him that he will not be able to return for supper this evening, but must work late at the office. He will try to inform Madame.'

'Thank you, Mademoiselle. Just tell Frau Herbach that there'll only be one for supper tonight. I shall be out too, I'm having supper with Colonel and Mrs Leslie.'

'*Bien*.' Mademoiselle withdrew, and a few minutes later Miranda heard the front door close behind her.

The house was quiet and peaceful and Miranda stretched out on the window-seat and relaxed in the warm afternoon sunshine, feeling pleasantly drowsy and temporarily free from that haunting sense of uneasiness that had twitched furtively at her nerves ever since she had started on the journey towards Berlin.

Her eyes closed, and she was on the verge of sleep when a sound from outside the window aroused her.

There were bushes immediately below the drawing-room windows, except in front of the single french window, and something or someone was crawling between those bushes and the wall. Miranda knelt up cautiously on the window-seat and looked out. The next minute she had leaned out over the sill and grasped the belt of a grubby pair of corduroy shorts.

There was a shrill squeal, and Miranda jerked her captive to its feet.

'Wally Wilkin! What are you doing here?'

Miranda shook him, and the large crêpe-hair moustache and beard with which his countenance was adorned fell off and was lost among the bushes.

'*Now* look wot you done!' said Wally indignantly.

'Never mind about those whiskers. What do you mean by crawling round the house like this, young Wally?'

'I'm detecting,' replied Wally sulkily.

'You're what?'

'Lookin' fer cloos.'

'Oh you are, are you. What sort of clues? And why here?'

'' Cos I 'av to keep an eye on me suspecs. That's why.'

'Oh, I see. This is a game you're playing.'

'Game? *Naw!*' said Wally indignantly. 'I jus' told you: I'm seein' if I can solve this 'ere case.'

'What case?'

121

'Why the murder, o' course!' explained Wally in disgust. 'That old bloke on the train.'

'Well, Dick Barton, would it be too much to ask you to take your magnifying glass and go and detect somewhere else? I hate to seem inhospitable, but I could do with a bit of sleep this afternoon.'

Miranda relaxed her grip, but Wally made no move to escape. He leant his grubby elbows on the windowsill and lowering his voice to a hoarse and confidential undertone, informed her that it was his ambition to join the secret service when he grew up, and that this being so, it was necessary to put in a bit of practice.

'That's the stuff!' approved Miranda. 'And have you solved this case yet?'

A sudden look of caution came over the grubby, freckled face, and the blue eyes were all at once shrewd and wary: 'Maybe I 'av, and maybe I 'aven't,' said Wally slowly. 'I ain't talking yet. But I gotta cloo.'

'Have you, indeed! And what have you done with it?'

'It ain't that sort of cloo. It's a thing I knows; not somethink I 'as.'

'Is that so?' said Miranda, politely. 'And what are you doing crawling round in the bushes, Detective Inspector? Collecting more clues?'

Wally nodded, and remarked with satisfaction that it was very useful having most of his suspects living next door to each other. Adding a rider to the effect that he could crawl round all three houses without showing up at all.

'Do you mean you've been snooping round our houses?' demanded Miranda. 'Wally, you're going to land the father and mother of a walloping one day if Colonel Leslie or Major Marson catches you!'

'They're out,' said Wally smugly. 'I can get up to that balcony, too. An' Mrs Leslie's! I did yesterday. S'easy!'

'You *what*? Why, you little horror! Don't you ever do it again!'

'I may 'av to,' said Wally darkly.

'Then let me tell you, Inspector Wilkin,' said Miranda energetically, 'that if ever I find you've been climbing up to the balconies and snooping in at the bedroom windows again, I shall go after you with a good stout stick. So now you know!'

'*Women!*' said Wally bitterly.

'I'm sorry,' said Miranda, softening. 'But I can't have you snooping round people's rooms, Wally. It isn't' — she hesitated for a word and finished rather lamely — 'British.'

'The secret service 'as to snoop,' said Wally austerely. 'Where'd us British be if we didn't? Beat by the Russians an' the Japs, and the F.B.I., that's wot!'

'It's quite a point,' conceded Miranda. 'But even a detective inspector has to have a search-warrant before he can search anyone's house, you know.'

'Okay,' said Wally resignedly. He scrambled about in the bushes, and having retrieved the crêpe-hair beard, regarded it doubtfully, remarking that it couldn't be much good for she had recognized him at once.

'Try something a bit less conspicuous next time,' recommended Miranda.

'I *could* try paintin' myself green so I wouldn't show up in the bushes?' suggested Wally. 'Camyflage — like them "commandos" use. There's a big tin o' green paint in the garidge of the Marsons' 'ouse: I saw it when I was detectin' this morning — I could swipe a bit o' that, easy.'

'Don't attempt it,' advised Miranda earnestly. 'Just think how you'd show up against things like walls and gravel. If I were you I'd stick to plain-clothes detecting. All the real experts do.'

'P'raps you're right,' conceded Wally, stuffing his unsatisfactory disguise into his pocket.

'Hullo, Wally. What are you doing behind there?' inquired Lottie, appearing round the corner of the house.

'I bin talkin' to your aunt,' said Wally with dignity.

'She isn't my aunt. She's my cousin,' contradicted Lottie.

'She isn't, neither! "*She's*" the cat's mother!' retorted Wally triumphantly. He wriggled through the bushes and they disappeared in the direction of the sandpit, wrangling amicably.

Friedel brought in tea on a tray at 4.30, and an hour later Stella phoned to say that she would not be back for supper: 'Robert has to work late, so we thought perhaps we'd have supper at the Club,' explained Stella. 'You don't mind do you, darling? Oh, and another thing: Friedel asked me if she could go out for an hour or two this evening and I said she could. Of course, I didn't know I'd be out then. You won't mind keeping an eye on Lottie, will you? Friedel will put her to bed. It's just that someone has to be in the house ... Sweet of you, darling. I must fly. I'll try not to be too late.'

There was a click and Stella had rung off.

'Well, that's that!' said Miranda. She would have to let Mrs Leslie know that she couldn't come, for if Stella had already given Friedel permission to go out, she, Miranda, could hardly countermand it. She opened the phone book and dialled Mrs Leslie's number, but it was Colonel Leslie who answered the phone and accepted Miranda's explanation and apologies without demur.

Miranda put down the receiver and went in search of Friedel.

'I go out when I have put Lottie to bed,' said Friedel. 'And your supper I put ready at a quarter to eight, yes? I am not gone more than the one hour. By nine o'clock I am back. I will make the back door to lock and then only the front door needs by itself stay open.'

'Will you tuck me in please?' requested Lottie. 'I don't think I like German mattresses, do you? They only tuck in in bits.'

'They aren't German mattresses,' said Miranda. 'No self-respecting German would dream of sleeping on one. They're army-issue mattresses. Biscuits.'

'Biscuits?' said Lottie, fascinated. 'Do you mean you can *akshually* eat them?'

'No, of course not, silly! It's only because they look like big square dog biscuits.'

'Oh. Why doesn't the Army have proper mattresses?'

'Goodness knows!' said Miranda. 'Now are you all fixed?'

'No. Rollerbear has fallen out.'

Miranda stooped and retrieved the small white china bear that was Lottie's chiefest treasure. Rollerbear measured some three inches in length and had once decorated the top of some forgotten Christmas cake, and for some unaccountable reason Lottie loved him above all her other toys. He accompanied her everywhere and spent every night tucked under her pillow.

'Rollerbear doesn't like these mattresses either,' said Lottie. 'He falls down the sides, over'n over. Good-night, Cousin 'Randa.'

'Good-night, puss-cat. Sleep tight.' Miranda switched off the light and went out, leaving the door ajar.

Across the landing was the big double bedroom that was Robert's and Stella's. The door was not quite shut and Miranda noticed that the bedroom light had been left burning.

She walked across the landing and pushed open the door, but either her eyes must have played a trick on her or else the head-lights of a passing car had flashed across the windows, for the room was in darkness.

Miranda closed the door, turned off the landing light that shone too strongly into Lottie's half-open door, and more from habit than for any other reason, changed her grey suit for the dress of topaz-coloured wool that she had worn the previous day, before going downstairs.

The drawing-room curtains had not been drawn and the room was in darkness, but beyond the windows the garden was full of cold spring moonlight and black shadows. Somewhere in the house a door shut quietly and Miranda turned away and went into the hall.

Friedel came out of the kitchen and said that the soup was on the table and that she had put cold meat and salad on the side-board. She had locked the back door, and would be back soon.

Miranda went into the dining-room and sat down to her solitary meal, and presently she heard light footsteps crossing the hall and the click of the front door as it closed. Friedel had gone, and she was alone in the house.

Alone in the house ... Now why should that thought suddenly disturb her and bring with it a return of the vague, troubling feeling of apprehension that had been absent from her all that sunny afternoon and quiet evening?

Besides she was not alone; Lottie was asleep upstairs.

Miranda turned her attention resolutely to the cooling soup, and having finished it, carried the empty plate to the sideboard and helped herself to cold meat and salad, making as much noise about it as possible as a protection against the silence.

The clatter of plates and knives comforted her in some obscure fashion; they made a pleasant, ordinary, everyday sound. She mixed herself a french dressing from the ingredients that Friedel had left on the table, and was pouring them over her salad when she heard soft footsteps on the landing upstairs.

For a fleeting moment her heart seemed to leap into her throat; and then she realized who had caused them and was correspondingly annoyed. She got up from the table, marched over to the door and called up to the top landing: 'Get back to bed, Lottie! It's quite time you were asleep. If I hear you out of bed again I'll come up and spank you. That's a promise!'

There was the sound of a hurried, surreptitious movement and then silence.

Miranda waited for a moment or two and then returned to her interrupted meal.

The sound of her own voice and the realization that someone else was awake in the house, even though it was only a child of seven, had temporarily dispelled her feeling of disquiet. But it did not last.

The uneasiness crept back again, and grew and spread with the silence of the quiet house. The tick of the dining-room clock seemed absurdly loud, for the noise it made was the only sound in that silence; and once again, as in the corridor of the Berlin train, Miranda found herself fighting an impulse to look over her shoulder.

126

She put down her knife and fork and was angrily aware that she had laid them down softly and with exaggerated care, and that she was holding her breath. Why should she suddenly feel that she must not make a sound — that any sound would seem frightening and overloud in that waiting silence? What was she listening for?

A board creaked overhead and Miranda's teeth clenched on her lower lip.

The quiet house, despite the stillness — or perhaps because of it? — began to fill with noises. The ticking of the clock; the sudden inexplicable creak of floors and furniture that becomes audible only by night; a moth fluttering against a windowpane, and an occasional stealthy scrabbling that sounded as though someone or something was crawling up the gutters, but that came from the central-heating pipes.

But Miranda was listening for none of these things.

She turned quickly and looked behind her; but there was no one there, and beyond the open doorway of the dining-room the hall stretched emptily away to the shadowed alcove where the telephone stood.

Miranda picked up her knife and fork again, feeling ashamed of herself for having given way to that foolish impulse, but she could not force herself to eat, and after a moment or two she laid them down once more and stared around her.

The dining-room furniture seemed to stare back at her, remote and uninterested, its varnished immobility mocking her tense and quivering awareness. She could see herself reflected dimly in the smooth panels of the sideboard, the polished table-top and the gleaming surface of a silver salver: a white, heart-shaped face with wide, terrified eyes, red mouth and dark wings of hair. A frightened girl in a sleek topaz-coloured dress.

The hideous hanging lamp above the dining-room table filled the room with harsh light, and there was no possible hiding-place in it. Even the curtains reached only as far as the window-sill, and their thin cotton folds could not have concealed a kitten.

Nevertheless, from somewhere someone was watching her. She did not know why she knew it. She only knew that she did know it; and with an absolute certainty that left no room for doubt.

Miranda stood up suddenly, pushing her chair back so violently that it fell with a crash to the floor. The noise, with its suggestion of uncontrolled hysteria, steadied her and made her realize that she was behaving in a panic-stricken and unadult manner, and that if she were not careful, would presently be rushing out of the house screaming. The house was locked up and no one could enter it except by the front door into the hall, which was clearly visible from the dining-room.

She forced herself to pick up the fallen chair and replace it, and feeling unaccountably fortified by the act, walked firmly across the room and out into the hall.

There was no one there. The staircase leading up to the shadowed landing was empty and nothing moved on or above it. Miranda turned towards the darkened drawing-room.

After the brightly lit hall and dining-room, the moonlight beyond the drawing-room windows appeared faint and wan, but as Miranda's fingers groped for the switch she thought she saw a flicker of movement outside the french window.

The switch clicked under her fingers, and as light flooded the room the windows were once again dark. But in that fraction of a second she had ceased to be frightened: 'Wally!' said Miranda, speaking aloud in the silence. 'I bet it's Wally!' Her curving mouth set itself in a determined line that boded no good for Master Wilkin, and switching off the light she tiptoed to the french window, unlocked it and slipped out into the garden.

The night was cold and very still. No breath of wind stirred the branches of the fir trees and not a leaf rustled, and Miranda too stood motionless; waiting until her eyes were accustomed to the uncertain light and listening for sounds of stealthy movement that would betray the whereabouts of that fervent embryo detective, Master Wallace Wilkin. And this time, vowed Miranda, I shall tell his father, and I only hope that Wally will have to take his meals off the mantelpiece for the next week as a result!

She held her breath to listen, but the garden was quiet and nothing moved. Perhaps Wally — if it had been Wally — had run for it as soon as he saw the drawing-room light go on. Or had that faint flicker of movement been only an owl or a bat? One thing at least was certain; she could not stand here indefinitely. She would walk once round the garden and then, if she found no one, would go in and lock the front door and turn on the wireless and every light in the house until Friedel or Robert and Stella returned.

Miranda walked down the sandy path that led past the dining-room windows and turned right-handed to skirt the lawn, but when she reached the cherry trees at the far end of the garden she paused, and on an impulse sat down on the wooden seat that encircled a tree near the path.

The windless night was full of stars and lights: stars in the sky and the red stars that warned aircraft away from the tall steel radio pylons. Twin stars, green and red, that moved across the sky and were the wing lights of an aircraft heading for Tempelhof airfield. A spangle of coloured lights that outlined the distant Funkturm ...

The path was a tangle of moonlight and tree-shadows, and the garden was fragrant with the faint, elusive scent of spring. The silent night was not frightening and hostile as the silent house had been, for the Leslies' drawing-room windows made friendly squares of soft, orange light against the blue of the moonlight, and Miranda could hear voices and laughter and the sound of a radio playing dance music.

She leant back against the rough bark of the cherry tree, and a few pale petals, dislodged by the slight movement, drifted down like snowflakes into her lap.

For no reason at all she found herself thinking of Simon Lang, and the discovery gave her the same feeling of resentment that Simon Lang himself seemed to produce in her. She had not meant to think of him, but it was as though he had walked across the

129

garden and stood in front of her, blocking out the moonlight and the white ghosts of the cherry trees, and refused to go away.

Miranda shut her eyes, and found that she could not picture him clearly. She could make a list of features, but none of them added up to the same Simon. He was, as he had told her, an unobtrusive person. He was certainly a singularly quiet one; his voice and manner and movements providing a gentle and pleasant façade that concealed the real Simon Lang.

The real Simon Lang, Miranda suspected, was a person who knew exactly what he wanted and invariably got it; and who, as a general rule, simply did not find it necessary, and could not be bothered, to use force or noise in any form in order to achieve it. He had interested her from the first moment she had set eyes on him, though she had not paused to discover the reason for this. And at the present time there was a more important question: why was he interested in her?

Had he been almost anyone else, Miranda would have instantly supplied an obvious answer. But in the case of Simon Lang she was regretfully compelled to reject that simple solution, since she did not in the least believe that Simon was attracted by her personal charms. Did he, then, believe that she knew more about the murder of Brigadier Brindley than she had admitted? Or was he, as Robert suggested, using that as a blind? — allowing someone else to suppose that he suspected her, in order to put that someone off their guard?

It was a possible solution, and an unpleasant one. But why should she, Miranda, be interested in Simon Lang?

Miranda frowned at the shadows of the cherry trees and was unable to find an acceptable answer.

Someone turned off the radio in the Leslies' house, and a few minutes later their lights went out, leaving the house in darkness. Presently Miranda heard the sound of cars being started up and realized that the Leslies must have decided to take their party on to the Club or to some Berlin nightspot. Three cars, one after another, purred down the road on the far side of the house. And as the sounds faded and dwindled away into silence, Miranda shivered and awoke to the fact that she was wearing a thin woollen frock and the night was cold.

A chill breath of wind sighed across the garden, bringing down a shower of white petals and bearing with it the threat of a stronger wind to follow, and she stood up to brush the fallen petals from her lap and resume her interrupted tour of the garden.

11

Once or twice Miranda stopped to peer left and right into the shadows, but the gesture was a purely perfunctory one.

If Wally had been there, he had gone, for the garden was so still that she would have caught the slightest rustle of movement. But all she could hear was the sound of her own breathing and the faint, faraway purr of traffic from the distant Herr Strasse.

Overhead the white pencils of Russian searchlights, paled by the clear moonlight, swept across the sky and picked out scattered, drifting shreds of cloud, as Miranda walked quickly along the path by the hedge that formed a boundary between the two gardens. She was cold, and anxious to get indoors once more to the comfort of the friendly lamplight, for now that the Leslies' house was in darkness, the moonlit garden seemed darker and somehow daunting.

The sandy path was bone white in the moonlight except where an oddly shaped shadow blotted it near a clump of lilacs by the gap in the hedge. A shadow that, when she reached it, was not a shadow at all ... but the body of a woman who lay face downwards with her feet towards the house and her head hidden by the darkness of the gap——

For a long moment that seemed to have no beginning or end, Miranda stood staring down at the sprawling, silk-clad legs and the blur of silvery-grey fur; numb with horror, and caught once more in the web of a waking nightmare. Then all at once she was on her knees beside it, tugging at it, trying to lift it, her voice a harsh scream.

132

'Stella! Stella! What's happened? . . . Oh no! . . . Oh God, no! . . . *Stella* . . . !'

The limp arms were outstretched, fingers clawed in the damp earth, and the body was slack and unbelievably heavy as Miranda put her arms about it and dragged it, panting, up and away from the black shadow of the hedge.

The head lolled back against her shoulder and the moonlight bathed it in white light. And it was not Stella. It was Friedel . . .

Miranda's immediate reaction was one of violent relief. It wasn't Stella! That, for the moment, was all that mattered, and she let the heavy head drop back onto the grass, and laughing a cracked, hysterical laugh of relief, fell on her knees again beside it.

A thin wet trickle, black in the moonlight, crept across the white face from some wound concealed by the woman's hair, and reached and darkened one staring eye. But the eye did not blink or close, and it was only then that Miranda realized that she was looking at a dead body. She had known it when she had first laid a hand upon it, but she had not really believed it until now.

A sudden, shuddering horror brought her to her feet: and then all at once she was running. Running desperately across the lawn and to the shelter of the house.

She had no clear recollection afterwards of entering the house or of fastening the french window behind her, but she had done so, and reached the telephone and had somehow managed to dial a number.

The distant muffled bell purred only twice and then someone lifted the receiver. 'Lang here,' said a quiet voice.

'*Simon!*' the word was a sob. Miranda's voice was shaking and she could barely control it. It seemed to her that she had shouted his name but to Simon it was no more than a soft, indistinguishable sound.

'Who is it? I can't hear you.'

Miranda fought to steady herself, gripping the receiver in both hands until the fingernails of her left hand cut into the flesh below the thumb.

'Miranda. Simon, please come quickly! Friedel's dead, and I'm all alone — *Simon!*'

Simon did not waste time asking questions. He said: 'I'll be along as soon as I can. Ring Dr Elvers, that'll save me time. You'll find his name in the book. Or get any doctor.'

'It's no good!' said Miranda frantically. 'She's dead! The blood went into her eye and——' But Simon had rung off.

Miranda stood shivering, still clutching the receiver to her ear. And as she stood there, she heard a sound. It was a very soft sound, but quite unmistakable, and she stopped shivering and stood rigid; staring with widened, terrified eyes at the receiver in her hand.

She had told Simon Lang that she was alone in the house. But it was not true. There was someone else there. Someone besides herself and Lottie. Someone who had listened to her conversation with Simon and then very quietly replaced the receiver of the telephone extension that stood beside Robert's bed in the big front room upstairs . . .

Miranda dropped the receiver and whirled round to stare up at the landing above the hall, her heart beating suffocatingly. But the landing was in shadow and from where she stood she could not see the door of Stella's bedroom.

She backed away towards the cloakroom. There was a bolt on the inside of the cloakroom door. She could shut herself in and wait until Simon came.

And then, suddenly, she remembered Lottie. Someone was hiding upstairs in one of the darkened rooms — and Lottie was up there too, asleep.

Miranda ran across the hall and raced up the staircase, heedless of what might be awaiting her in the shadows above the lighted hall, and flung open the door of Lottie's room. She found the switch and pressed it, and the room was flooded with soft light.

Lottie was sound asleep, curled up with her hands folded under her chin. She did not move or wake, and Miranda pulled the key

134

from the outside of the door with trembling fingers and locked herself in.

She knew that she should turn off the light again in case it should wake Lottie, but she could not bring herself to wait in the dark, and she found a small green cardigan and draped it over the light instead. The effect was dim and eerie, but at least it was better than darkness, and she leant weakly against the door, struggling to steady herself and regain control over her breathing.

Once she thought she heard a stair creak and someone moving somewhere in the house, but though she strained her ears to listen she could not be certain of the sound or its direction.

Whoever had been in Stella and Robert's bedroom would not stay there: that much was certain. And it would be quite simple for anyone to leave, for they had only to walk down the stairs and out of the front door. Or if that was too public, the drop from the balcony outside the bedroom windows was not so great, and the small back landing, from which one flight of stairs ascended to the attic and another descended to the kitchen quarters, lay only a few yards to the right of the bedroom door. Once down the back staircase there would be no difficulty in leaving the house, since the locks were Yale ones and could be opened from inside.

Oh, why didn't Simon come?

Miranda left the door and went quickly to the window, but there was no sign of any approaching car. Only the moonlight, and the yellow glow of the street lamps gleaming intermittently through the fretted branches of the trees that a rising wind was beginning to sway and shiver.

She dropped the curtain back into place and as she turned away her eye was caught by her own reflection in the looking-glass above the small dressing-table. There were marks on the pale topaz-coloured wool of her dress. A dark stain near the shoulder.

Miranda put up an unsteady hand and touched it.

So it had happened again! The pattern had repeated itself. Once again there was blood on her dress — and now there was blood on her hand too ... *'Circumstantial evidence'*.

135

She could not let it happen again! She could not. Who would believe her this time? She must change her dress ... hide it .... burn it! She began to tear at the fastenings with frenzied, frantic hands.

A fingernail caught and tore agonizingly in the catch of the zip-fastener, and her hair tangled about the dangling charms on her bracelet and wrenched free as she pulled the dress over her head and threw it from her as if it had been something alive and crawling. Her breath was coming in sobbing gasps and her hands were wet with sweat.

A car turned into the road and its headlights licked the windows with brief, brilliant light; and then it had jerked to a stop outside the house. Quick footsteps sounded on the flagged path below and Miranda heard the front door open.

Simon Lang! And she had sent for him herself. She had lost her head and sent for the one man who already had reason to suspect her of murder. She must have been mad! She should have said nothing; pretended to know nothing; changed the stained dress and waited for someone else to discover the murder. Instead of which she had run headlong into suspicion and danger as once before she had run wildly down the corridor of the night train to Berlin ...

'Miranda!' Simon's voice echoed strangely in the silent house. She heard him cross the hall and jerk open the drawing-room door.

'Miranda!'

Lottie stirred and murmured in her sleep and once again the instinct to protect the sleeping child overcame the nightmare numbness that had held Miranda in its grip. She turned the key in the lock and went out onto the landing, closing the door softly behind her.

Simon was standing in the hall immediately below her, his body, seen from above, looking curiously foreshortened by the drop, and the pupils of his eyes so dilated that his eyes looked black, like a cat's that has come in from the dark. He stood quite still for a

136

moment, looking up at her; and then she saw his face change and he came up the stairs, taking them three at a time, and was standing in front of her, his hands gripping her shoulders, as he had stood in the corridor of the train on the night that Brigadier Brindley had died.

He said sharply: 'Are you all right?'

'*Ssssh!* You'll wake Lottie,' said Miranda automatically. She swayed and would have fallen but for Simon's grip on her shoulders.

Simon shook her savagely. The action was so unexpected that it acted upon Miranda's numbed faculties like a dash of cold water, and she gasped and jerked herself away.

'That's better,' said Simon ungently.

He caught her arm and pulled it through his, and holding it tightly against him, turned and walked her down the stairs and into the hall.

'Now let's have it,' said Simon, swinging her round to face him.

His eyes narrowed suddenly. In the dimness of the unlighted landing he had not noticed her unorthodox attire, and had imagined her to be wearing some form of evening dress. Miranda looked down, following the direction of his startled gaze, and her white face coloured hotly. She had forgotten that she wore no dress and was standing in the full light of the hall clad in the scantiest possible underwear.

She tried to pull away, but Simon's fingers tightened about her arm as his eyes took her in from head to foot — the tangled disorder of the dark curls, the white arms and shoulders, the absurd wisps of lace-trimmed, apricot-tinted transparency, long slender legs and small high-heeled slippers. And suddenly there was a cold anger in his eyes that frightened her.

'What on earth,' said Simon softly, 'are you dressed like that for? Come on — out with it!'

'I – I meant to burn it.' Miranda's voice was a jerky whisper despite her effort to control it, and her eyes were wide and enormous.

137

'Burn what?'

'My dress. There was blood on it. You see I – I touched her. And – and it was like the other time; and I thought you would think — that everyone would think ...' Miranda's voice trailed away hopelessly and stopped.

Simon said: 'I see.' There was, curiously enough, relief in his voice. He released her arm and Miranda sat down abruptly on the bottom step of the stairs.

Simon turned on his heel, and going over to the coat rack by the cloakroom door, took down a coat at random and returning, tossed it at Miranda.

'You'd better put that on.'

It was a Burberry of Robert's and far too large for her, but Miranda struggled into it, wrapping it about her as she sat on the hall stair.

Simon said curtly: 'Where is she?'

'In the garden.' Miranda jerked her head towards the open door of the drawing-room and the moonlit windows beyond. 'By the gap in the hedge near the lilac bushes.'

He turned and walked quickly across the hall and into the drawing-room, and she heard him open the french window and go out. After that there was silence for what seemed a very long time ...

Miranda leaned her head against the newel post and shut her eyes. She felt utterly exhausted and strangely apathetic. None of this was real. It could not be real, because things like this did not happen to ordinary people like herself. They only happened to strange beings whose faces adorned the pages of the more sensational Sunday papers. She would wake up presently and find that the whole thing was a nightmare.

A slight sound aroused her and she opened her eyes. Simon Lang was standing in front of her, frowning down at her, and he did not look in the least like a nightmare.

'She's dead all right,' said Simon. 'Who is she?'

'Friedel. The housemaid.'

Simon leant down and pulled her to her feet and walked her across to the dining-room.

The lights still burned above the table and the room was in every way as Miranda had left it halfway through her supper. It seemed as if months of time must have passed since she had last sat here, and yet her half-eaten meal was still on the table and the hands on the clock-face pointed to five minutes past nine. Friedel had said she would be away only an hour. She would be back by nine. But Friedel was dead and her body lay in the cold spring moonlight beyond the curtained windows of the dining-room.

Miranda began to shiver again, and Simon pushed her down into a chair and held a glass to her mouth. She drank obediently and choked as the fiery liquid caught her throat.

He stood looking down at her with a frown in his eyes, and after a moment or two he pulled up a chair, and sitting down facing her said: 'Tell me what happened.'

'I was alone in the house,' began Miranda haltingly. 'It was Mademoiselle's day out, and Robert phoned to say he wouldn't be back until late, and then Stella rang up and said she would have supper with him at the Club and would I look after Lottie as Friedel wanted to go out for an hour or two. I said good-night to Lottie, and Friedel said that my supper was ready, and then -- then she went out.'

'What time was that?'

'About a quarter to eight I think. I don't think I looked at the clock ...'

She looked at it now. Not much more than an hour ago! It wasn't possible — it wasn't possible——

Simon's voice jerked her back to the present.

'What happened then?'

'I heard someone moving about upstairs and I thought it was Lottie. I called up to her to get back into bed. And then ...' She stopped.

'And then?' prompted Simon.

'I – I was afraid.'

'Why? What were you afraid of?'

'I don't know. I thought that someone was watching me. I was quite sure of it. I didn't hear anything, it was just a – a feeling. And after a bit I couldn't bear it any longer, so I went into the hall to see if anyone was there; but there wasn't anyone. And then I thought I saw something move outside the drawing-room window, and I thought it was Wally . . .'

'The Wilkin child? Why?'

'Because he had been playing round here before, and I'd caught him only this afternoon crawling through the bushes under the windows. I thought he was at it again and that this time I'd catch him and give him a good smacking, so I went out and – and found her.'

Miranda's voice wavered uncertainly and her hands tightened on the arms of her chair.

'Where?'

'Near the lilac bushes, in the gap by the hedge. I told you.'

'She was on the edge of the lawn,' said Simon. 'Did you move her?'

'Yes . . . I forgot that. I tried to lift her. I – I thought it was Stella.'

'*Stella?* You thought it was Mrs Melville? Why?'

'She was lying face downwards, you see. And – and her head was in the shadow and she was wearing Stella's coat.'

Simon Lang did not say anything for what appeared to be a very long time. He sat quite still and looked at Miranda, his face entirely expressionless and his eyes intent and unreadable. And once again, as earlier in the evening, she became aware of the clock, chipping off splinters of time into the silence.

She put up a hand to loosen the enveloping folds of Robert's Burberry from about her throat, jerking at it as though it impeded her breathing.

Simon said: 'So you thought it was Mrs Melville. What did you do when you found out that it wasn't?'

'I dropped her, and ran in and telephoned you.'

'Why? Why not a doctor? Or Major Melville?'

'I don't know,' said Miranda wearily. 'I suppose because I knew that she was dead and I remembered your number. You gave it to me. I can't quite remember what I thought.'

Simon Lang looked away from her for the first time and his speculative gaze travelled over the table.

'What time was it, would you say, when you went out into the garden?'

'I don't know. I didn't look.'

'But you must have some idea. It can't have taken you very long to drink a plate of soup — put it at five minutes. When did you think you heard Lottie moving?'

Miranda pressed her hands to her face, trying to think back. 'I put the soup plate on the sideboard and helped myself to meat and salad and – and I mixed some dressing. It was after that I thought I heard Lottie.'

'Let's say another five minutes. And then?'

'I told you. I went to the door and called up to her.'

'And came back to the table but did not touch your food. Why?'

'I told you,' repeated Miranda. 'I felt — I felt jumpy and frightened, so I sat here for a bit and – and listened, I suppose.'

'For very long?'

'Not very. Not as much as five minutes. Five minutes is a very long time when you're sitting quite still and you're frightened.'

'Then it was probably about eight o'clock — five past at the most — when you went out into the garden. But it was almost half-past eight when you telephoned me. What were you doing in the garden for twenty minutes, Miranda?'

Miranda stared at him, her eyes wide and frightened, and once again she put up a hand to tug at the cloth about her slender throat. 'Nothing. I mean I – I looked for Wally. I stood and waited for a bit, thinking I would hear him move. Then I listened to the party in the Leslies' house until I saw their lights go off and heard them leave.'

Simon let his breath out in a curious little sigh. He said: 'So you knew that there was no one in the next house.' It was more in the

141

nature of a statement than a query, but Miranda did not appear to notice that. The brandy that Simon had given her was taking effect and she was feeling less tense and considerably more at ease.

'Yes. And I began to feel cold and I couldn't hear anyone moving, so I decided that I would go round the rest of the garden and then lock myself into the house and play the radio until the others came back. So I walked round and ... I've told you the rest.'

Simon said: 'Twenty minutes is a long time, Miranda. Too long. Are you quite sure that you've told me everything?'

'Yes,' said Miranda flatly. She could feel the colour flooding up into her face; it was a childish and Victorian habit that she had failed to outgrow and over which she had no control.

'And that's all you did in the garden? Just walked once round it?'

'I sat on the seat under the cherry tree for a bit. I was thinking.'

'What about?'

'Nothing,' said Miranda quite definitely. 'Just thinking.'

Simon gave a little shrug and dropped the question.

'Are you quite sure that there was no one else in the house?' He saw the look on Miranda's face and said: 'So there *was* someone. Who was it?'

'I don't know,' said Miranda in a shuddering whisper that made her teeth chatter: 'It was when I was telephoning you. You rang off, and just afterwards I heard someone put down the receiver of the extension in Stella's room. There must have been someone up there, listening.'

'And you've no idea who it was?'

'No. I was too frightened to think. I tore upstairs to Lottie's room and locked myself in; and then you arrived. That's all.'

'You didn't hear anyone leave the room?'

'I'm not sure. I thought I did. They could have gone down the front stairs — or the back ones. But – but then I saw that I'd got blood on my dress and I suppose I lost my head.'

Miranda laughed: a dreary little laugh with no mirth in it. 'I thought what a fool I was to have sent for you — or for anyone!

It was exactly the same all over again you see. That's what made it so awful. And so – so horribly impossible. It was a sort of repeat performance. Do you remember saying that whoever killed the Brigadier must have had blood on them? Well I was the only person who had blood on them. And now I've got it again! Silly, isn't it?'

She laughed again, loudly, and Simon said curtly: 'Stop it, Miranda!'

'I'm sorry. I feel a little odd.'

'You're tight,' said Simon unkindly.

He got up and stood looking down at her for a moment, his hands in his pockets. 'You'd better go upstairs and take that coat off, and get back into your dress,' he said. 'I'm going to do some telephoning and there will be quite a few people round here soon. You'll have to answer a good many questions, and if your story is true there's no point in your not wearing the dress you had on when you found that woman. In fact, it won't look so good if you're not. Do you know where I can contact Major Melville?'

Miranda didn't answer the question. She stood up quickly; so quickly that for the second time that evening she knocked over her chair, but this time she did not notice it. She said breathlessly: 'It *is* true! Why should you say it isn't true?'

'I haven't said so,' said Simon evenly. 'Where is Major Melville?'

'I don't know. Yes I do. Stella said they'd probably have supper at the Club.'

Simon walked past her and out of the room, and Miranda stooped mechanically and replaced the fallen chair. Her heart was hammering again and once more she felt as though she was in the grip of a nightmare. *'Twenty minutes is a long time, Miranda ...'*

Were innocent people ever hanged for murders they had not committed? *'If your story is true.'* How could you prove a thing like that if people would not take your word for it? She had read books in which people who discovered murdered bodies instantly panicked and either attempted to dispose of them, or concealed evidence and were, on that account, suspected of committing the crime. And she had always thought scornfully that of course any innocent person would instantly ring for the police, and only a hysterical or a guilty person would keep quiet about it. But perhaps those panic-stricken characters had been right after all. She, Miranda, had sent for the police, in the person of Simon Lang. But she might well have been better off if she had done nothing, concealed evidence, and professed blank ignorance of the whole affair.

12

Miranda awoke next morning with an aching head and a dull sense of disaster.

She sat up wearily and frowned at the clock by her bedside, wondering if it had stopped, for the hands pointed at ten minutes to eleven. But the small strip of bright sunlight that pierced between the curtains confirmed the lateness of the hour, and she crawled out of bed and crossing to the basin turned on both taps and splashed her face with water.

Her eyes felt heavy from lack of sleep; her head ached abominably and her brain seemed singularly sluggish. She began to dress slowly, remembering as she did so the details of the past night ...

Friedel Schultz was dead; murdered. Someone had hit her over the back of the head with one of the iron pokers from the boiler-room. Her death must have been more a matter of chance than judgement, for had the blow fallen an inch higher it would have stunned but not killed her.

Within an hour of her death a wind had risen and blown steadily and with increasing force until shortly before midnight, when it had culminated in a brief and violent storm. There would be no trace of footprints on the sandy paths or by the lilac bushes on this bright morning to betray where the murderer had stood, or come, or gone; and Miranda herself had dragged Friedel's body from where it had originally lain ...

They had questioned her about that for hours: Simon Lang and the grey-haired man who had spoken to them in the waiting-room at Charlottenburg station, and a third man whom she could not remember having seen before, but who had evidently

145

interrogated Stella and Mademoiselle on their first morning in Berlin.

There had been a doctor too, and a couple of medical orderlies with a stretcher who had carried the body of Friedel away from the house. There had been people with lights and cameras; though by the time these had arrived the little breeze that had driven Miranda from her seat by the cherry trees had freshened to a wind that had blown the sandy paths clean, and there was nothing to photograph except Friedel herself, lying on her back at the edge of the lawn where Miranda had left her.

Simon had failed to contact either Robert or Stella, and they had returned in the middle of it all, though not together: Stella arriving shortly after ten o'clock and Robert half an hour later.

Mademoiselle had returned at half past eleven. She had been to see a film at the A.K.C. cinema in the Reichskanzler Platz, and had walked home after coffee and biscuits at a café.

It had all been a nightmare. The lights above the dining-room table shining down on the remains of Miranda's supper and the faces of the three men who questioned her. The arrival of Stella, who had walked into the hall just as Friedel's limp body was being carried in from the garden.

Simon had gone out to intercept her and explain the ugly situation in as few words as possible, but Stella had not appeared to hear him. She had only stared at Friedel and said in a queer high-pitched voice: 'But she's wearing my coat! Why is she wearing my coat? Where's Miranda?'

'I'm here,' said Miranda shaking off the hand of the grey-haired man who would have detained her, and running into the hall: 'She must have borrowed it Stel', and thought she could put it back before you got home. But I thought it was you who'd been killed ... I saw the coat, and I thought it was you!' Miranda's voice wavered.

Stella's eyes widened until they were violet circles, and the last vestige of colour drained out of her pale face leaving it a dreadful greenish white. She put up a hand to her throat and said in a dry

146

whisper: 'You thought it was me!' And then she had fainted, falling to the floor in a sprawling, untidy heap.

Hours later — or was it only minutes? — she had been carried up to her room, where she had been very sick, and finally the doctor had given her an injection of morphia and she had gone to sleep. But that had not been until after Robert had arrived back.

Robert, it appeared, had intended to work late at the office and dine in the Mess, but the Colonel had rung him up shortly before seven-thirty and suggested that he bring the work over to his house for discussion since another matter relating to it had just cropped up, and stay to supper there: whereupon Robert had borrowed a fellow officer's car and had driven to the Lawrences' house.

He had listened to an account of the evening's happenings with incredulity. Then he had seen Miranda sitting pallid and exhausted, facing her interrogators over the dining-room table, and he had lost his temper.

'What the hell do you mean by devilling the girl? Can't you wait to do your bullying in the morning?' stormed Robert. He strode over to the table and put his arms around her, and Miranda, turning, had clung to him and burst into overwrought tears.

Robert picked her up bodily, and having favoured the assembly with an unprintable opinion of them, carried her out into the hall and up the stairs. Stella's bedroom door stood open, and Stella was facing it, her fair hair dark with water where the doctor had bathed her forehead and face, and looking as though she was about to be sick again. Robert put Miranda roughly on her feet and left her at a run, and she saw him catch Stella into his arms. Then the doctor closed the door on them, and she was alone on the landing and Lottie had awakened and was demanding a drink of water.

Miranda dried her wet cheeks with the back of her hand and attended to the matter, and having retrieved Rollerbear from the floor and succeeded in settling Lottie off to sleep again, went slowly downstairs once more.

Simon Lang was still sitting in the dining-room, but the others

147

had gone. He was engaged in playing patience with a doll-sized pack of cards that Lottie had left on the windowsill, and he looked up briefly as she came into the room and then thoughtfully placed the queen of diamonds on the king of clubs before speaking.

'I think some of these must be missing,' he said. 'Why did you come down again? Your cousin is quite right. As far as you are concerned there is no real reason why you should answer any more questions until the morning.'

'I don't intend to,' said Miranda wearily. She sank into a chair, resting her elbows on the table and her chin in her hands. 'But I can't go to bed yet. I shouldn't sleep. Besides, Mademoiselle isn't back yet. Someone will have to let her in.'

'Someone will. I'm afraid that I must break it to you that I shall have to stick around here until the governess turns up.'

'Why?'

'Oh just a matter of routine you know. Someone has got to ask the usual questions: where was she, what was she doing at such-and-such a time, and all the rest of it.'

'Why can't you ask her that in the morning?'

Simon Lang looked along the lines of cards, added a three of clubs, and said softly: 'She might have a different story by the morning.'

Miranda got up abruptly and went over to the sideboard, returning a moment or so later with a glass in her hand.

Simon lifted an expressive eyebrow. 'Do you usually drink whisky with lemonade?'

'No. I don't drink it with anything,' said Miranda bleakly, 'but I'm going to drink it now. Robert says it's the world's best pick-me-up, and I need one.'

'Robert was not aware that you would ever try it out on top of a straight double-brandy,' observed Simon. 'Leave it alone, Miranda, and go and get yourself some hot milk instead; or some black coffee.'

Miranda drank off the contents of her glass with deliberation and suppressing a grimace of distaste, pushed it away from her and said: 'Where are the others?'

'They've gone.'

'And – and Friedel?'

'She's gone, too. Miranda——'

'My name,' said Miranda stiffly, 'is Brand.'

'But then I don't know you well enough to call you by your name,' said Simon gently, his attention still apparently on the array of cards spread out before him. 'Don't be childish, Miranda. Who introduced you to Brigadier Brindley?'

The question was so unexpected that for a moment Miranda wondered if she had heard aright. Simon looked up and waited, his eyes on hers.

'I – I don't remember. Robert, I suppose — or Stella. No it wasn't. It was Colonel Leslie: I remember now. It was in the dining-car of the train from the Hook. He was sitting opposite the Leslies and I sat next to him because we could only sit four to a table, and as Mademoiselle and Lottie were with Stella and Robert, I sat at the next one.'

'Did you get the impression that they had known each other before, or had only just met?'

'I don't really know. It's very difficult to tell with army people, because even if they have only just met they know so many people and places in common that they sound as if they know each other well. Mrs Leslie must have known him before, because she said that Stella——' Miranda stopped, frowning. 'No, it wasn't that of course.'

'What wasn't which?'

'Nothing really. Only something I got the wrong way round. I thought she meant the Brigadier but she didn't. It was Johnnie she meant.'

'Who meant? And who is Johnnie?' inquired Simon patiently.

'Johnnie Radley: Stella's first husband. He was killed at Tobruk.' Suddenly she found herself telling Simon of that curious conversation in the Kurfürstendamm. Perhaps it was the unac-

149

customed effects of a stiff whisky on top of the brandy that Simon had given her, or perhaps she only wished to talk in order to keep herself from thinking of Friedel's dead face in the moonlight and the feel of that slack, heavy body in her arms — and of her own perilous position.

Simon listened without comment and without once raising his eyes from the tiny coloured playing-cards before him. He continued to deal and place them, and when she had finished he swept the cards together and remarked in an abstracted voice that there were two missing.

There were low voices in the hall, and Robert and the doctor came down the stairs and into the dining-room. Robert looked bewildered and angry, and his handsome face was unusually pale. He ignored Simon and asked Miranda why on earth she wasn't in bed?

'Mademoiselle isn't back yet,' said Miranda tiredly. 'And I thought that Stella ...'

'Stella's asleep. And it's quite time you were too. Run along now, darling; I want to talk to Lang. I'll see to Mademoiselle.' He turned to the doctor. 'Can't you give her something? Not a knock-out drop, just something that will help her sleep.'

'She won't need it,' said Simon dryly. 'All she needs is a couple of aspirins to ward off a hangover.'

Robert said furiously: 'What the hell do you mean by that?'

'Only that the kid has about a quarter of a pint of mixed whisky and brandy inside her at the moment,' said Simon equably, 'and as she appears to be unused to spirits it should prove a fairly effective soporific.'

The doctor silently handed over two aspirins and Miranda swallowed them obediently and stood up. Robert put an arm around her slim shoulders: 'I'll see you up to your room.'

Miranda smiled a little crookedly and said: 'I'm all right,' and turning her head saw that Simon had risen too and was watching her. She thought that she had never seen a blanker or more expressionless face. And yet there was something there — perhaps in the eyes that met hers so steadily — something watchful and intensely interested and, yes, angry . . .

She freed herself gently from Robert's hold and turned and went out of the room.

But she had not gone to sleep until long after midnight. She had not even undressed. She had sat on the edge of her bed with her chin on her hands and stared ahead of her, and listened to the murmur of voices from the dining-room. She had heard Mademoiselle return, and Mademoiselle's excitable tones raised in angry expostulation — the governess became exceedingly foreign when agitated, and her speech became a mixed torrent of English and the German-French of St Gallen.

Miranda, listening to her, gave a little shiver of distaste. She found Mademoiselle repellent, and felt towards her much as Aunt Hetty did towards cats. Even the smell of the caraway seeds that Mademoiselle would nibble between her strong yellow teeth could make her nerves curl in disgust.

Mademoiselle had been with Stella for three years, ever since Lottie was five. She had proved a hard worker, and willing to help with housework, mending and laundering; she never seemed to take holidays, had no near relatives, and in a day when reliable household help was difficult to obtain, had turned out to be worth at least four times her modest salary. Stella frequently said that she did not know how she would manage without her, and blessed the chance that had brought her to their door inquiring for employment.

Three years ago Miranda, who had recently left school, was living in a girls' club in London, having obtained work with a model agency. And later, when she was earning a steady income, she had taken a small flat with a girl of her own age who was studying at R.A.D.A. So she had not seen very much of Stella, and little or nothing of Mademoiselle until she had accepted the Melvilles' invitation to go out with them to Berlin, and had met them all in the lounge of the Station Hotel at Liverpool Street. But since then her first instinctive dislike of the elderly Swiss spinster, with her dyed hair, her peculiar eyes and perpetual aroma of caraway seed, had grown into aversion. And tonight, sitting in her bedroom with her aching head in her hands, Miranda listened to Mademoiselle's plangent tones echoing up from the hall below and shivered with distaste.

Presently Mademoiselle had come upstairs and gone to her room, and later Robert had crossed the hall with the doctor and Simon Lang. Miranda could not make out what they were saying, but Robert's voice sounded weary and cross, the doctor's soothing, and Simon's unendurably placid.

It was past one o'clock before Miranda again removed the topaz-coloured dress that was smeared with Friedel's blood, and fell into an exhausted and uneasy slumber; but the hall was bright with mid-morning sunlight when she came downstairs again.

She could hear Stella's voice behind the closed door of the drawing-room, and as she hesitated someone crossed the landing above and came quickly down the stairs. It was Mrs Leslie, hatted and gloved and carrying a small suitcase. She stopped when she saw Miranda and looked surprised.

'Hullo, my dear. They told me you were asleep. Have you had any breakfast? It was kept hot for you. I've been helping the governess to pack.'

'Pack what? Is she leaving?' inquired Miranda, wishing that her head did not ache so.

'Oh no. It's only the child. Lottie is going over to the Lawrences' for a day or two until this horrible business is cleared up. Katy Lawrence rang me up this morning and asked me to arrange it. She didn't like to ring this house in case Mrs Melville or you were asleep, so I came over and fixed it with Robert. Of course it's the obvious thing to do — get the child right out of the way. The governess is to sleep here and bicycle over every morning to look after her during the day. It's no distance, really.'

Miranda said: 'Who's Stella talking to?'

'Captain Lang — or some other man from the local equivalent of the Gestapo,' said Mrs Leslie with a trace of acid. 'We've had a swarm of them all over the place this morning, including the German police. They had Edward and myself answering a lot of idiotic questions before breakfast; *and* the servants and the batman! They even wanted a list of our guests last night, and in what order they had arrived. I never heard such nonsense! I'll tell the cook that you're up and she can bring you something to eat in the dining-room.'

'I don't want anything to eat,' said Miranda with strong revulsion.

'Nonsense! You'll feel far better once you've had some food and hot coffee,' said Mrs Leslie bracingly. 'You're looking a wreck. At least twenty-four!'

Miranda smiled and Mrs Leslie said: 'That's better,' and went off to the kitchen to speak briefly and with authority to Frau Herbach.

'Silly woman!' said Mrs Leslie, returning. 'Scared out of her wits and wants to leave. Says she'll be the next victim. And this is the nation that ... well, never mind. Ah, here's the coffee: have some of that at least. I'll take the suitcases over to my house.'

'Is Lottie at the Lawrences' already?' asked Miranda, following Frau Herbach and the tray into the dining-room.

'No, she's over at my house playing with that child with the freckles who was on the train with us. Katy Lawrence is going to fetch her later. I expect I shall be seeing you. Brace up!'

She turned away and left Miranda to her belated breakfast.

Someone had forgotten to turn off the central heating in the dining-room, and since the room was full of sunlight and very hot, Miranda went over to the nearest window and opened it. The drawing-room windows, a yard or so to the left, were also open, and Stella's voice was clearly audible. There was a break in it, as though she had been crying.

'... Oh, I know I behaved like a fool! But I *had* to know. I couldn't bear not knowing! You see, he'd known her in Egypt and I knew that she had written to him.'

Simon Lang asked a question, but Miranda only caught the

153

intonation of his quiet voice and did not hear the words.

Stella said: 'It was Mrs Marson. She was there too — at the Lawrences'; I think all the wives were — and she said something to Sally — Mrs Page — about her being a grass-widow for the evening because her husband was dining out at some Mess in the American sector. So then Mrs Bradley asked Sally if she'd like to come up to their flat for supper, but she said she already had a date, and Mrs Bradley laughed and said: "Trust you for that!" And – and — when Robert, my husband, rang up and said he wouldn't be back to supper because he would be working late on some scheme, I . . .'

There was a brief pause, as though Stella were striving to control herself, and when she spoke again, it was in a flat, level voice.

'I didn't mean to do anything silly. It was just that I didn't want to go back to the house because . . .' Her voice wavered momentarily. 'Because Miranda was there, and I wanted to be alone and think. So I rang up and said I wouldn't be back, and I drove out somewhere — to that place where the swimming-pool is — and parked the car and walked about the grounds and thought about everything. And then I suddenly decided to ring up the office and – and make sure. I drove to the Officers' Club and telephoned from there. But there was no answer from his office and he wasn't in the Mess either.'

Simon Lang must have moved nearer the window, because this time Miranda heard him say: 'What time was that?'

'Just after half-past seven.'

'Quite sure?'

'Yes. I looked at the clock when I'd finished telephoning. It was about a minute past the half hour.'

'And then?'

'Then I went out and got into the car and drove to the road where the Pages' flat is,' said Stella in a hard, defiant voice. 'I parked the car where I could watch the entrance. And I saw Sally — Mrs Page — come out and get into a taxi — and I followed it. But I lost it at the traffic lights.'

'Had you waited long?' Simon's voice was entirely matter-of-fact, and he might have been discussing the weather. It evidently had a steadying effect upon Stella, for her voice sounded less taut and more normal.

'No. Only a minute or two. It's not far from the Club, so it must have been about twenty to eight.'

'Mrs Page was dining at the Leslies',' said Simon. 'So by that reckoning she must have arrived at their house not later than ten minutes to eight.'

'I know,' said Stella wretchedly. 'I've made a complete fool of myself. I see that now.'

'What did you do when you lost sight of the taxi?'

'I parked the car in a side street and just sat.'

'For how long?'

'I don't know. It didn't seem very long, but it may have been an hour — or two hours!' She gave a dreary little laugh. 'And then I had something to eat at a café in one of the back roads and came home, and ... Well, you know the rest.'

Simon said: 'Did you see anyone you knew? Or anyone you think might be able to identify you, between the time you left the Club and eight o'clock? That's almost the only time we're interested in.'

'No,' said Stella wearily. 'No one at all. So you see I haven't got an alibi. Captain Lang ...'

'Yes?'

'Does Robert have to know?'

'Not unless you tell him yourself,' said Simon. 'It might not be a bad idea you know,' he suggested, gently deprecatory.

'I can't!' Stella's voice had a hard edge to it. 'He asked me this morning and I said that I had just decided to see Berlin and have supper at a German café for – for fun. I only told you because ...' She stopped, and then said in a voice that was puzzled and a little angry: 'I don't know why I should have told you.'

Because people do tell him things, thought Miranda wryly. Things they don't mean to tell him——

She leaned against the windowsill and looked out across the sunny strip of lawn. Last night's rain had battered the cherry trees, but though the ground below them was strewn with fallen petals, new buds were opening to take their place, and the garden looked fresh and clean and a little smug. It did not seem possible that a woman had died a violent death in it only a few hours ago.

Mademoiselle came round the corner of the house wheeling her bicycle, and seeing Miranda at the window, paused and inquired if she had slept well. She herself had not closed her eyes, so great was her alarm, and her sorrow for the poor, poor woman so foully done to death — without doubt by the agents of the Soviet. Always there were killings and kidnappings in Berlin by the Russians: one had told her so only yesterday.

She was interrupted by Stella who leant out of the window to ask if she was sure she knew the way to the Lawrences' house?

But yes, said Mademoiselle. She knew quite well the direction and would have departed earlier had it not been for the time wasted by the imbecile gendarmes and their so foolish questions. Mademoiselle concluded her remarks with a resounding sniff and wheeled her bicycle away, and Stella said: 'Hullo, 'Randa. I didn't realize you were up. How are you feeling?'

'Terrible! Come and have some coffee.'

'I can't,' said Stella with an attempt at a smile. 'I'm being given the third degree.'

'Do you mean to say that the imbecile gendarmes haven't finished with their so foolish questions yet?' inquired Miranda, raising her voice with intent.

Stella frowned and said sharply: 'Don't be silly, Miranda!' She drew in her head and Miranda heard Simon Lang laugh, and then the window shut with a bang.

Miranda poured herself another cup of black coffee and sipped it slowly. She was trying to explain something to herself. She, Miranda, had for a brief space behaved like that fictional character who plays into the murderer's hands by concealing evidence instead of yelling for the police. Which was understandable, since

156

she had, after all, received a series of violent and unpleasant shocks, and could be forgiven for reacting to them a little wildly.

What was not understandable was why, in the bright light of morning, an uncomfortable proportion of the panic that had driven her to tear off the stained dress, and had whispered the words *'Circumstantial evidence'* in her ear, should still remain with her? Because, of course, it was nonsense. Suspicion could not possibly rest on her for the simple reason that unless they suspected her of homicidal mania, she had no shadow of motive for killing Brigadier Brindley or Friedel Schultz; and no possible connection with either of them. And yet she was still afraid. Why?

Because of Simon Lang! The answer presented itself to her as suddenly as though someone had spoken the words aloud.

Simon Lang could see a possible reason why she might have committed both crimes. A motive that had escaped Miranda herself, but was, none the less, a feasible one; since she did not believe that he would waste time on impossibilities. It followed, therefore, that somewhere in all this there was some connection between Brigadier Brindley, Friedel and herself, and a possible motive for the murder of both Brigadier Brindley and Friedel by Miranda Brand.

She heard the drawing-room door open and Stella walk quickly across the hall and run up the stairs, and a moment later the sound of her bedroom door being shut with a bang. Miranda put down her coffee cup and, leaving the room, walked resolutely across the hall and into the drawing-room.

Simon Lang was leaning against the window frame, his hands deep in his pockets, looking out into the garden. He turned his head as she entered and acknowledged her presence with something that might conceivably have been called a smile, and when she did not speak, turned back to his contemplation of the garden.

Miranda seemed suddenly to have forgotten what it was she had wanted to say. She crossed the room slowly and stood beside him, looking out on the green, sunlit space and trying to imagine it as

157

it had looked last night; and would look again when the sun had set: a place of darkness and mystery and shadows.

Something of what was passing in her mind seemed also to be in Simon Lang's, for he said under his breath: '*"Is the day fair? Yet unto evening shall the day spin on ..."*' He did not finish the quotation, and Miranda spoke the next two lines almost without knowing that she had done so: '*"And soon thy sun be gone; then darkness come, and this, a narrow home."*'

Simon turned and looked at her, his eyebrows up and an odd gleam in his eyes.

Miranda shivered suddenly in the bright sunlight and said: 'It all looks so ordinary, and so safe. It doesn't seem possible that anything like that could have happened out there.'

Simon said: 'You've forgotten the first line of that poem.'

'No, I haven't. You left it out. *"O passer-by, beware!"* I was the passer-by: but how is one to know?'

Simon did not reply and the room was very silent; as silent as the quiet garden outside.

Miranda sighed and turned away from the window. 'I wanted to ask you something,' she said slowly. 'You have a theory about me, haven't you? A possible reason why I might have murdered two people who were complete strangers to me.'

She looked directly at Simon Lang, but her eyes were dazzled by the bright sunlight beyond the window, and his face seemed to be oddly out of focus and once again entirely without expression: as though a blind had been drawn down over it. He did not trouble to deny or confirm her statement, but returned her gaze evenly and in silence.

'What reason could I possibly have had?' urged Miranda. 'I didn't know either of them.'

Simon said quietly: 'That might not have been necessary.'

'I don't understand.'

'Don't you? I wonder.'

Simon was silent for a moment or two, then he said meditatively: 'Men commit murder for a variety of reasons. But generally

158

speaking, there are only two reasons why women do; and they frequently commit them for a combination of the two. It is just conceivable — only just — that you might qualify on account of those reasons.'

'I don't understand!' repeated Miranda angrily.

'If you don't, then there's no need for you to worry,' said Simon.

'But I tell you, I'd never even met Brigadier Brindley before that afternoon on the train,' insisted Miranda.

'No, I don't think you had,' said Simon unexpectedly.

'There you are then! As for Friedel, I hadn't spoken more than a dozen words to her.'

Simon looked at her speculatively for a moment or two, then he said quietly: 'Whoever killed the Brigadier need not have known him for more than a few hours.'

'And Friedel?'

'That was, I think, a mistake,' said Simon. He glanced at his watch and said: 'I must go,' and turned and walked to the door.

Miranda ran after him and caught at his arm: 'But you haven't answered my question!'

Simon looked down at the slim fingers that clutched his sleeve. 'No,' he said reflectively. 'I don't believe I have.'

He detached her fingers quite gently, as though he were removing some small creeping object that he did not wish to harm, and the hall door closed quietly behind him.

Miranda made a sound like an infuriated and frightened kitten, and turning her back on the door, ran upstairs to find Stella.

13

Stella's bedroom door was not only closed, but locked. Miranda knocked softly, and receiving no answer, tried the handle.

A voice that she did not immediately recognize as Stella's said sharply: 'Who is it?'

'It's me,' said Miranda with a fine disregard for grammar. 'I only wanted to see how you were bearing up.'

A key turned in the lock and the door opened. Stella said: 'I'm sorry. I didn't hear you knock. Come in. Has Captain Lang left?'

'Yes,' said Miranda uncommunicatively.

Stella moved over to her dressing-table, and sitting down in front of it began to fidget aimlessly with bottles and brushes, and Miranda, watching her reflection in the glass, saw with something like horror that she looked old. Sallow-skinned and haggard, and desperate. Stella looked up, and catching sight of Miranda's face in the glass, started violently. The bottle she had been touching overturned and spilt a stream of scented lotion over the table, and Miranda ran to her and put her arms about her.

'What is it, Stel'? What's the matter?'

Stella flinched at her touch and then sat still, submitting to the embrace. But Miranda could feel that her body was tense and trembling, and see that she was staring at her own reflection in the mirror as if it were some stranger she saw there. She said in a hoarse whisper: 'I'm afraid, 'Randa. *I'm afraid!*'

Miranda's arms tightened about her and she tried to think of something to say that would convince Stella that Robert would never leave her for Sally Page or anyone else. She said to gain time: 'What have you got to be afraid of, darling?'

'Of being murdered,' said Stella in a whisper.

The answer was so unexpected and so shocking that Miranda released her and took a quick step backward.

'What on *earth* do you mean?'

Stella's hands clutched at the edge of the dressing-table. 'Someone meant to kill me. *Me* — not Friedel!'

Miranda opened her mouth to say 'Don't be ridiculous!' but a sudden recollection of what Simon had said to her less than ten minutes ago checked the words on her tongue. At the time, preoccupied with her own angle, she had not stopped to think what he had meant when he said that Friedel's death had probably been a mistake.

After a moment she said: 'Nonsense!' but the word lacked conviction and Stella brushed it aside.

'It isn't nonsense! It was night, and she was wearing my coat. Don't you see — someone thought it was me! Even *you* did. You said so! Someone thought I should be here alone, as you were. You should have been out — Mrs Leslie told me so — but I ought to have been here. I tell you, someone meant to kill me, 'Randa!'

Miranda said: 'Darling, why? *Do* be sensible! Why should anyone want to kill you? Surely it's obvious that someone had it in for that wretched woman, and the fact that she had borrowed your coat had nothing whatever to do with it?' She was trying to be reasonable and comforting, but she did not believe her own words, because if Simon Lang thought that Friedel's death was a mistake, he must have a very good reason for thinking so. But who would want to kill Stella? Surely you would have to hate someone very much to wish to kill them? Simon had said that women usually killed for one of two reasons; though he had not specified those reasons. Was one of them hate? Who hated Stella? Who would want her out of the way?

Two names leapt to Miranda's mind: Norah Leslie and Sally Page ...

'No!' said Miranda aloud. *'No!'*

'You can believe what you like,' said Stella in a shaking voice,

161

'but I know that someone meant to kill me. I tell you I *know!*'

But Miranda had been speaking to herself — or to Sally Page: pretty, young, foolish Sally, who imagined herself to be in love with Stella's husband. Or to Norah Leslie, who hated Stella for some hidden reason of her own. But neither of them was capable of murder, and it was all nonsense that Stella had been the intended victim. It *must* be! Simon was wrong, and Friedel had been killed for some reason unconnected with either or any of them.

She tried to make Stella see this, but Stella was frightened beyond the reach of reason. Her insular dislike of foreigners and foreign countries, her jealousy of Sally Page, and the shocking reality of the two brutal murders with which she had been brought into contact, had combined to bring her to the verge of a complete physical and mental collapse. She would only repeat, 'I know that it was meant to be me,' in reply to all Miranda's soothing arguments.

Miranda said patiently: 'How can you be so sure? Do you know of any reason why anyone should want to kill you?'

'*Yes* . . .' Miranda barely caught the whispered word. Stella was not even looking at her; she was staring in front of her as though she saw someone or something that Miranda could not see, and there was a stark terror in her eyes that made Miranda's heart miss a beat.

Miranda said quickly. 'If you mean Sally Page, I think . . .'

'*Sally?*' interrupted Stella, her gaze returning to Miranda. 'What on earth has Sally Page to do with it?' Her voice sounded genuinely startled.

'Nothing,' said Miranda hastily. 'Stel', this reason you know of — why someone should want to kill you — what is it?'

Stella's face changed. It became blank and expressionless, and her violet-blue eyes were no longer terrified, but guarded and wary. She did not answer for a moment, and then she picked up a powder puff from the dressing-table and spoke to Miranda over her shoulder.

'Of course I don't know of any reason. How should I? It's just

162

that that woman was wearing my coat. That's all. Don't let's talk about it any more for heaven's sake, 'Randa. Oh God, what a mess I look! I must do something to my face before Robert gets back.'

'Where is he?' asked Miranda, only too glad to change the subject.

'Seeing a lot of people about this Friedel business. He'll be back for luncheon. You might go down and see if the cook is doing anything about it. She's been behaving in a most peculiar manner. Where the Germans acquired their reputation for toughness I can't imagine. They seem to me to collapse into tears and hysteria at the drop of a hat! Oh well, I suppose I can't talk. Go and see about it will you, darling? Robert should be back any minute now!'

But Robert had already arrived, for Miranda found him in the drawing-room with Harry and Elsa Marson. The three had been talking together in low tones, but they broke off as she entered and turned quickly to face her.

Standing together in the cool cream and green of Stella's drawing-room, they seemed to Miranda to look curiously alike, despite their wide physical dissimilarities. And for a brief moment that fleeting impression of likeness puzzled her, until she realized that it was solely a matter of tension. They had turned simultaneously, and as they stood facing her in silence, their three faces bore the same look of strained wariness. It lasted only for a moment, and then the tension relaxed and Robert said: 'Oh, it's you, 'Randa. I thought——' He bit off the sentence and turned to Mrs Marson: 'Elsa, have a brandy and soda instead of that sherry. You look as if you could do with it. We all could.'

'Thank you, no,' said Mrs Marson. 'I think it is time we go now.'

She looked shockingly ill, thought Miranda. Something had happened to her face since they had first met on that fateful journey to Berlin. It seemed to have aged, as Stella's too had aged. Yet that was not all. Her face seemed thinner and somehow more un-English, and she had taken to a lavish use of make-up, as though to provide a mask with which to conceal that change. But the bright patches of rouge on her cheeks only served to accentuate

163

their thinness and the curious grey pallor of her skin, and no amount of paint and powder could disguise the dark patches under her eyes or dim their feverish glitter. She too looked as Stella had looked — haggard and raddled and afraid. Miranda wondered if her own face bore that same look of fear?

Harry Marson said: 'Hullo, Miranda. This is a bloody business isn't it — in more senses than one.' He finished the contents of his glass at a gulp. 'We've had the *Polizei* and the F.B.I. and the Gendarmerie and old Uncle Sherlock-Holmes-Cantrell and all swarming over us since early dawn. Or that's what it feels like. The entire allied police force appears to be interested in the demise of your late parlourmaid, and it's probably only a matter of time before we're all lined up answering questions for a squad of comrades from the N.K.V.D. as well!'

Robert said quite pleasantly: 'Shut up, Harry,' and Harry Marson shot him a quick look and reddened under his tan. He cleared his throat uncomfortably and said: 'Well I suppose we'd better be getting along. Give you a lift to the office after lunch — fair exchange and all that.'

'Make it about three,' said Robert.

'Okay. Come on, Elsa.'

They went out through the french window and took the short cut across the Leslies' garden to their own house.

Stella came down to luncheon looking smooth and poised and soignée. It did not seem possible that this was the same woman who had crouched before her looking-glass, hysterical and terrified, so short a time ago. She had changed into a leaf-brown suit that brought out the copper tints in her blond hair, and had made up her face with care. But her hands still trembled slightly and the carefully applied mascara could not hide the redness about her eyes.

Robert went to the foot of the stairs to meet her. He took her into his arms and held her close to him for a moment, her head thrown back so that he could look into her eyes. Then he kissed her gently and released her.

164

'Well done, darling,' said Robert approvingly.

A little flush of colour rose to Stella's cheeks and the tension in her face and body seemed to relax. She smiled at him warmly and lovingly, and tucking her hand through his arm, turned towards the dining-room.

A little after three o'clock a horn sounded in the road. 'That'll be Harry,' said Robert. 'Darling, I'm going to be late again this evening. I'm sorry. It's specially beastly just now, but there is a bit of an international flap on, and the C.O. is up to his eyes in work and worry. I'll be back as soon as I can, but it may not be until around eight o'clock. Goodbye, my sweet. Try not to worry too much. Everything is going to be all right, and as soon as all this has blown over I shall see if I can't scrounge a bit of leave and we'll go down to Italy for ten days. Would you like that?'

'No,' said Stella with a crooked smile. 'Frankly, darling, I'd prefer ten days in a boarding-house at Blackpool or a cosy chalet in some Butlin holiday camp. Bracing Britain is good enough for me, and I feel I never want to see another hysterical foreigner in my life!'

Robert laughed and stooped to kiss her. 'Butlins it shall be! And if only I were a man of means instead of an impecunious chap who has still to qualify for a minimum pension, I'd hand in my papers and take to breeding pigs tomorrow! Never mind, my sweet, one day we shall retire to some nice, safe semi-detached on a bus route, and keep hens in the back garden.'

'It sounds heavenly,' said Stella with a laugh. 'But why the semi-detached? Why not Mallow?'

'My dear girl,' said Robert, reaching for his hat, 'by the time I can afford to retire or am heaved out — whichever comes first — the local housing committee will have grabbed it under some by-law and converted it into Workers' flats. And about time too! With the cost of living well over the roof, the place is a mark one white elephant.'

The car horn tooted again impatiently and Robert pulled Stella to him and kissed her again, holding her for a moment with his

165

cheek against hers. He looked past her to Miranda, his eyes anxious, and said: 'Look after her, 'Randa.'

Stella released herself with a little laugh. 'It's Miranda who needs looking after darling, not me. 'Randa was in the thick of it all.'

'Well, look after each other then.' He reached out and ruffled Miranda's dark hair affectionately, kissed her cheek, and was gone.

Two men came to interview Stella during the course of the afternoon: one of them Colonel Cantrell, whom Miranda had first seen in the waiting-room of Charlottenburg station, and the other a German policeman. But they did not ask to see Miranda, and she returned to the garden and sat on the edge of Lottie's sandpit with an anxious eye on the drawing-room windows.

Why were they worrying Stella again? Was it because she could produce no alibi for the previous night? But Stella of all people would not kill someone in mistake for herself. Unless Simon was wrong and there was no question of a mistake? Or did they perhaps think that for some reason of her own Stella might have killed Friedel and had the brilliant idea of dressing her in her own coat in order to create the impression that she herself had been the intended victim — thereby providing herself in some sort with an alibi, to compensate for the fact that she could produce no evidence to prove where she had been during that short margin of time in which Friedel must have met her death? They might reason like that; but then they had not seen her, as Miranda had, in her bedroom that morning. Stella was afraid. Afraid for her life. Genuinely and terribly afraid. And despite her subsequent denial, it was quite obvious that she had a special and secret reason for that fear.

Mrs Marson . . . ? *Had* it been Elsa Marson who had spoken to Friedel on the landing in the hostel that first morning in Berlin? Where had she been last night, and what had she been doing in the Soviet Garden of Remembrance? Miranda sighed and abandoned the problem in favour of wishing herself back once more in the tiny, comfortable flat off Sloane Street.

166

Colonel Cantrell and the German policeman left after half an hour, and towards five o'clock Stella suggested a visit to the swimming-pool at the Stadium, where Lottie and the Lawrence children were to have a swimming lesson. She had not referred to the afternoon's interview, but her eyes were over-bright and there was a hectic flush of colour in her cheeks that made Miranda feel anxious. Stella was making an obvious effort to appear her normal self, and was gay and talkative and had confined her conversation to an amusingly malicious account of the Wives' Meeting at the Lawrence house.

'I wonder if we need any petrol?' said Stella, starting the car and backing it out cautiously. 'I think there's a spare gallon somewhere.'

Miranda leant forward and peered at the gauge: 'No. You've got two gallons in the tank. It isn't far, is it?'

'Only a couple of miles, I think. If that.' Stella sighed and said: 'Do you remember when we bought this car? It was in 1950, for Robert's leave. We went to Dorset. Oh, those peaceful English lanes and hedges! And here I am, driving it down an autobahn in Berlin. It seems all wrong, somehow.'

'Don't worry, darling,' comforted Miranda. 'You'll drive it down a lot more English lanes one day. It's done a nice, comfortable wodge of British mileage — 17,332 miles no less — so I see no reason why it should not tot up a few on autobahns before getting back to hedges again.'

'It won't be hedges,' said Stella gloomily. 'It will be some beastly bamboo forest or a rubber plantation, and I expect we'll be made to paint it a dreary shade of jungle green.'

The eastern entrance to the Stadium area, where Hitler's Youth Rallies and the Olympic Games of the Nazi era had been held, led into a road that skirted a vast amphitheatre and passed between green playing fields to a large block of buildings, one of which housed the big indoor swimming-pool.

Stella parked the car, and they walked between tall gates and along a wide path, and turned down a short flight of stone steps and past a large outdoor pool which was three parts full of dark, stagnant water and flanked by a bronze bull and his mate, wading knee-deep in rigid bronze ripples, and eventually reached the huge indoor pool.

After the sharp evening air outside the atmosphere seemed to them intolerably steamy and stifling, for the pool was a heated one. But they endured it for an hour, after which Mrs Lawrence, who had also been watching her offspring having a swimming lesson in the pool reserved for children and beginners, invited them back to her house for a drink so that Stella could say good-night to Lottie.

The house lay not more than half a mile from the west entrance of the Stadium area in a quiet, tree-lined road, and it was after half-past six by the time they reached it and were ushered into the drawing-room by Katy Lawrence, who hunted the children off to supper in charge of Mademoiselle and apologized for the absence of the Colonel.

'He's having a foul time, poor pet,' said his wife, dispensing sherry. 'There's some terrific flap on. George thinks I don't know a thing about it, but of course I do. They're all getting a lecture, or a "briefing", or whatever they call it, this evening by someone from the Headquarters — Toddy Pilcher. Rather a pompous little man, I always thought. And then there's this talk by the C-in-C tomorrow night. George says Toddy insisted on a projector in the lecture room. Lantern slides — I ask you! Sounds madly Women's Institute to me. Was that the doorbell? Let's hope it's Monica Bradley with that stuff for the Thrift Shop at last!'

But it was Sally Page who was ushered in by a whitecoated batman. Sally wearing that same look of strain and weariness that Miranda had seen on Stella's face; and Mrs Marson's. And on her own as it looked back at her from a mirror. Yet on Sally it was neither ugly nor ageing: she merely looked fragile, childlike and pathetic, and the faint smudges of sleeplessness under the forget-me-not blue eyes only served to enhance their size and colour.

Sally had only called to say that she could not, after all, help in the Thrift Shop the following week, but that she had swopped weeks with Esmé Carroll and did Mrs Lawrence mind? She stayed to drink a glass of sherry and press Stella and Miranda to go back with her to her flat that evening.

'*Do* say you'll come!' begged Sally prettily. 'I do so want you to see my flat. And Andy would simply love to see you: he wants to show you some photographs he's taken of me. And besides I want your advice about what colour to have the drawing-room painted. I hear that your drawing-room is lovely, Mrs Melville. You *will* come, won't you?'

Miranda saw Stella's face pale and her mouth tighten, and noticed that her voice was distinctly metallic as she said crisply: 'I know Miranda would love to go, but I'm afraid I can't manage it this evening.'

Left with no option — since she could hardly refuse in face of Stella's positive statement that she would love to go — Miranda accepted, and Sally smiled disarmingly at her, and having got her way, turned to the subject of Friedel's murder. Whereupon Stella stood up abruptly saying that she would run up and say good-night to Lottie, and left the room. Miranda endeavoured to change the subject, but without success, since her hostess was far too interested in the whole affair to discourage such an entertaining topic of conversation.

'We had the police round this morning,' said Sally, ending a long and enthusiastic dissertation on the latest murder. 'Well, not really the police I suppose, but that nice Lang man, and another creature who just sat there and never uttered — rather good-looking, with dark hair. They wanted to know what we were doing last night. I mean to say — *honestly*! As if any of us were likely to go round hitting German housemaids on the head with pokers! Not that I haven't thought it mightn't be a good thing, because you've no idea what a clueless creature the Labour Exchange people have foisted on us ...

'She says her name's Sonya, and I'm quite sure she's a Russian spy. I mean, she wears Russian boots and stumps about in them

169

all day and simply *never* washes. She's supposed to be a cook, but she can't even boil a potato, and when I complained she said she didn't understand English cooking — only German. So of course I said, "*Let's* have some German cooking," because I'm all for fancy foreign dishes. But it seems that German cooking is just the same as English cooking, only worse: I mean all you do is to pour masses of grease over everything and that's it.'

She paused for breath and Miranda, fearful of the conversation returning to the subject of Friedel, said: 'Well, personally, I think you're very lucky to have cooks and housemaids at all. If there is one thing I do detest, it's peeling potatoes and washing up greasy dishes.'

Mrs Lawrence, however, was not to be drawn into a discussion of the servant problem. She said: 'But why were you questioned about last night, Sally? Did they explain?'

'Oh yes. But it wasn't very exciting, really. It was just in case either of us had seen anyone lurking about, or noticed anything like a car standing at the end of the road. Things like that. And alibis of course. Simon Lang said it would help to clear up things if we could each produce an alibi.'

'Why "each"?' inquired Mrs Lawrence, puzzled. 'Surely Andy was dining in the American sector?'

'Well, he was,' said Sally, 'but it was *too* stupid — I can't think how he could have made such a silly mistake — but it seems it was the wrong night, so he came back and went to bed.'

'Does that mean he hasn't got an alibi?'

'Oh no; I'm afraid that as suspects we're both out of the running,' said Sally regretfully.

Miranda, noting the tone, thought with some irritation that Sally, whose reading seemed to be entirely of the escapist variety, would rather have enjoyed appearing as a witness in a murder trial: she probably saw herself as the frail and sensitive heroine of this type of fiction, and would have found it pleasurably exciting to be a suspect.

'Andy couldn't get the lift to work,' explained Sally, 'so he routed out the caretaker, who is rather an old sweetie, and the old

170

boy fixed it for him. Andy asked him in for a beer, and very fortunately noticed that the time was just eight o'clock by that dining-room clock of ours; because he told Herr Hübbe that he could only have missed me by about a quarter of an hour or so and now he would have to cook his own supper.'

'And what about you?' inquired Mrs Lawrence. 'Did you have to produce an alibi too?'

'Oh yes. Mine's all right too. I arrived at the Leslies' at ten to eight and I said, "I do hope I'm not late" — not that I thought I was, but you know how one says that sort of thing — and Colonel Leslie looked at his watch and said, "You're about dead on time; it's ten to eight." And the good-looking man with the dark hair wrote something in a notebook and said, "That agrees with Colonel Leslie's account," so I suppose they were checking on the Leslies as well.'

'But *why*?' demanded Mrs Lawrence. 'What possible reason can they think any of you could have for murdering an unknown German servant-girl? The thing's absurd!'

'I couldn't agree more. But Andy has a theory that the police, or the S.I.B. or M.I.5, or whoever it is who is doing all the fussing around over this, think that there is some connection between the murder of that Brigadier and this German woman's.'

'Quite ridiculous,' pronounced Mrs Lawrence firmly: 'Of course they don't think anything of the sort!'

'Then why is it that they have questioned all the same people?'

'What people?'

'"Lang's Eleven",' put in Miranda; and instantly regretted having spoken.

'Lang's eleven? What *do* you mean? What eleven?'

'Nothing really,' said Miranda unhappily. 'Only that there were eleven people who might have murdered the Brigadier, and most of them seem to have been questioned again over this murder.'

'Not most of them,' corrected Sally Page. 'All of them.'

'How do you know that?'

'I asked,' said Sally, simply. And ticked them off one by one on

171

the fingers of her rather large, schoolgirlish hands. 'Myself and Andy, Elsa and Harry Marson, the Leslies, Miranda and that Swiss female, Mademoiselle something-or-other, and Mrs Melville and Bob, and——'

'Bob . . . ?' for a moment the unfamiliar name puzzled Miranda.

Sally flushed. 'Robert. We used to call him Bob when he was in Egypt. Then there's Mrs Wilkin of course. They even checked up on her, believe it or not!'

She laughed her pretty, shallow laugh, and Mrs Lawrence said: 'Wilkin? *Not* the mother of that frightful freckled child?'

'You mean Wally,' said Miranda. 'The original Giles cartoon, isn't he? Where have you come across Wally?'

'My dear, he has been infesting my house all day! It seems he's a special friend of Lottie's. Mademoiselle did her best to chase him off the premises, but I think he came back over the wall.'

Sounds of woe from above penetrated to the drawing-room and Stella reappeared looking worried. 'That was Lottie,' she said apologetically. 'She's left that tiresome little china bear of hers behind at the swimming-pool, and she won't go to sleep without it.'

'Oh dear,' exclaimed Mrs Lawrence, 'and I'm afraid the car has gone off to fetch George. But I'll get the driver to go up and look for it as soon as he gets back.'

'Please don't bother. I could go, if it comes to that. But Mademoiselle has offered to run up on her bicycle. It's no distance at all, really, and I do think she might have seen that Lottie had that toy. It's all right for her to go, isn't it? I mean, they will let her in?'

'Of course. She'll probably be stopped at the gate and asked what she's doing, but they know her. She took the children there for a walk this afternoon and George gave her a pass in case anyone asked questions. In a month or two, when they've moved all those offices and things into the Stadium area, they'll probably get madly security-minded. But no one bothers much at the moment. They stop a car with a German registration number and ask questions, I believe. But all our cars go through on sight,

172

because of the B.Z. on the number-plates — for British Zone.'

'Then that's all right,' said Stella, thankfully. 'I must admit that the last thing I want to do is to drive back to the baths and hunt around for twenty minutes or so for a minute china toy. But thank goodness Mademoiselle is made of sterner stuff. I only hope she's got a bicycle lamp. It's getting dark. 'Randa, if you're going to see Mrs Page's flat, I think I'll get along home and have a hot bath before Robert gets back. Good-night, Mrs Lawrence, and thank you again for having Lottie. It's really very good of you.'

Mrs Lawrence saw her to the door, while Sally Page went off to telephone Andy and tell him that she was bringing Miranda back to the flat. She appeared to take an unconscionable time over it, and when at last she returned she looked flushed and defiant: the reason for this becoming immediately apparent on their arrival at the flat, when Miranda realized, too late, that Sally's only object in asking her there had been to use her as a buffer between herself and Andy. There had apparently been a major matrimonial row between the two young Pages, but owing to Miranda's presence, Andy was compelled to play the willing host and dispense drinks and social smalltalk.

The flat proved to be large, dim and depressing, and Sally seemed to have made little effort towards improving it. The drawing-room, which was chilly and uncomfortable, smelt strongly of turpentine. 'The painters have been in,' explained Andy gloomily.

Sally urged Miranda to stay to supper or, alternatively, to accompany Andy and herself to the Club. But Andy made no attempt to second the invitation, and when Miranda firmly excused herself, he said that he would drive her back; adding curtly that as it was Sonya's day out, Sally had better get down to cooking something for supper.

He was morose and monosyllabic on the journey to the Melvilles', and to Miranda's relief he refused her half-hearted invitation to come in for a drink, and having dropped her at the gate drove away at speed without waiting to see her to the door.

173

The bell had been answered by Robert.

'Hullo, 'Randa, you're just in time for supper. Frau Herbach insisted on leaving before it got dark, so I've been trying my hand at a bit of amateur cookery. However, not to worry; it will be quite edible. All I've actually done is to heat up the stuff she left ready. Tell Stella to get a move on while I dish up the result.'

He vanished in the direction of the kitchen, and Miranda started up the stairs. She was halfway up when she remembered that earlier in the evening she had left her handbag in the front pocket of the Melvilles' car; and since it contained her lipstick and powder puff, she turned and went down again to the hall, lifted the garage key off its hook near the hall door, and went out, leaving the door open behind her.

A wandering gust of wind blew down the road, momentarily shaking the branches of the trees before the street lamp near the gate and sending leaping shadows across the house wall. The road looked long and dark and deserted, and Miranda shivered and walked quickly down the short path to the left of the house.

The garage was cold and airless and smelt unpleasantly of petrol and mildew, and the single overhead bulb only served to throw the interior of the car into deep shadow. Miranda reached in and switched on the dashboard lights, but the bag was not there, and she realized that Stella must have taken it in when she returned from the Lawrences'.

Switching off the dashboard light she slammed the car door behind her, and in the same moment thought she heard a sound behind her: a swift, stealthy, scrambling sound. Miranda whirled round, her hand still clutching at the door of the car, and stood rigid, listening. But the gust of wind that had blown along the street had died away, and the night was quiet again and nothing moved.

The car threw a dense black shadow across a pile of empty wooden packing-cases stacked against the far wall, above which a small window, its panes festooned with cobwebs, cut a dark square in the whitewashed brick. Beyond the open doorway the

174

path lay dark and empty, and the light streaming out from the garage caught the lilac bushes lining the short, concrete ramp that sloped up to the level of the road, and silhouetted their motionless leaves against the surrounding shadows, as though they had been canvas scenery lit by stage footlights.

Miranda did not move. Her fingers, clenched about the metal door handle, felt stiff with cold, and her heart was beating in odd, uneven jerks. Had she really heard a sound, or had it only been an echo from the slamming of the car door? Was there someone crouched among the empty packing-cases, or waiting outside behind the lilac bushes? — waiting until she switched off the light and turned to lock the door? Waiting for her as they had waited for Friedel?

The silent garage and the quiet night outside seemed to be waiting too, and in the silence she could hear the sound of her own uneven heartbeats.

A swift, flickering shadow swept across the small, cold walls and brought a choking gasp to her throat, but it was only a large moth attracted by the naked light. And suddenly the taut thread of terror slackened and she took a deep breath, and walking quickly over to the garage door, turned off the light with shaking fingers, and locking the door behind her, fled back up the path to the house.

Stella was coming down the hall stairs, but she checked at the sight of Miranda's white face; one hand gripping the banister and the other suddenly at her throat, her eyes wide with terror: *'What is it? What's happened?'*

'Nothing. I – I went down to the garage to get my bag out of the car, and I thought I heard someone or something. Probably only a cat or an owl. But my nerves are in poor shape these days, and I panicked and ran back here at the double. That's all.'

Stella swayed and Miranda ran up the stairs and put an arm about her.

'I'm sorry,' apologized Stella: 'But you gave me a fright; rushing

175

in like that. I thought for a moment that something awful had happened.'

'Something awful has,' announced Robert, appearing abruptly from the direction of the kitchen: 'I've let the soup boil over. You've no idea the mess it's made. For God's sake, darling, come and mop up the ruin!'

The strain left Stella's face and she laughed, and releasing herself from Miranda's arm ran down to him: 'Let's have supper in the kitchen. Then we can serve everything out of saucepans and save on the washing up.'

'Let's not,' said Robert. 'There's burnt soup all over the top of the stove, and it smells hellish. Let's eat in the dining-room, and stack.'

'It does smell horrid, doesn't it?' said Miranda, wrinkling her nose. 'Rather like petrol.'

'That's me,' said Robert. 'Only it's turpentine. I spilt about half a pint of it over my trousers. Our dear governess uses it to discourage moths, and she had left her bottle, improperly corked, on the bathroom windowsill. I knocked it for six.'

'It goes well with burnt soup,' commented Miranda lightly, going upstairs to tidy herself for supper.

Apparently a modicum of soup had survived, for by the time she reappeared in the dining-room Robert had produced three plates of it and Stella was already sipping hers cautiously.

'What were you panicking about in the garage for, Miranda?' inquired Robert.

'I was looking for my bag. And I wasn't panicking — or at least not much.'

'Well the next time you want to go scouting around in the dark, call me first, and I'll go along as bodyguard — heavily armed with the offensive weapon which is at present nestling in my cupboard under a discreet pile of underpants. I have even taken the precaution of loading the thing since last night.'

Stella's face was suddenly white. 'Robert! You don't mean — you don't really think——'

'Of course not, darling. It was only a weak attempt at humour. All the same, I'd rather you both laid off wandering around after dark — for the sake of your nerves if nothing else. Did you find your bag, 'Randa?'

'No. I turned on the dashboard light and hunted around, but——'

'I took it in,' interrupted Stella. 'I meant to tell you, only Robert and his soup put it out of my head. It's in the drawing-room.'

'That's a relief. It's got my only lipstick in it — which accounts for my rather pallid appearance at the moment.'

'Rubbish!' said Robert, turning to look at her. 'If you did but know it, Miranda my pet, yours is one of the few faces that looks better the less you do to it. It's the planes or something. I suppose that's why you photograph so well. As for lipstick, you don't need any. You have a mouth like that plummy pre-Raphaelite female in the Tate Gallery — Mona something. The one dressed up in a pair of brocade curtains and ropes of red beads, clutching a hideous feather fan.'

'Robert, this is most unexpected of you!' said Miranda, surprised. 'I'd no idea you frequented the Tate!'

'I don't,' admitted Robert, clearing away the soup plates and proceeding to carve cold mutton: 'The comparison is not my own. I was idly gazing at a reproduction of the masterpiece in question, "courtesy of the Tate", on the cover of some arty-crafty publication at Katy Lawrence's on Sunday, and happened to mention that the damsel reminded me dimly of someone. It was your friend Lang who remarked that she had your mouth. And how right he was! She has.'

Miranda coloured and Stella looked at her sharply, but forebore to comment.

'Which reminds me,' said Robert handing round the mutton, 'How was it that you knew that chap's telephone number, young 'Randa? I gather you rang him up and yelled for help.'

'He gave me his number,' said Miranda shortly, angrily conscious of her heightened colour.

Robert lifted an amused and mocking eyebrow. 'And you carried it about clutched in one hand ever after, I suppose?'

'No,' said Miranda coldly. 'I didn't need to. I've got a freak memory for numbers. If I've seen them written down, I can visualize them again as if I was looking at a photograph.'

'Oh damn!' interrupted Stella. 'Now I've spilt the mayonnaise! Quick Robert, get me a cloth from the kitchen!'

In the ensuing tumult Simon Lang was forgotten, and Miranda, profoundly grateful for Stella's timely interruption, hastened to change the subject.

14

'Where's Mademoiselle?' inquired Robert, stacking dirty plates in the serving-hatch. 'Is she having supper with the Lawrences? I thought she was supposed to eat here.'

'So she is,' said Stella. 'I hope you've left her some soup.'

'Not a drop — unless she cares to scrape some off the linoleum. But there's any amount of cold mutton and salad left.'

Stella looked at the clock and frowned. 'It's nearly ten o'clock,' she said in a troubled voice: 'I'd no idea it was as late as that! She *must* be back by now. She's probably in the kitchen.'

'No she isn't,' reported Robert, peering through the hatch.

'Then I think I'll just run up and see if she's in her room. You know how she sulks sometimes.'

'I'll go,' said Miranda. 'You put your feet up on the sofa while Robert brews some coffee. You look all in.'

Miranda tapped on Mademoiselle's door, and receiving no answer turned the handle and went in. The room was in darkness and she turned on the light and stood looking about her curiously. It was meticulously neat; the bedcover drawn smoothly and without a wrinkle and the dressing-table almost bare — a severely utilitarian hairbrush and comb, a solid pin-cushion and a small box of hairpins being all that lay upon it. There were no photographs or any form of personal souvenirs, and it might have been a hotel bedroom for all the impression that its owner's personality had left upon it.

Miranda switched off the light and went downstairs again. 'She's not there,' she reported.

'I think perhaps I'd better ring up the Lawrences',' said Stella anxiously.

But Mademoiselle was not at the Lawrences'. She had not returned there and Lottie had eventually gone to sleep without Rollerbear.

'Damn the woman!' said Robert crossly. 'I suppose she's punctured a tyre or something of the sort, and hasn't got the sense to ring up and let us know. I suppose I'd better go out and hunt her up.'

He collected a coat from the hall and went off to the garage; to return an hour later, but without Mademoiselle. The German sentries on the Stadium's gates had been changed about the time she would have left, and the ones now on duty had no recollection of seeing any woman on a bicycle. 'She's probably met a pal, or gone off to some lecture,' said Robert irritably. 'After all, there's no particular reason why she should come home early now that Lottie isn't here. She's probably going to seize the opportunity and take every evening off!'

'But Rollerbear!' said Stella unhappily. 'She knows how Lottie feels about that creature. Surely she would — Robert don't you think we should do something?'

'Such as what?' inquired Robert shortly.

'I don't know,' said Stella helplessly. 'Ring up the hospital perhaps. She might have had an accident or – or something.'

'Nonsense!' said Robert crisply. 'We should have heard soon enough if anything like that had happened. No, the blighted woman has undoubtedly gone on the toot for the evening. We'll leave the front door unlocked and she can let herself in. And I hope you'll rub it into her tomorrow that the next time she takes an impromptu evening off she rings up first!'

But in the morning Mademoiselle's room was still empty and her bed had not been slept in, though the coverlet was rumpled as though someone had sat on it. Her brush and comb, toothbrush and nightdress were missing, and the hall door, which Robert had left on the latch, was now locked. Mademoiselle had apparently returned sometime during the night, collected a few necessities, and left again as quietly as she had come. But she had left behind her one memento of her arrival. On the centre of the bare dressing-table, where her brush and comb had previously lain, stood a small china bear.

There was something white lying in the shadow just behind the door, and Miranda stooped mechanically and picked it up, but it was only a much crumpled face-tissue. 'Elizabeth Arden', noted Miranda with a mild sense of surprise. She had not suspected Mademoiselle of such expensive tastes. Somehow one connected her complexion more with face flannels and carbolic soap.

'I don't understand!' said Stella angrily. 'If she wanted to go, why didn't she say so? Why didn't she explain? She might at least have given me a month's notice instead of going off like this and leaving me in the lurch. Besides, we owe her for nearly three weeks. Robert, you don't think there's anything behind it, do you?'

'Of course there's something behind it,' said Robert crossly. 'She's tired of being interrogated by the police, and someone has offered her a better job at a considerably higher salary. We weren't paying her much, and you can bet your bottom dollar that some dame in the French or American sector has been advertising for a governess at three times the amount, and the old witch saw it and has snapped it up.'

'But to go off being owed money!'

'My dear girl, if she'd told you she wanted to go, you'd have insisted on her giving a month's notice — you know you would! And the chances are she couldn't wait. I hold no brief for the woman, but I can follow her line of reasoning.'

'Well I think it's beastly of her!' burst out Stella angrily. 'After we've paid her fare out here and everything! Can't we report her to the police or something, and at least get the money for her fare refunded?'

'I doubt if we'd have a leg to stand on,' said Robert moodily. 'The employee is always right in these days. Anyway I have no intention of wasting time and money in prosecuting the woman. Let her go — and the hell with her!'

But it appeared that the authorities took an entirely different view of the matter.

The following day, answering a ring at the doorbell, Miranda was confronted by Simon Lang. He walked in without ceremony, tossed his hat onto the hall table and said without preamble: 'What's this about the Melvilles' Swiss governess having run out on them?'

Miranda stiffened. 'Hadn't you better ask my cousin?' she asked coldly.

'I tried to, but he's out on some conference. I'd like to see Mrs Melville, please.'

'She's out,' said Miranda briefly.

'Then you'll have to do instead. *Has* the governess disappeared?'

Miranda said carefully: 'Mademoiselle Beljame has left. Yes.'

'When?'

Miranda hesitated, frowning, and Simon said with unwonted terseness: 'Don't be silly, Miranda! This is serious.'

'Why?'

'*Why*? Well apart from anything else we have two unsolved murders on our hands, and your Mademoiselle Beljame is a possible suspect.'

'Do you — do you really think that she might have done it?'

'What I think is beside the point,' said Simon Lang. 'At the moment I want to know when Mademoiselle Beljame went, where she is, and why the hell it wasn't reported immediately!'

'But we don't *know* where she is,' said Miranda breathlessly. She sat down somewhat abruptly on a hall chair and explained the circumstances, and when she had finished he asked to be shown Mademoiselle's room. It had, however, been swept and dusted only that morning, the bed-linen removed and the blankets neatly folded.

'Who did this?' demanded Simon.

'We did. Stella and I. We do the rooms now that Friedel — until

182

we can get a housemaid. Mademoiselle did her own of course, but as she wasn't here we did it. Her trunk is under the bed. I thought we ought to pack her things in it, but Stella said to leave them as they were, and if she wanted them she could jolly well come and pack them herself.'

Simon opened the cupboard, and looked into the drawers, but Mademoiselle's scanty possessions had little to tell him.

'Why wasn't this reported at once?'

'I don't think it occurred to us,' said Miranda candidly. 'We just thought she'd heard of a better job and left. It happens pretty often in Berlin, I gather; you just ask any of the wives! Stella wanted to tell the police. But only because of having paid her fare out, not because she thought there was anything fishy about it.'

Simon made no comment. He sat down on the edge of the bed and looked about the room with the shadow of a frown between his brows, and after an appreciable interval he said: 'If she went into the Stadium area last night we ought to be able to fix the time she went in and the time she left, because of the guards on the gates. Except that it is possible — though damn difficult — to get out of that place without using one of the entrances, providing one is prepared to risk taking a bit of skin off oneself.'

He stood up. 'Where can I find Mrs Melville? I'd like to see her.'

'She went out to do some shopping at the Naafi,' said Miranda, following him out onto the landing and watching indignantly while he locked the door behind him and calmly pocketed the key. 'I think she was going to the Lawrences',' she added as an afterthought as they reached the hall. 'You might find her there.'

'Thank you,' said Simon, picking up his hat. He paused by the hall door and looked at the catch of the Yale lock, and then said: 'How many other exits are there from this house? Apart from the windows, of course?'

'Two; the back door and the french window in the drawing-room. But we bolt those every night.' Miranda looked at his still face and said breathlessly: 'But if Mademoiselle did it — the murders I mean — she couldn't get away! No one can get in or out of Berlin without endless passports and identity cards and bits of paper.'

Simon Lang transferred his speculative gaze from the Yale lock to Miranda's face and said: 'You've forgotten the Russian zone. It provides an admirable bolt-hole for every variety of bad hat.'

'Then you think she's in East Berlin?'

'No,' said Simon meditatively, 'I think she's——' He stopped and gave a slight shrug of his shoulders and said: 'No matter,' and turning away, opened the door and went down the short path that led to the gate, and drove away.

Stella returned just before lunch. She had met Simon Lang at the Lawrences', and she seemed cheerful and almost exhilarated. 'He thinks Mademoiselle may have had something to do with the murders,' she explained, 'and that she's taken fright and made a bolt for it. I only hope it's true!'

'Why?' demanded Miranda, startled.

'Because if only it *is* her it means that it wasn't——' Stella broke off abruptly and bit her lip. 'I mean,' she said carefully, 'that if it was Mademoiselle, then the whole matter is cleared up and we won't have any more of those ghastly police inquiries and people snooping around the house asking questions. It means that it's all over, and we can breathe again and enjoy ourselves, and nothing else frightening can happen.'

Miranda said quickly: 'For goodness sake cross your fingers when you say things like that! We don't know yet that she was the one.'

'She must be!' insisted Stella passionately. 'She's *got* to be! If she isn't, why did she run away?'

'Perhaps because she had heard of a better job — as Robert suggested. It may still be that, you know.'

'I don't believe it,' said Stella obstinately. 'Of course she's the murderer! Why don't you want it to be her?'

'I do want it to be her,' confessed Miranda. 'That is, if it has to be one of us, I can't think of anyone I'd rather it was. I've never liked the woman. She gives me the creeps; I don't know why. Like spiders! The whole house feels a better place now that she's out of it. Those awful caraway seeds! Do you remember the time your

184

mother gave me a slice of seed cake when I was about twelve — the day we took a picnic to the Roman camp — and I was instantly sick all over the chocolate éclairs?'

Stella made a grimace and laughed. 'Yes I do. Beastly child! But that was years before Mademoiselle arrived on the scene. I wasn't even married to Robert then. Lottie wasn't born.'

'Oh, I know: I wasn't suggesting that I disliked caraway seeds because of Mademoiselle. Only that I probably disliked Mademoiselle because of the caraway seeds! I hope that she just disappears into the Russian zone and that we never hear of her again. The Russians are welcome to her! All the same, we may well hear that she is merely pursuing her governessing in some innocuous home in the American sector; and if so we are right back where we started from and still under suspicion.'

But by tea-time no trace had yet been found of the errant governess, and a representative of the K.R.I.P.O., the German police force, speaking correct but halting English, had called to ask more questions and to interrogate Frau Herbach, the cook.

Robert returned shortly after tea in a bad temper. He had not seen Simon Lang, but Colonel Cantrell, the A.P.M., had apparently rung him up at his office and been brusquely outspoken on the subject of his failure to report the disappearance of Mademoiselle Beljame. Robert was normally an easy-going and even-tempered person, but Colonel Cantrell's comments having been forceful in the extreme, he was feeling sore and sulky, and Miranda hastened to accept an unexpected invitation by the Leslies to go swimming, and hoped that by the time she returned the atmosphere in the house would be less electric.

There were not many people at the indoor pool, for although the water was kept at a comfortable temperature and the big building was warmed throughout, it was still too early in the year, and too cold, for people to think of swimming.

Sally Page, her pretty figure showing to advantage in a brief swimming suit of white satin, was sitting at the far side of the pool, her feet dangling in the water, talking to Elsa Marson.

185

Mrs Marson, wearing a gaily coloured bathing-dress and a scarlet cap, was obviously in better spirits, and it occurred to Miranda that this was the first time that she had ever seen her laugh. Elsa Marson had always seemed pale and anxious, but this evening there were patches of bright colour in her cheeks, her eyes were sparkling and she looked as though some load of anxiety had been lifted from her shoulders. Catching sight of Mrs Leslie and Miranda she waved, and slipping into the water swam across to them.

'What's the water like?' asked Norah Leslie, peering cautiously over the edge.

'Too warm,' said Elsa. She turned to Miranda: 'Sally says that it was the Melvilles' Swiss governess who did the murders, and that she has run away to hide herself in East Berlin. Is it true?'

'What's that?' said Mrs Leslie sharply. She swung round to look at Miranda, her face pale and startled.

Miranda inquired tartly as to where Sally Page had obtained her information, but Norah Leslie was not to be deflected: 'Is it true?' she demanded. 'Did that woman really do it? Who said so? How did they find out?'

'We don't know that she did,' said Miranda briefly. 'Sally's only guessing.'

'Then she *has* disappeared?'

'Yes,' admitted Miranda reluctantly. 'But we think she may have merely gone off to some better-paid job. You know what it's like in Berlin. I gather that in spite of all the talk of unemployment, anyone who hears of a better job, or feels peevish for any trivial reason, is apt to walk out without a word of warning, and the first their employer knows of it is when the cook or the housemaid or the nurse fails to turn up. Mademoiselle may have found it catching.'

'But she *has* disappeared?' insisted Mrs Leslie.

Miranda did not answer. She looked across the pool to where Sally Page dangled her pretty feet in the vivid blue water and wondered where Sally had obtained her information. There was a quick way of finding out.

Miranda stepped back, took two running steps and dived cleanly into the pool. But it seemed that Sally had no desire to speak to her, for when Miranda surfaced Sally had already risen and was running lightly along the edge of the pool towards the diving-boards. Miranda swam to the side and sat watching her as she climbed one ladder after another until she reached the highest board, thirty feet or more above the water. Her tall, slender figure seemed absurdly small seen from below, and Miranda, who had no head for heights, shuddered and felt a little sick as young Mrs Page walked calmly out upon the narrow plank and looked down at the clear blue depths below, her hands at her sides.

Sally tested the spring of the board, waiting, it seemed deliberately, until the attention of the other bathers was focused upon her. Then she turned and walked back again, swung round and ran lightly along it, and springing upwards and outwards, somersaulted once in the air and finished with a perfect swallow dive. Her body entered the water like a silver arrow, so smoothly that it appeared to cause only the slightest splash, and one or two spectators applauded vigorously.

It was a surprisingly competent performance, and Miranda felt a glow of admiration. She was a tolerably good swimmer herself and could dive prettily, but she knew that she would never have dared walk out upon that slender plank so near the high ceiling, and that she did not possess either the nerve, judgement or coordination of brain and muscle to execute such a dive.

Sally rose to the surface, shook the water out of her eyes and swimming easily to the edge of the pool hoisted herself out of the water and walked quickly away in the direction of the changing-rooms.

Colonel Leslie, employing a stately breaststroke, swam across to Miranda and paused beside her, keeping himself afloat by duck-paddling. 'Norah tells me that your cousin's governess has bolted, he remarked. 'Very useful of her. I should imagine that this lets us all out. Well, no one can say that it has not been an interesting experience.'

'What has?' asked Miranda bleakly.

'Being a murder suspect.'

'I don't think they know yet that it was her.'

'No. But provided she doesn't turn up again, the supposition will be that it was. The various police forces of this city are fairly efficient, my dear, and as they have been unable to trace her as yet, we can be reasonably sure that she is well and truly behind the Iron Curtain.'

Miranda looked at him in some surprise, but he appeared to be unaware of any discrepancy in his words. Yet if it were true that he had only just this moment heard of Mademoiselle's disappearance, how could he know that she might not already have been traced? However, as she did not want to talk of Mademoiselle, she said: 'I expect so,' in a colourless voice. Mrs Leslie swam across to join them, and after a few minutes of desultory conversation, offered to race Miranda a length, and having lost by a couple of yards, left the water and went off with her husband to talk to some friends on the steps at the far end of the pool.

It was almost an hour later that Miranda, who had become involved in a game of water-polo, strolled down from the changing-rooms in the wake of the Leslies, who had gone on ahead some ten minutes earlier in order to collect their car, which they had parked a good distance away, telling her that they would pick her up by the gate that gave access to the swimming-pools. The air outside felt very cold after the overheated atmosphere inside the building, and the clear spring evening was faintly scented with fruit blossom and the fumes of petrol.

A reclining nude in bronze, several times larger than life, stood near the edge of the open-air pool against an angle of the wall that bore the word *Herren* largely lettered upon it — the word apparently directing attention not to the bronze statue, but to a shadowy flight of steps that descended to a door in a narrow area behind it. The bronze itself, like the wall and the stone-paving below, was pockmarked with bullet holes, and Miranda looked at it critically as she passed.

The entire Stadium was littered with similarly pockmarked

statuary, and she was pondering over the Nazi passion for outsize representations of the unclothed male and female body, when she was surprised to see that the Leslies had gone no further than the other side of the open-air pool — the one flanked by the bronze cattle — where they seemed to have been waylaid by one of the swimming instructors, a Herr Kroll.

Herr Kroll, talking excitedly, was gripping the Colonel's arm with one hand and gesturing with the other, and presently all three of them bent to peer down into the dark, stagnant depths of the water below. Miranda heard Colonel Leslie say, 'Rubbish!' and Herr Kroll retort, '*Nein*! I tell you, no! It is not the rubbish!' and presumed that the instructor had been explaining how the sea-green tiles of the pool were protected from cracking in the winter frosts by a grid of ropes, each the thickness of a man's body, that were made from bales of straw and lay, partially submerged, on the surface of the water, where they moved sluggishly to every breath of wind and thus prevented ice from forming. Either that, or he was telling them a tale that Harry Marson had told her; about how the Russians, when they had first occupied Berlin and used some of the nearby buildings as stables for their horses, had found no better use for this huge, pale-tiled pool than to use it as a dumping place for manure.

A last ray from the setting sun gilded the flanks and tipped the long, curving horns of the bronze bulls with gold, and across the dark green water of the pool the ruined columns of a bomb-damaged wing of the building began to take on the outlines of some pyloned temple of the Nile Valley. Miranda quickened her steps, and joining the group at the pool side, demanded to know what all the excitement was about?

Colonel Leslie, who had been bending down to peer short-sightedly into the water, straightened up and said irritably: 'Herr Kroll here thinks there's something down there — a body; or something equally ridiculous. He swears he saw a face. Well, if he did it isn't there now, for I'm damned if I can see anything. Come along, Norah.'

'No, wait a minute, Ted. I believe I can ... *There*! Over there! I'm sure I ...' Mrs Leslie gripped Miranda's arm and pointed: 'Look — down there, just below that ... No. It's only a hank of straw. Funny, I could have sworn I saw a face too.'

'Probably your own reflection,' grunted her husband, bending again, hands on knees, to peer in the direction in which she had pointed. 'Your eyes are better than mine, Miranda. See if *you* can see anything.'

The sun slid below the horizon, and a little breeze awoke and sighed through the branches of a group of pine trees that stood near the edge of the lawn behind them, momentarily ruffling the quiet surface of the pool so that a half-submerged rope of straw immediately below Miranda drifted a little way and disclosed the pale, distorted reflection of her own face looking up at her, Narcissus-like, from a patch of dark water.

The breeze passed and the water steadied again ... And it was not her own face that was staring up at her from the pool, but another face. A ghost out of the terrifying, shadowy past. A pallid face, open-mouthed, with wide, staring eyes and lank, straw-coloured hair. Suddenly and horribly familiar ...

A second catspaw of wind ruffled across the pool, and the heavy blond hair drifted before it and was once again only a swathe of sodden straw. And below it lay the grey face and black, scanty locks of Mademoiselle Marie Beljame.

Miranda did not know how long she stood there looking down at that drowned face, for she had stepped back into the past and was a child again — several hundreds of miles and fifteen years removed from the battered city of Berlin.

Every sound of the quiet evening came clearly to her ears with an unnatural distinctness; but now each one possessed a different and terrifying meaning. The muffled shouts and laughter of the few remaining bathers from the indoor swimming-bath were the cries of fleeing, panic-stricken people. The whisper of the breeze through the pine needles was a frightened man whispering orders in the shadow of fog-shrouded whin bushes. A passing car was the drone of an enemy bomber, and the faint lap of water against the sea-green tiles at the far side of the wide pool was the lap of waves against a pebble beach . . .

She became aware that the swimming instructor was shouting, 'You see now how I am right?' That Colonel Leslie was swearing and that Norah Leslie had screamed — though mercifully only once — and that other departing bathers were hurrying up to swell the group and add their voices to the babble of sound.

The sky behind the tall, spidery lines of the wireless masts had turned to a clear green flecked with gold and the bronze cattle that stood at the head of the pool were no longer warmly gilded, but dark and clear-cut in the gathering twilight.

Miranda stepped back from the rim of the pool, moving very carefully, as a person may move on a surface of ice. Edging her way through the rapidly growing crowd, she reached the top of the flagged steps, and turned down the wide path towards the entrance gates, past the shell of the ruined, roofless wing where the budding boughs of young trees thrust up through the fallen rubble around a small, white, concrete square that was a newly built fire-station.

A car was coming up the road past the hockey field, and as it reached the junction of the road opposite the gates to the swimming-pool, and slowed for the turn, Miranda broke into a run.

Simon Lang jammed on the brakes, and after one quick look at her face threw open the car door, and she stumbled in and sank down beside him.

Simon did not ask any questions. He leant across her and shut the door, and turned the car into the road that ran past the Sports Centre; bringing it to a stop by the curb a few yards from the gates to the pool, with the engine still running.

There was a babble of voices from the path beyond the gates, and as Colonel and Mrs Leslie and a tall woman in a persian lamb coat came into view, Miranda said with stiff lips: 'They're looking for me.'

There was a queer singing sound in her ears and she felt cold

191

and oddly light-headed. She was aware of Simon calling across the road something about giving her a lift home, and the car moved forward again before she heard the reply.

Simon said lightly : 'I imagine, from their expressions, that they are all under the impression that I have arrested you.'

Presently he brought the car to a standstill by some trees and switched off the engine. He turned to look at her and said abruptly: 'Do you want to be sick?'

Miranda shook her head. The gold had faded from the sky, and dusk was gathering over the scattered lawns and gardens and buildings of the Stadium. Simon lit a cigarette and sat relaxed and silent, leaning back against the worn leather seat and letting her take her own time, and after a while Miranda said jerkily: 'Mademoiselle Beljame——' and he turned his head and looked at her; his face indistinct in the twilight and his quiet eyes reflecting the faint glow of his cigarette.

'I *knew* her!' whispered Miranda: 'I didn't realize it before. I never recognized her. I don't know why I never recognized her. It was the hair, I suppose: and she looked so old, and – and I never thought of it. I only knew that I didn't like her. I suppose that was why I didn't like her.'

She stopped, and after a moment or two Simon said quietly: 'Who was she?'

'I don't know. But years ago, when I was a child, my parents were killed in Belgium, while we were trying to reach the coast. The road we were on was bombed and our car was wrecked, but I must have been thrown clear. I don't remember much after that; except how Mother looked, and – and my father. I wasn't very old, but I knew they were dead. There were a lot of other people who were dead too. There was a head in the middle of the road; only a head. It had its eyes open and it was looking at me. It's funny that I should have forgotten that until now. I thought — I thought I didn't remember it. But it's come back again . . .

'I was frightened of the head, and I picked up my doll and ran away screaming. Then sometime later on — or perhaps it was days

192

later, I don't remember — a woman spoke to me in French. There was a man with her and they took me with them and gave me some food, and the woman pointed to my doll and said: "That is how we will do it." I thought she meant to take it away, but she didn't. I was afraid of them; but there was no one else. I think we must have walked a long way, but we only walked at night and hid in the daytime. Then we joined some other people, and one night we got into a boat and there was a lot of shooting and it was dark and misty, and the woman got left behind ...

'When we got to England the man was ill, and I was left on my own. I heard people talking in English so I spoke in English too, and I remember someone saying: "Good God — the child's English!" I didn't see the man again: I think he died. I'd forgotten about the woman, but – but now I've remembered her again. It was Mademoiselle Beljame ...'

'Why have you remembered now?' asked Simon quietly.

'Her hair,' said Miranda in a whisper. 'She had a lot of thick yellowish hair, and she wore it banded across her forehead; not strained back and dyed black, like Mademoiselle's. The straw looked like hair, and – and her face was puffy, and not so old. And then I remembered where I had seen eyes like that before. They weren't the same colour: I don't know how I could have forgotten that. Someone – someone only the other day — said that you never forgot a physical defect. But I had forgotten it. Until – until now.'

Simon said: 'Where is she?'

Miranda turned to look at him, her face no more than a small white blur in the shadows, and tried to speak and could not.

Simon reached out a warm hand and laid it over the two cold ones that were clutched together so tightly in her lap, and her chilled fingers turned and clung desperately to his. He said: 'Tell me, dear.'

'In – in the open-air pool near the swimming-bath.'

She felt rather than saw the sudden involuntary movement of Simon's body, but his hand remained steady and his voice un-hurried.

193

'She's dead then.' It was a statement and not a query.

Miranda nodded dumbly, and when she spoke again he had to bend his head to catch the words.

'The swimming instructor, Herr Kroll, found her. Or – or perhaps it was Mrs Leslie . . . I don't know. They were arguing and pointing, and Colonel Leslie told me to see if I could see anything . . . and – and at first I thought it was only the reflection of my own face, but then the wind moved some straw and . . . And I saw her face——'

Simon did not ask any further questions. He released her hands and restarted the car, and before the sudden flood of light from the headlights the violet evening turned to night as the car swept down a long curving road bordered by trees, and turned in the direction of the Herr Strasse.

There was a rigidly enforced speed limit in Berlin, but Simon must have disregarded it, for in an astonishingly short time the car drew up before the Melvilles' house. He had not spoken during the swift journey from the Stadium, but now he turned to look at Miranda; his face unwontedly grim in the reflected glow of the headlights.

'You are not to say a word of this to anyone — about recognizing her. Anyone at all. Do you understand?'

Miranda nodded wordlessly. He studied her face for a moment or two, and what he saw there evidently satisfied him, for he laid the back of his hand against her cheek in a brief gesture that was somehow more intimate than a kiss, and then leant across her and jerked open the door of the car: 'And another thing,' said Simon. 'Don't go out of the house until I've seen you again. No matter who asks you. And if for any reason you are alone in the house, lock yourself into your room. Is that understood?'

Miranda nodded again and stepped out into the dark road, and Simon gave a little jerk of his head in the direction of the gate: 'Go on. I want to see that you get safely into the house.'

Once again it was Robert who opened the front door for her, and turning to look back, she saw the car move away down the road.

194

'Who was that?' inquired Robert, shutting the door behind her. 'That wasn't the Leslies' car, was it?'

'No,' said Miranda, looking curiously dazed. 'Captain Lang gave me a lift back. He – he wanted to ask me some questions.'

Robert laughed — he appeared to have recovered his good temper. 'Still Suspect Number One, are you? Don't worry, darling! It's my guess that Lang is merely using this business as an excuse for enjoying your society. And who can blame him? Cheer up, 'Randa!' He put an arm about her shoulders and gave her a companionable hug as Stella leaned over the landing rail to ask if Miranda had brought the Leslies in for a drink.

'No,' said Miranda; and was spared explanations by the ringing of the telephone bell. Robert released her and went over to answer it, and she saw his face stiffen and after a moment relax again. He said: 'Yes. She's here,' and turned towards Miranda holding out the receiver: 'It's for you.'

It's Simon, thought Miranda, her hands suddenly unsteady, but he can't have got there as soon as this: he can't have found her yet!

She took the receiver and steadied her voice with an effort, glad that Robert had walked quickly away. But it was only Sally Page, ringing up to ask if she would like to make a fourth to dine and dance at a nightclub on Grünewald Strasse with Andy and herself and a young American; they could pick her up in about twenty minutes.

Miranda, feeling weak from a mixture of shock and emotional reaction, murmured excuses and thanks, and rang off. She went to bed early that night, but could not sleep. The past that she had buried deep in oblivion for so long had returned to her, and when at long last she dropped into an uneasy sleep it was to dream of a blond woman with curious eyes, who smelt of caraway seeds and dragged her by the hand through a clinging fog down a long road pitted with shell holes . . .

15

'Pssst!'

The bushes underneath the drawing-room window rustled, and a twig, accurately aimed, flipped against the pages of the morning paper that concealed Miranda's face.

Miranda lowered it hurriedly.

'Pssst!' said Wally Wilkin, his flaming hair and excited eyes appearing briefly above the level of the sill.

'Hullo, Inspector. On the trail again?' inquired Miranda, folding away the paper.

'Sssh!' begged Wally frantically, casting an agonized look towards the half-open door into the hall. Miranda rose and shut it and returned to the window-seat: 'Well, Rip Kirby — what is it now?'

'That there governess,' hissed Wally. 'They found 'er!'

Miranda's hands clenched suddenly on the window ledge. 'Who told you? How do you know?'

'Cos I was there! In the water she was. I saw 'em pull 'er out. Coo, it were a treat!'

'Wally, *no!*'

'Dad takes me up to see the 'ockey, an' 'e thinks I gorn 'ome in the other lorry. But I nips off to 'ave a bathe. Then up comes a chap wot tells everyone to clear off, and I sees there's a guard on the gate and that 'tec's there with 'is busies; so I 'ides, and I seen 'em fish 'er out. Drowned she was, and all tangled up in that grass — and 'er bike too. An' listen — I know oo done it, cos I——'

There was a sound of women's voices from the hall, and Wally disappeared with the speed of a diving duck as the drawing-room

196

door opened and Elsa Marson came in, followed by Stella carrying a sheaf of cherry blossom and white lilac.

'Do look, 'Randa! Aren't they lovely? Mrs Marson has just brought them over. Isn't it sweet of her? Would you be an angel and put them in water for me? She's offered to give me a lift to the Lawrences', because Robert has the car this morning and I have to take over some clean clothes for Lottie.'

Elsa Marson looked curiously at Miranda, and from her to the window, and her eyes were all at once wide and wary. She walked quickly across the room to lean on the windowsill and look out into the garden, and said with an attempt at a laugh: 'I see that I have only brought coals to Newcastle. I did not realize that you had cherry trees in your garden.'

'But no white lilac,' said Stella. 'Our lilac isn't out yet, and it will be several days before we can pick any. I think your garden must get more sun than ours.'

'Perhaps,' said Elsa Marson, her gaze roaming quickly about the garden. Miranda looked out, but Wally had vanished and the leaves were unmoving in the morning sunlight.

A bell rang in the hall and Stella deposited her fragrant burden on the coffee table and said: 'With any luck that will be a new housemaid. The Labour Exchange swore they'd send round a few suitable applicants. Or do you suppose it's someone ringing up to ask us to forward Mademoiselle's belongings?'

She went out into the hall, shutting the door behind her, and Elsa Marson said in a bright, conversational voice: 'You know, I really thought that you were talking to someone in here when we came in!'

'Did you?' Miranda's tone expressed polite interest and Mrs Marson coloured and turned away from the window to walk aimlessly about the room, fingering photographs and ornaments and talking at random of the weather and the recent kidnapping by the Russian police of a German from West Berlin: 'It says in the papers that they have their agents everywhere — all through the city. Why do we not put a stop to it? Why cannot we protect these people? *Why?*'

197

Her voice rose unnaturally, and a small porcelain horse that she had been fidgeting with slipped from her fingers and smashed in pieces on the parquet floor. Mrs Marson stared at it in horror and plunged down upon her knees to gather up the broken bits.

The door opened and Stella was back, her face white and excited. Mrs Marson began to apologize for her clumsiness, but Stella said: 'The horse? It doesn't matter,' and looked across the room at Miranda: 'Captain Lang is here.'

Simon had been up all night, and had not slept for over twenty-four hours. But there was nothing in his face or manner to betray the fact. Stella said abruptly: 'He says that they have traced Mademoiselle.'

There was a little crash as the broken pieces of china that Mrs Marson had gathered up fell back onto the polished floor.

Simon said: 'Can I help?' He crossed over to her and stooping down began to pick up the pieces, an expression of polite concern on his face.

Stella said urgently: 'Where is she, Captain Lang? Don't keep us on tenterhooks! Has she only gone to another job? Or did she make a bolt for it to the Russian zone after all?'

Simon straightened up and placed the small white pieces neatly into an ashtray. 'She's dead,' he said laconically.

Stella said: 'No! Oh, no!'

She pressed the back of one hand against her teeth as though to stop herself from screaming, and did not notice that Miranda had shown no surprise at the news.

'Why do you not stop it?' cried Elsa Marson hysterically. 'Why is there no protection? It is the Russians, I tell you! The *Russians*!'

Her voice rose to a scream and Stella took her hand away from her mouth and said desperately: 'Please don't, Mrs Marson!' She turned to Simon Lang.

'How did she — die?'

'She was drowned.'

The rigidity went out of Stella's body. 'Oh, thank God!' she said on a long breath of relief.

She took an uncertain step towards the nearest chair and sinking down into it, hid her face in her hands, and after a moment or two let them drop and looked up: 'I'm sorry. That was a beastly thing to say. But I didn't mean it like that; I thought for a minute it was another murder.'

'It was,' said Simon Lang briefly.

Stella's hands tightened on the arms of her chair until the knuckles showed white, but she did not move or speak.

Simon said: 'She was hit over the head with something like a spanner, and either fell, or was pushed, into the water, somewhere around Tuesday evening or Tuesday night.'

He turned away to gaze abstractedly at an excellent reproduction of Velasquez's 'Lady with a Fan' that hung on the wall beside him, and added as though as an afterthought: 'Her hands were covered with green paint.'

For a moment no one spoke and then without warning Mrs Marson began to laugh. She rocked to and fro in shrill, hysterical mirth that grated abominably upon their taut nerves and went on, and on . . .

Stella came to her feet in one swift movement and crossing over to her, grasped her by the shoulders and shook her. Mrs Marson gasped, gulped and dissolved into tears, and Stella put an arm about her and glared defiantly at Simon Lang: 'I'm going to take her home,' she said: her face was quite white and her eyes were blazing.

'A very good idea,' said Simon politely. 'Perhaps you wouldn't mind staying with her until her husband or some responsible person can keep an eye on her? And after that I'd like to see you: we'll have to go over the details of Tuesday evening again, I'm afraid.'

'Of course. Come along, dear, I'll take you home.' Stella led the sobbing Mrs Marson from the room and the door closed behind them.

Miranda said in a shaking voice: 'What did that mean?'

'What did what mean?'

'The green paint. Why did it frighten her so?'

'Because there is a can of green paint in Major Marson's garage. They have been painting their garden furniture.'

Miranda said helplessly: 'I don't understand!' and sat down abruptly on the window-seat as though her legs could no longer support her: 'Simon, what is it all about? Please tell me! You know, don't you?'

'Yes,' said Simon slowly. 'I know. Not quite everything yet, but enough to go on with.'

He looked at her thoughtfully for what seemed a long time. His eyes were slightly narrowed and there was an expression on his face that puzzled her — though it was probably familiar to Lieutenant Hank Decker of the United States Army and other devotees of poker.

After a moment or two he sat down beside her, and thrusting his hands in his pockets said: 'What is it that you want to know? I'll try and answer at least some of the questions.'

'I want to know about Mademoiselle. I've been thinking and thinking about her. I even dreamt of her last night! Was she really the woman I think she was, or did I only imagine it?'

'No. She was the same woman.'

'How do you know? Perhaps – perhaps I was mistaken?'

Simon shook his head. 'No you weren't. We spent most of last night and a good bit of this morning going through endless files and records and documents and dossiers. It was all astonishingly simple really, and one wonders why on earth no one spotted it before. Do you remember the story Brigadier Brindley told you at Bad Oeynhausen?'

'About the Nazi couple who murdered their servants and got away with millions of pounds worth of diamonds?'

'The Ridders. Yes. But it was not the Ridders who murdered their cook-housekeeper and valet. It was the cook and the valet — Karl and Greta Schumacher — who murdered the Ridders. They probably planned it for weeks beforehand. We shall never know about that, but the chances are that the building of the new garage and the lime pit at the bottom of the garden gave them the idea——

'On the night that Herr Ridder returns to Berlin with the diamonds he is killed by the Schumachers. Frau Ridder is probably already dead and her jewels, plus any other available loot, packed in a small suitcase. The Schumachers dress the bodies in some of their clothes — they were much of a size — making sure that a few identifiable metal objects are included with them for the purpose of identification; the buttons off the valet's coat for instance, and his wristwatch, and a locket and chain and ring belonging to the cook, and one or two similar things that lime would not destroy—— Greta Schumacher probably shaves Frau Ridder's head and chops off a hank of her own hair to bury with her, just in case.

'Then they bury the bodies in quicklime, and make their getaway. Once the lime has destroyed the flesh that deformed hand of Frau Ridder's will not show, since the bone formation was apparently normal. But even then the imposture might well have been discovered if it hadn't been for the tremendous events that were taking place at the time. The British Army was in full retreat, Belgium suing for an armistice, and France crumbling to pieces. The authorities had a great many things on their hands in those days!'

Miranda said: 'Brigadier Brindley said there was a child. Did they kill it too?'

'No one knows. There seems to be no evidence to show that it was even in Berlin at the time. But its body was never found. I think myself that they may have taken it with them and that it died or was killed on the road, which is why they picked up a stray child as a substitute. They may have needed a child; it was probably part of the plan.'

Miranda said slowly: 'Then it was the housekeeper — Frau Schumacher. How did they get away?'

'I don't suppose anyone will ever know that. The chauffeur may conceivably have been in the plot. Or they may have stuck a gun in his ribs, or had some convincing lie ready. They probably meant to get across Europe to Lisbon, and so to South America, but found that it was too dangerous and decided to try for England instead. I don't suppose they ever realized you were British. You say the woman spoke to you in French, so the odds are that you answered her in the same language.'

Miranda nodded. 'I expect so. I spoke more German and French than English in those days.'

'Then that's the answer. You were a stray child and they needed a child. But your chief attraction was undoubtedly the fact that you were clutching a large doll. What better way to smuggle out a lot of stolen valuables than for a child to carry them inside a toy?'

'But the Dutch diamonds?' said Miranda.

'No one knows what they did with those, or even if they knew anything about them. They may not have done. The stuff they got away with was a sufficiently spectacular haul! Well, there you are. Some of that is guesswork, but there's quite a bit of evidence to support it, and it all adds up. Do you mind if I smoke?'

Simon drew out a flat gold cigarette case and offered it to Miranda, who shook her head. He lit a cigarette himself and flicked the spent match out of the open window.

'Go on,' said Miranda impatiently. 'That isn't all.'

'You told me some of the rest yourself. Greta Schumacher was left behind when you and her husband escaped across the channel. Karl Schumacher died of double pneumonia, and no one connected a dying refugee with an obviously English child. The jewels and money were not found until some time later, and by the time their ownership was proved the trail was cold and there was nothing to connect the Ridders with you, or you with an unknown dead man: you apparently insisted that the doll was yours and that no one had touched it. In the end it was decided that the Ridders had at one time been among the refugee party, and had hidden the stuff there temporarily, meaning to retrieve it, but had probably been killed in an air raid. Various trails were followed up, but none of them led anywhere.'

Miranda said: 'But Mademoiselle — Frau Schumacher? How did she—— What happened to her?'

'We haven't got much of a line on her yet,' confessed Simon. 'But as far as can be made out she ended up in a prison camp where one of her cell mates was a Swiss woman called Beljame, who either died or was assisted to die, and Mademoiselle — Frau Schumacher — eventually turned up in England with her papers and calling herself by that name. She was, of course, looking for a husband and a child, and a doll stuffed with jewels. And also, possibly, a fortune in Dutch diamonds! She must have struck a trail at last, for your cousin Robert says she turned up on the doorstep one day with some story about having been told that they needed a governess-cum-household help.'

'Supposing they hadn't?'

'Domestics were pretty rare in those days,' said Simon. 'She drew a card to an open straight and pulled it off.'

'She did work well,' said Miranda, slowly. 'And they paid her so very little: that was the main reason why they kept her on.'

'When did you first meet her — as Mademoiselle?' asked Simon.

Miranda frowned, trying to think back. 'Only about two years ago, I think. And then only for very brief intervals. I hardly spoke to her. I had a job in London and didn't get to Mallow often. But I never liked her. She looked quite different — thin and old and black-haired. I couldn't have recognized her. But she still ate caraway seeds, and I suppose, without knowing it, the smell of them must have reminded me of that awful time. It wasn't until I started for Berlin that I really began to feel on edge and to feel — oh, I don't know!'

'Aunt Hettyish?' supplied Simon with a grin.

'Yes!' Miranda turned a surprised look on him. 'How did you know that?'

'You explained the expression to me once,' said Simon. 'I thought it very apt.'

'Well, it's true. I didn't connect it with Mademoiselle. I only knew that for some reason or other I felt on edge and - and frightened. It was a horrid feeling. I suppose it came from being boxed up with her for so long, and my subconscious or something getting uneasy about it. But how could I be expected to guess at such a fantastic coincidence?'

'It wasn't a coincidence,' said Simon. 'It was a careful piece of planning by Mademoiselle Beljame, *alias* Greta Schumacher. But what we *don't* know is why did she stick to the Melvilles after she found out that the jewels had gone? — which she must have done fairly soon. However, the chances are that the answer to that is quite simply because it was a job, and since she had nowhere else to go she might as well live that way as any other. It was what followed that was the fantastic coincidence. Your cousin Robert meets a man who had known his father, and asks him to have supper with you all at the Families' Hostel. And during the meal Brigadier Brindley, who had actually stayed at the Ridders' house, told the story — probably for the five-hundredth time — of the missing diamonds.'

Miranda shivered in the warm spring sunlight. 'And she had to sit there and listen to it!' she said in a whisper.

'Yes. It can't have been very pleasant. But there was worse to come. He mentioned, didn't he, that Frau Ridder had a physical defect, and added that of all things a physical defect was the one thing one did not forget?'

'Yes,' said Miranda. 'But he was wrong. I forgot.'

'You were only a child, and very frightened; so to you it was only an unimportant detail in a welter of horrible things. But I think that the ex-housekeeper thought that the Brigadier's remark was aimed at her — remember, she had actually seen and spoken to him in the Ridders' house! Supposing he had recognized her? She may even have thought that he told the story in order to surprise some reaction from her. I think that she must have decided then and there to take precautions against his denouncing her when she reached Berlin, and his talk of sleeping tablets gave her the opportunity.'

Miranda said: 'Then it *was* Mademoiselle who killed him!'

'I think so,' said Simon, slowly. 'You all told me that she and the Brigadier and Mrs Melville each took sleeping powders. But though a good many people saw the Brigadier and Mrs Melville take theirs, no one seems to have seen the governess take hers. My guess is that she put it in the hot milk that she gave to Lottie, to ensure that the child slept soundly.'

'But — Friedel?' said Miranda. 'Why Friedel? There was no reason for that.'

'That's something else I don't know yet,' admitted Simon. 'I think that it's perfectly possible that she did kill Friedel, but that she killed her by mistake — and in mistake for someone else.'

'Stella,' whispered Miranda.

'It could be. On the other hand — always supposing she did do it — she may have mistaken her for you.'

'*Me?*' Miranda's face was suddenly white and startled. 'But why me? You're joking!'

'You know, this doesn't strike me as being a joking matter,' observed Simon pensively.

'But why me? It doesn't make sense!'

'I think you may have had something that she — or someone — wanted. *That——*' Simon reached out and touched the charm bracelet that encircled Miranda's slim wrist: 'The ankh. It was one of the items inside your doll, if you remember. I don't suppose she realized that you had it until you drew attention to it yourself.'

Miranda stared at the little metal charm with a shrinking distaste. 'But why should she want it?'

'I don't know. I'm not even sure that she did. It's just a theory as yet. But I'm interested in that charm; because you weren't wearing the bracelet when you arrived in Berlin. *Or* when I spoke to you that afternoon at the Families' Hostel.'

Miranda wrinkled her brows. 'I must have been! I always wear it. No . . . You're right. I couldn't make the catch work; it's stiff. So I put it in my pocket.'

'And someone noticed that you were not wearing it, and searched your room for it.'

'How can you know that?'

'I don't. It's just an idea. But since I knew that your room hadn't been searched officially, I realized that you obviously had something that someone wanted badly. And having heard at least half a dozen versions of the Brigadier's story, and its sequel, I made a guess at what it was.'

Miranda looked from the little metal charm to Simon's face, and back again. 'It can't be true! Why try to kill me when it would be so much simpler to steal it?'

'Perhaps it wasn't so easy to steal?' suggested Simon. 'You've just told me that you always wear it. And possibly time was short.'

Miranda said: 'No, you can't be right. You've forgotten the coat. Friedel was wearing Stella's coat.'

'Yes, I know. But your coat is squirrel, isn't it? By moonlight the difference in colouring would be negligible. And there's another point that appears to have escaped general notice. Both you and Friedel had dark hair, but Mrs Melville is a blonde.'

Miranda said in a low voice: 'Stella thought that someone had meant to kill her.'

'I know she did. She was almost scared out of her wits, wasn't she? I realized that. But it was better to let her go on being scared, in order to allow the murderer to think we were off on a false trail.'

'Stella said that there was a reason — ' began Miranda and stopped.

Simon looked up quickly. 'What's that? What did she say?'

'Very little,' said Miranda slowly. 'She said that she knew that someone had meant to kill her, and when I told her not to be silly and asked her if she knew of any reason why anyone should want to kill her she – she said "Yes".'

'Are you sure of that?' demanded Simon.

'Quite sure: she said it in a sort of whisper, as though she were talking to herself. Afterwards she said she hadn't said anything of the sort; but she had — I heard her. And she was more than just frightened. She was terrified!'

Simon Lang said 'Oh' in a preoccupied voice, and remained silent for a moment or two, watching a thin spiral of smoke curling up from his cigarette, and presently Miranda said: 'If it was

Mademoiselle who killed the Brigadier and Friedel, then the case is over.'

'That's where you're wrong. Because now Mademoiselle herself has been killed.'

'I was forgetting that,' said Miranda unhappily. She turned to stare out of the window and said abruptly: 'Is it Elsa Marson?'

'Now why should you say that?' inquired Simon with an odd note in his voice.

Miranda turned to face him: 'Because I saw her at the hostel the day we arrived, talking to Friedel in German. I wasn't sure then, but I am now. It *was* Mrs Marson. And I saw her again in that Russian cemetery place. She had gone there to meet someone, hadn't she?'

'Yes,' said Simon slowly. 'She had. And for that reason it's possible that Friedel was killed by someone who had no connection with the murder of Brigadier Brindley, and who killed her knowing quite well who she really was.'

'Who was she?'

'She was Mrs Marson's sister,' said Simon surprisingly.

'Her *sister*!' Miranda stared at him, open-mouthed. 'How long have you known that? Did she tell you?'

'Since yesterday. She told us everything. Elsa's mother was French and her father German. They parted in 1938 and the mother took the younger child with her and resumed her maiden name. Elsa's elder sister and brother remained in Germany with their father. When the war broke out the mother's family supplied her with falsified identification papers that mentioned a French father, deceased, and got them away to England. The mother died in the last year of the war, and Elsa got a job as private secretary to the head of a firm of importers.

'Major Marson met her and married her, thinking that she was French and an only child. She was afraid to tell him that her father was a German and a Nazi. Then last year the regiment was sent to Berlin, where Friedel saw her by chance and was struck by her resemblance to a photograph of their mother; and also to their elder brother. She stopped her in the street one day and taxed her with it, and Elsa lost her head and admitted it. After that, Friedel blackmailed her.'

'Threatened to tell Harry, I suppose. Beastly woman!'

'Yes. After paying over various odd amounts, Mrs Marson borrowed money and paid Friedel a large sum, in return for which her sister had promised to leave Berlin. But when the Marsons returned from leave Friedel was still here. She rang up Mrs Marson and arranged to meet her at the hostel, which is where you saw them. You interrupted them, and so Friedel, who had got a job with Mrs Melville, arranged another meeting that night. She told Mrs Marson that their brother was in East Berlin. He had played ball with the Communists and risen to a position of some importance, at a shady level, but he was getting frightened and wanted to escape to the West. He also wanted money. More money than Elsa could supply. And he thought he knew how to get it. He had something to sell that he thought the Americans or ourselves would be prepared to pay pretty highly for. And he was right!' added Simon grimly.

'What was it?' inquired Miranda.

'That, my dear Miranda, is still a Top Secret: and likely to remain so. But I think you saw Mrs Marson take it over.'

'Yes I did. I thought she was doing a bit of black-marketing. But why go to all that bother? Why didn't he just walk out with it himself? It seems quite easy to go from one zone to the next.'

'Because he hadn't the nerve,' said Simon. 'By chance, and a talent for lock-picking that must amount to genius, he knew he could get his hands on a bit of pure dynamite. He didn't mind walking into West Berlin with empty hands, but he was scared of a good deal worse than death if he was caught trying it with that packet on him. And I can't say that I blame him. He and his sister made a deal with Mrs Marson. She was to go on that bus tour, collect the goods, and hand it to Friedel. We kept an eye on Elsa Marson, because for all we knew she might have been working for the Russians. It looked like it, and we wanted to see who contacted her.'

Miranda said: 'I thought I saw someone, the evening we were all looking at the ruin of the Ridders' house. Was that one of your people watching her?'

'I expect so,' said Simon without interest. 'When Friedel was killed, Mrs Marson lost her nerve and made a clean breast of it. As it turned out, she and her brother had done us a signal service.'

'Then he *has* got away?'

'Not as yet; which leads me to believe he has been liquidated.'

'Poor Elsa — what hell she must have been through! So she didn't have anything to do with Mademoiselle or the Ridders after all?'

'Apart from confusing the issue, no.'

Miranda said: 'But there's something else, isn't there? The green paint. If there hadn't been, you wouldn't have suddenly brought it up like that.'

'Like what?' inquired Simon softly.

'You said it on purpose,' said Miranda accusingly 'Didn't you? You wanted to see what she'd do.'

'I must be getting very obvious in my old age,' said Simon regretfully. 'Or else you are too acute for your tender years.'

'Then I *was* right?'

'Almost. You see that picture?' Simon gestured with his cigarette towards the dark Velasquez print. 'It makes a very adequate looking-glass, and people are more likely to display their emotions when they think they are unobserved. It is beginning to dawn on Mrs Marson that the Russians may get to hear of her part in taking that package out of East Berlin, and the mention of green paint in connection with Mademoiselle instantly suggested to her that the governess and her killer had been lurking round her house. I wasn't interested in Mrs Marson's reactions. But I *was* interested in Mrs Melville's. I wanted to know if green paint meant anything to her. It did.'

'Nonsense!' said Miranda sharply. 'You're imagining things!'

'Am I?' said Simon softly. 'I don't think so.'

Miranda stood up abruptly. 'What are you hinting at?' she demanded breathlessly.

Simon leaned out over the windowsill and dropped the end of his cigarette into the bushes. 'That wasn't a hint, it was a statement of fact.' He leant his head against the window frame and looked up at Miranda, his hands deep in his pockets.

'That mention of green paint meant something to Mrs Melville. It gave her a clue to something that had puzzled her, and it frightened her badly — so badly that I thought for a moment that she was going to faint. But she hid it very well. Mrs Marson's hysterics helped her out there, and I have no doubt at all that had I been facing her she would have kept a better control over her features. But I had my back to her, and you and Mrs Marson were both looking at me and not at her.'

Miranda said angrily: 'Why are you trying to make her out to be a hypocrite?'

'My dear Miranda,' said Simon mildly, 'there is a considerable difference between being an actress and a hypocrite. A good many men and women can act very well if they have to. Some are better than others; that's all.'

'You don't know Stella!' said Miranda shortly.

'Do you, I wonder? Sit down and be sensible.' Simon reached up and caught her wrist, and pulled her down again onto the window-seat. 'How can you be sure that you know anyone well enough to tell what they might not be capable of under pressure? I'm not accusing your Stella of anything. I am merely pointing out that she knows something, or thinks she knows something, about that green paint on Mademoiselle's hands. She may decide to tell. I can only hope so. To possess a vital piece of knowledge in connection with murder is a very dangerous thing. After all, a murderer can only hang once.'

Miranda stared at him, whitefaced. 'You mean that – that anyone who knew something that might point to the murderer might be murdered too? That's what you mean, isn't it?'

'Of course. It occurs in almost every detective story, and you'd be surprised how often it also happens in real life.'

Miranda put out a shaking hand and clutched at his sleeve.

'*Wally!*' she said breathlessly.

Simon's brows twitched together in a sudden frown. 'The Wilkin brat? What about him?'

'He was here this morning. He said he saw the body being taken out of the pool last night——'

'I know he did,' said Simon grimly. 'And the bicycle, too! It had green rubber hand-grips that had been daubed with fresh green paint — Wally's work! He'd done it to get his own back on Mademoiselle, who'd caught him lurking round the Lawrences' house on the evening that she disappeared. He was looking for Lottie it seems, and Mademoiselle, who also had a score or two to settle, went after him with a stick and evidently landed a few shrewd shots on target. The paint was Wally's revenge.'

'Then why,' demanded Miranda hotly, 'didn't you say so at once, instead of scaring the daylights out of Stella and poor Elsa Marson with your sinister hints?'

'I've already told you why,' said Simon patiently. 'I wanted to know if by any chance green paint meant anything to anyone here. It ought not to have done, since only the police — and Wally of course — knew anything about it. You see, it wasn't applied until dusk on the evening of the day Mademoiselle disappeared. And as it was dark when she set off for the swimming-baths to look for Lottie's china bear, she wouldn't have noticed it; though she must have realized that there was something sticky on the handles, once she got started. But then rubber is apt to become tacky with age, so she probably thought it was that; or if she did drive up to the fact that it was paint, she obviously decided to deal with it when she got back. Only she never did get back.'

'I still don't see why you should have thought that Stel'——'

'Use your head, Miranda!' interrupted Simon brusquely. 'No one except Wally, Mademoiselle, and the murderer — who presumably touched the handles when the bicycle was tipped into the

211

pool — could have known anything about that paint. Unless someone else brushed against it by accident, either when it was parked at the Lawrences', or by the gate into the swimming-pool area.'

'Wally may have told someone!'

'I doubt it. I caught the young demon watching us fish the body out of the pool. Which was when he owned up about the paint — he hadn't much option, as his clothes were liberally bespotted with it! I tore a king-size strip off him in more senses than one, and told him that if he said one word about the affair, he'd be for the high-jump!'

'He didn't tell me that,' said Miranda. 'But he said he knew who had killed her. Supposing he was hiding there on Tuesday night too—— Supposing ...'

Simon stood up as swiftly as though he had been jerked to his feet and his quiet voice had an unexpectedly harsh ring to it: 'Did he give you a name?'

'No,' said Miranda, her own voice unsteady. 'We were interrupted and he bolted.'

Simon said a single wicked word in a tone that held so much concentrated rage that Miranda flinched and her eyes widened with shock. But it seemed that his fury was directed neither at her nor Master Wilkin, but against himself. 'Why didn't I think of that?' whispered Simon. 'It ought to have occurred to me that there might be some particular reason for that kid's interest in the pool and why he should happen to be hanging about there. I should have jollied the little blighter along — instead of scaring him into clamming up like an oyster. I ought to be hung, drawn and quartered——!'

'But you can't ... but you don't think that he *really* knows, do you?' quavered Miranda.

'We can always find out,' said Simon briefly. He turned and walked quickly across the room, but at the door he stopped suddenly and came back to her.

'What I told you last night still goes. You are not to tell anyone anything of all this until I give you permission. *Anything*, do you understand?'

'Yes,' said Miranda unsteadily.

He stood looking down at her with an odd mixture of doubt and irresolution on his normally blandly expressionless face, and said something under his breath that Miranda could not catch. And then he swung round, and she was alone.

16

Stella returned, looking white and exhausted, barely five minutes after Simon's departure. She seemed surprised that he had gone. 'I thought he wanted to see me,' she said, sinking wearily onto the sofa. She leaned her head on her hand and shut her eyes.

'Why don't you take a couple of aspirins and have a day in bed?' suggested Miranda. 'You're looking like a ghost.'

'Am I?' Stella got up and went to peer at herself in a little Venetian-glass mirror that stood on the chimneypiece. 'I do look a bit of a hag, don't I? I feel as if I'd aged ten years since I arrived in Berlin. Oh dear, that Marson woman!'

'How is she?'

'I telephoned her unfortunate husband and he came right over. I should think Colonel Lawrence must be going crazy, what with his officers' time being gummed up by police inquiries and hysterical wives.'

'Was she very tiresome?'

'Awful!' said Stella feelingly. 'She appears to have got a bee in her bonnet about Soviet spies. She thinks Mademoiselle may have been one. She also thinks that the Russians mean to kill her in revenge for something or other. I think she must be out of her mind!'

She leant tiredly against the chimneypiece, her back to Miranda, and said: 'It's because of the green paint. Captain Lang said something about green paint, and Mrs Marson seems to think that this proves that Mademoiselle had been snooping around their house.'

The words were said casually enough, but Miranda was suddenly aware, with a startled sense of shock, that Stella was watching her in the Venetian-glass mirror: watching her with an inexplicable and furtive intentness. Miranda flushed hotly and looked quickly away. It was true then, what Simon had said! Stella did know something about that green paint — and she wanted to know if Miranda also knew. She had mentioned it deliberately while watching Miranda's face reflected in the little mirror, as Simon Lang had watched hers in the glass of the Velasquez print.

Stella ... Miranda stared blindly out of the window and thought about Stella, and all that she knew about her. She had said so confidently to Simon: 'You don't know Stella!' and he had replied, 'Do you?' *Did she?* She had known Stella for so long, yet how well did she really know her?

Stella had been there, part of the background of her childhood and schooldays — taken for granted. She was in many ways a curiously childlike person; a charming, rather spoilt child, simple, direct and not particularly clever. Gay and lighthearted when things went well, tearful and dazed at the unreasonable injustice of life when they went wrong. She was pretty without being beautiful, and always well dressed; always smooth and scented and shining. She had been widowed and remarried, and although she hated army life and the prospect of living in foreign countries she had again married a soldier. She loved England and Mallow — and Robert.

A sudden thought took root in Miranda's mind and grew swiftly into a certainty. Robert! Stella adored Robert. She would, thought Miranda, quite literally die for him if it were necessary. She would certainly lie for him and scheme and fight for him, and protect him. Simon had said that most people could act if circumstances forced them to it, and Miranda had thought instantly and scornfully 'Not Stella!' But even a bird will pretend to a broken wing and act a part to perfection, limping and fluttering, in order to lure an enemy away from its nest.

For some obscure reason Stella was afraid for Robert. Far more afraid than she had been for herself. She had been convinced that someone had meant to kill her: and been reduced by that knowledge to helpless and shuddering terror. But she was not helpless now. She was wary and alert and watchful.

Turpentine! thought Miranda suddenly. Robert had spilt some turpentine . . . when was it? — on Tuesday evening, of course! Was that what Stella had thought of? Had it puzzled her, and had the mention of green paint made her think that he had perhaps used it to clean stains from his clothes? What did Stella know, or think that she knew?

Whatever it was, she was wrong! Robert could not possibly have been involved in the murder of Mademoiselle. And for a very simple reason. He had no means of knowing that Mademoiselle would be at the swimming-pool late that evening, since her presence there was purely fortuitous. He had been at a conference that had not ended until about seven-thirty, and had been given a lift home by Harry Marson: and from then, until they had gone up to bed, he had been with Stella or herself or both of them.

But even if Robert had not possessed an alibi and had actually been seen near the pool that evening, Miranda would still have been sure that he could not possibly have murdered Mademoiselle. It was not a question of proof, but of instinct. There was no hard core to Robert. He was charming and attractive, and despite an occasional display of temper or irritability, essentially easy-going — she would not use the word 'weak' even to herself.

Robert wouldn't *care* enough to commit murder, thought Miranda, trying to explain her conviction to herself. Things don't matter enough to him. He will always avoid something unpleasant rather than face it — if facing it means taking any drastic action. He loves Stella, but not as Stella loves him. He lets himself be loved. He will always let things happen, never do them — or even do anything towards making them happen. Why is it that I can see that, thought Miranda, and Stella can't? The answer presented itself to her almost before the question had formed in her mind. Because Stella was in love with him and wore the bandage of her love across her eyes. She could not reason; she could only feel.

Stella's voice cut sharply across the silence.

'What are you thinking about, Miranda?'

Miranda turned quickly and said in some confusion: 'Nothing. I mean I was just thinking about all this ghastly business, and——' The sound of voices and laughter from the hall interrupted her, and she realized gratefully that Robert was back. It must be later than she had thought.

'I only hope there's some beer,' said Stella anxiously. 'He seems to have brought someone back with him. I wonder——' She stopped suddenly and Miranda saw her stiffen. The door opened to admit Colonel and Mrs Leslie, Robert, and Sally and Andy Page.

'Stella darling, have we a spare can of petrol?' demanded Robert, crossing to her side and kissing her lightly. 'Andy very kindly offered me a lift home, and then ran out of petrol about a quarter of a mile back. We were forced to abandon ship, and Colonel Leslie picked us up. There's a two-gallon can in the garage, isn't there?'

'Yes, I think so,' said Stella.

'Good. Well let's have a drink first. What about a glass of beer, sir? Or there's gin if you prefer it. Sherry for you, Norah?'

'Thank you.' Mrs Leslie looked across at Stella and said: 'I must apologize for this invasion, but your husband insisted.'

Stella smiled a stiff, social smile that did not reach her eyes, and murmured some polite formula as Norah Leslie accepted a cigarette and sat down on the sofa and Sally Page perched gracefully on the arm of a chair, one long slim leg swinging from the knee, and said, smiling appealingly at Stella: 'It's our fault really, Mrs Melville. I can't get Andy to have the petrol-gauge mended, and so this sort of thing keeps on happening.'

'Nonsense,' said Andy irritably. 'It's only happened once before — on the day we first discovered that the thing was bust. I can't understand it happening again. I filled the tank up only a day or two ago. It's all this coffee-partying of yours that eats up the petrol.'

'Far more likely to be a leak in the tank,' retorted Sally. 'I don't see what else we can expect with a museum piece like that.' She turned again to Stella: 'I keep telling Andy that a fifth-hand pre-war car is a false economy. A decent car might cost a good bit more to start with, but it would save pounds in the end! Don't you agree, Mrs Melville?'

Stella was saved the necessity of replying by the unexpected appearance of Harry Marson.

'Hullo,' said Harry, checking in the doorway and looking about the room, 'I seem to have gatecrashed a party.'

'Not at all,' said Robert hospitably. 'This is purely impromptu. The more the merrier. Have some beer?'

'Thanks, I will.' He turned to Stella. 'Elsa sent me over to ask if you could lend her something to read; magazines for choice. I've bunged her off to bed. She was feeling a bit mouldy.'

'Of course I will. I haven't got much in that line, I'm afraid, but she can have what there is.'

'Good of you,' said Harry Marson, and raised his tankard. 'Well — here's to crime!' He drank deeply and did not appear to notice the sudden strained silence that followed upon his words.

Miranda looked around the room. At Sally, sitting suddenly still, her slim foot in its neat shoe no longer swinging. At Mrs Leslie, with the cigarette ash falling unnoticed onto her skirt. At Andy Page, holding his tankard so tightly that the knuckles stood out white against the tanned skin. At the little muscle that twitched nervously at one corner of Colonel Leslie's mouth and belied the habitual boredom of his expression. At Stella, whose frightened gaze had darted momentarily to Robert and then away again, and at Robert, whose handsome mouth had tightened to a hard line . . .

The silence was becoming oppressive when it was broken by Mrs Leslie.

'You're spilling sherry all over the chair, Sally,' she said briskly.

Sally righted the glass that she had been holding at an acute angle, and stood up hurriedly: 'Oh dear! I *am* sorry, Mrs Melville.

218

How messy of me!' She produced a face-tissue from her handbag and scrubbed anxiously at the stain.

'That,' said Robert, 'will be ninepence. And if you go on scrubbing at it Sally, it will cost you an additional two bob for having the hole invisibly mended.'

Sally laughed and tossed the crumpled tissue in the general direction of the fire. The tension was eased and a babble of conversation broke out again. But Miranda was not deceived. In the short space of silence that had followed upon Harry Marson's ill-chosen toast she had realized that the Pages too knew of Mademoiselle's death: the Leslies must have told them. They were all attempting to behave as though nothing had happened, but sometime during that morning each one of them had heard that there had been a third murder, and they were acting — discussing trivialities in gay, artificial voices.

'Fiddling while Rome burns!' thought Miranda, exasperated, and she said in a hard, bright voice: 'Well, what do you think about our latest murder?'

Seven faces turned swiftly towards her as though they had been pulled on one string. Seven faces that were all at once blank and unsmiling.

Stella said: 'Miranda — please!'

'Why? What's the matter?' demanded Miranda crisply. 'Why shouldn't we talk about it? It's what we're all thinking about, isn't it?'

Robert got up quickly, and coming over to her put an arm about her. 'Take it easy, darling. We all know how you feel. And we all feel much the same.'

Miranda jerked herself away angrily. 'I'm not having hysterics, if that's what you mean. I just think that it's silly to put on an act and pretend, when – when we all know what's happened.'

Robert returned to his chair and poured himself out some more beer, and sat down again.

'Of course we all know,' he said deliberately. 'We've all been on the carpet again; separately and severally. But what you do not realize, Miranda my pet, is that there is a limit to what one can take in this line. We have all been surfeited with horrors of late, and this is in the nature of a last straw. It's not that we are being ostriches and burying our heads in the sand, but that we just do not feel like discussing it any more. So for the time being, darling, we'll just lay off it if you don't mind.'

'Hear! Hear!' approved Harry Marson. 'Speaking for myself, I have gone over and over it until my brain is bubbling, and I now propose to lay off it for good — God willing and the gumshoe boys permitting.'

He finished his beer and set down his empty tankard with a thump.

'I'm sorry,' said Miranda contritely. 'You're right, of course. It's only that I——' She checked herself with an effort.

'Forget it, darling,' said Robert lightly. 'Have some more beer, Harry.'

'No thanks. Time I was getting back.'

Stella routed out some magazines and a novel for Elsa Marson, and the party broke up: Harry and Mrs Leslie leaving through the garden and Robert accompanying the Pages to the garage in search of petrol.

Colonel Leslie, who had offered to drive the Pages to where they had abandoned their car, lingered for a few moments in the hall, waiting for them to return, and said kindly to Miranda: 'Cheer up, my dear. Don't let this get you down. It's a terrible business, but perhaps not as bad as Lang and his lot, and the *Polizei*, seem to think. She could have taken the bicycle in with her, instead of leaving it unattended outside the entrance gate, and been wheeling it along the edge of that pool when she tripped, or the bicycle skidded and took her in with it, and she hit her head as she fell. Those sagging great ropes of straw would have let her through, but held her down if she tried to struggle up. Pity that instructor fellow, Kroll, didn't spot her earlier — or later, after we'd left! He called us over to show us, you know. If it hadn't been for him, we wouldn't have been involved in it. And if we hadn't asked you to go swimming with us, *you* wouldn't have been either. I'm sorry about that ...'

'You needn't be,' said Miranda sadly. 'We'd still have been involved even if she'd been found by the Bürgermeister of Berlin and his entire family! Because she was Lottie's governess, and employed by Robert and Stella, and we all lived in this house.'

'I suppose so,' admitted the Colonel. 'Still, it was unfortunate that——— Ah! here, I think, is the petrol.'

Stella and Robert accompanied the salvage party to the gate, and Miranda, left alone in the empty hall, went back into the drawing-room. It was quiet and warm and still, and in the silence she could hear through the open windows the voices of Harry Marson and Mrs Leslie talking in the next garden.

The green and white room was heavy with the scent of flowers, and Miranda looked guiltily at the wilting sheaf of cherry blossom and lilac, and realized that she had forgotten all about Elsa Marson's offering. A wisp of damp face-tissue had been wrapped about the stalks, but the petals of the cherry blossom were limp and fading for lack of water, and as she picked them up a small shower of white petals fell from the flowers in her arms onto the carpet, and she thought with a touch of irritation that if Elsa Marson needed an excuse to call on the Melvilles in order to find out what was going on, she might at least have refrained from bringing over cherry blossom, when she must have been able to see quite clearly from her own house that the Melvilles' garden was full of it!

Miranda bent down to gather up the fallen petals and stopped with her hand an inch away from the fender.

Presently she straightened up slowly, leaving the petals un-touched, and having laid the flowers carefully on the table, sat down on the sofa, her brain whirling. She had remembered some-thing that had happened in this room during the last half-hour. Something that her mind must have subconsciously noted at the time, but put aside. And a fantastic, impossible theory began to form in her head ...

221

She sat quite still, staring blindly ahead of her while another small, unregarded incident, and another and another, detached themselves from the memories of the past few days and fitted themselves together, like pieces of a jigsaw puzzle, to form a picture.

I have been looking at it the wrong way round, thought Miranda. It's like looking in a mirror. You see something quite clearly, but you see it the wrong way round.

Even Simon had seen it the wrong way round. No, that was not true. He had seen it both ways. If Friedel's death was a mistake, then the first guess was the right one after all, and it should have been Stella who died in the garden. The diamonds had only muddled it: they, and the package that Elsa Marson brought out of East Berlin. They sounded more important and more interesting, and so the more ordinary thing was overlooked. And if that were true, then Mademoiselle was only the excuse and the opportunity. She was dead now, and her story was finished. But the other story had not finished yet——

I must tell Simon, thought Miranda. I must let Simon know.

There was still no sound from the hall and the house was so quiet that Miranda could hear a faint clatter of pots and pans from the kitchen where Frau Herbach was preparing lunch.

Seized with a sudden panic she jumped up and ran quickly across the drawing-room and into the hall, and dialled Simon's number.

A strange voice answered her. No, Captain Lang was not in, and the strange voice had no idea when he would return; who was speaking? Oh, Miss Brand. Would Miss Brand care to leave a message?

Miranda hesitated. She could hear Robert's voice from the path outside the drawing-room windows.

She said hurriedly: 'Yes. Tell him I want to speak to him.' And rang off.

At four o'clock Miranda rang Simon's number again. But he was still out, and the same voice assured her politely that Captain Lang would telephone her as soon as he came in: and with this she had to be content.

Robert returned an hour later with the unwelcome information that he would have to have an early supper, and leave again immediately afterwards to attend a talk by the Commander-in-Chief Northern Army Group on 'Allied Strategy in Europe'.

'I ought to have told you before,' apologized Robert, 'but what with all this flap on I'd completely forgotten about the damn thing. It's at eight-thirty, so I should be back by eleven at the latest; but ... ait up for me.'

... aid: 'Are you taking the car, or is someone fetching you?'

... tainly not taking the car! I don't see why the hell ... trol for this sort of show. One of the

... am. 'I'm sorry, my love. I ... one in the house.

The M.O.

17

The long afternoon wore away, and still Simon did not phone.

Stella flipped over the pages of a magazine and Miranda forced herself to read a book, and struggled to keep her thoughts from the impossible theory that had occurred to her that morni... won't think of it! she told herself desperately. I *won't*. I wo... of it until Simon comes. He will know what to do abo...

It was half-past three when a bell cut shrilly thro... and Miranda threw aside her book... door before Stella could ris...

She ran across th...
Simon Lang...

'Wh...

ng. I
n't think
ut it.

ough the silence,
ana was at the drawing-room
I'll answer it,' she said quickly.
he hall and lifted the receiver. But it was not

was it?' asked Stella as she returned to the drawing-room.

'It wasn't the telephone,' said Miranda. 'It was the front-door bell. One of the Wilkin children asking if we'd seen Wally.'

'He's probably up at the Lawrences' playing with Lottie,' said Stella.

'That's what I told her,' said Miranda, and shivered. Wally! Was he really at the Lawrences', or was he——? She pulled up her thoughts with a frightened jerk as they approached the edge of a yawning gulf into which she dared not look. I won't think of it, she told herself frantically. I won't think of it! *Wally*...! Oh, not Wally!

'Only the Germans,' said Stella bitterly, 'would install a door-bell that is practically indistinguishable from a telephone bell. Oh, what wouldn't I give to be home! The daffodils will be out in the orchard at Mallow, and the primroses...' She got up suddenly and went out of the room, and Miranda heard her slam the door of her bedroom behind her and knew that she was crying.

don't w

Stella s

'No, I'm ce
I should use my own pe
Volkswagens is calling for me.'

He lifted Stella's hands and kissed the
don't like having to go out and leave you two a
Thank God we shall have a batman again tomorrow
says Davies is fit for duty again, and until this business is cleared
up he can live in. I shall feel a lot better when I know that there
is a large and trustworthy chap around the place to discourage the
criminally-minded when I'm not on the premises!'

He turned to Miranda and said: 'Keep an eye on her for me,
'Randa. She's just about all in.'

'I will.'

Robert put his hands on Miranda's shoulders and turned her
about to face the light.

'You aren't looking too good yourself,' he said frowning. 'This
has been one hell of a holiday for you, hasn't it dear? I wish we
hadn't had to drag you into all this ghastly business.'

'Don't be silly, Robert,' said Miranda crisply. 'As if anyone
could have known what was going to happen! And if I had known,
I should probably have thought it sounded thrilling and insisted
on coming. It's only when one is actually involved in a murder case

that one realizes that it isn't thrilling at all, but only very terrifying and quite beastly.'

Robert said: 'When this is all over, you and Stella had better take the next boat back to England and spend a month or two recuperating in some nice, safe, rural spot where the only problem on the hands of the local constable is who pinched the postmaster's prize marrow off the lectern during the Harvest Festival!'

He kissed Miranda affectionately and went out into the cold spring night.

Stella shivered suddenly. 'Cold, darling?' asked Miranda. 'Why don't you go and have a hot bath and get to bed?'

'I'm not cold. It was only a goose walking over my grave; and if I did go to bed I shouldn't sleep, so what's the use?' She closed the hall door, released the catch of the Yale lock and pushed home the heavy bolts above and below it. Miranda saw that her hands were shaking so that she could hardly control them, and that her face was white and frightened. She looked up and seeing Miranda's expression, smiled a little uncertainly.

'I know it's stupid of me, but I feel better with the doors locked. Robert locked both the other ones and any windows large enough for a cat to crawl through! If only I'd known that he was going to be out, I'd have asked a couple of people in to play bridge.'

'Well, let's do it now,' suggested Miranda. 'Let's go over and collect the Leslies.'

'No, don't let's,' said Stella with another shiver. 'Nothing would induce me to walk through the garden, and I don't intend to let you go over, and be left on my own in this house even for two minutes! Anyway, Colonel Leslie is sure to be going to this lecture affair too, and I couldn't stand Mrs Leslie solo just now. Let's turn on every light in the drawing-room and see if we can find a good programme on the wireless instead.'

The drawing-room looked larger and less friendly with all the lights burning, and the wireless offered them a choice between a mournful and wailing concerto by a popular modern composer, a drama about racketeers on the New York waterfront, a reading

225

from *Murders in the Rue Morgue*, a political broadcast, and a variety of excitable gentlemen declaiming passionately in French, German, Italian and Russian.

Stella switched off impatiently and fetched a book. She seemed disinclined for talk, but Miranda noticed that although she kept the open book in her hands and occasionally turned a page, her eyes were unmoving and fixed in a blind stare as though they were turned inward on some frightening mental vision, and that every now and again she would shiver as if a cold intermittent draught blew through the warm room.

The house seemed strangely empty now that Robert had gone, but Miranda could not rid herself of a conviction that they were not alone, and that from somewhere near at hand an unseen pair of eyes was watching their every movement. Yet the curtains were closely drawn and gave no glimpse of the moonlit garden, and the door into the hall was shut. Could there be someone outside that door, waiting and listening? No, that was absurd! Every window and door was barred and bolted and there was no one in the house but Stella and herself. Nevertheless she found herself listening intently for sounds in the empty house or from the silent garden. Stella seemed aware of it too, for twice she turned her head and glanced uneasily over her shoulder. Her frightened tension reacted unpleasantly upon Miranda's own taut nerves and the thoughts that she had striven to keep at bay for so many hours came circling and swooping back again, closing in upon her like vultures gathering above a kill.

Had Stella too seen the thing that she had seen, and put the same interpretation upon it? Was she facing the same picture that had taken shape before Miranda earlier that day, and finding it equally feasible and frightening?

Why hadn't Simon telephoned? Had he ever received her message? If he had, surely only something urgent and alarming could have prevented him from getting in touch with her? He had gone to find Wally ... *Wally!* She had forgotten all about Wally! Supposing he too had – had disappeared?

226

Miranda's hands felt cold and unsteady. Like Stella's, she thought. We are both sitting here pretending to read and slowly scaring ourselves into idiocy. It's almost as if we were waiting for something horrible to happen. She looked across the room and saw Stella's desperate eyes upon her and tried to smile and could not.

Stella dropped her book to the floor and stood up abruptly. 'It's no good trying to read tonight,' she said in a high, strained voice. 'I can't concentrate. I think I'll get some knitting. It's a nice, soothing occupation!'

She went quickly out of the room leaving the door ajar behind her.

Miranda lowered her own book and thought, shall I try and ring Simon again? No. What's the use? I've done all I can.

She could hear Stella's footsteps in the hall, and a faint draught of cold air swung the drawing-room door open a little wider and ruffled the pages of the daily paper that lay on the window-seat. The faint rustle of the paper seemed absurdly loud in the silent room and Miranda started violently and bit her tongue, and closing her book with an impatient bang she reached for a cigarette. She very rarely smoked but at the moment, to smoke a cigarette, like Stella's knitting, seemed a soothing occupation.

The telephone bell rang shrilly in the hall and the cigarette box jerked from her grasp and fell to the floor, scattering its contents over the carpet.

Simon! thought Miranda with a gasp of relief. She jumped to her feet and started for the door, but Stella was already at the telephone.

'Hullo? . . . Yes, speaking.'

Miranda lingered near the open doorway hoping to hear Stella call her. But it was not Simon.

'*Who?*' Stella's voice sounded unnaturally high-pitched. 'Oh! Yes, of course I remember.' There followed an audible gasp and a long minute of silence. Miranda knew she should close the door and not listen to a private conversation, but she did not move.

There was something in Stella's voice that frightened her; and Stella was speaking again.

'*No!* ... No, I can't! not at this time of night! ... But *why*? ... Why not tomorrow? ... It's no good, I daren't! I tell you, I daren't ... not alone. Is Robert there? ... Can I speak to him? ... Oh. Oh, I see.'

There was another long pause and then Stella's voice; trembling and shrill, and completely unnatural.

'How do I know it is you? It might be anyone! ... Oh ... All right then. I'll ring you back.'

There was a click as the receiver was replaced and Miranda heard Stella ruffle through the leaves of the telephone book and presently dial a number.

'Hullo? — Oh it *is* you. I – I had to be sure ... Very well then. I'll do it ... Yes, as soon as I can.'

She rang off and came swiftly across the hall and into the drawing-room. Her face was colourless and her eyes feverishly bright, and she was breathing unevenly. She said: 'I have to go out. I don't think I shall be very long. You – you won't mind staying here alone, will you? You could ring up Mrs Lawrence or someone?'

'*Going out?* But where? Who was that on the phone? What's happened, Stella?' Miranda's voice was sharp with alarm.

'It was Colonel Cantrell. He says he has to see me at once. I said I wouldn't go, but he says it's a most important matter and that it can't wait. He wouldn't say much on the phone, but Robert is there; and so is Captain Lang, and I think one or two of the others. He said I was to take the car and drive over at once.'

Miranda said: 'But *why*? What's happened? Surely no one else is dead?' She heard the note of hysteria in her voice, but could not control it.

'I tell you I don't know! I'll try not to be too long.'

Stella turned away and went quickly across the hall to the cloakroom where the coats hung, Miranda at her heels. She took down a dark tweed coat from its peg, struggled into it, and reached for the garage key.

228

Miranda saw that her hands were trembling so that she could not fasten the heavy coat buttons, and she caught at Stella's arm.

'Don't go, Stel'! Let them come here. You can't go alone! It isn't safe, I tell you. It isn't safe!'

'I must,' said Stella, briefly. 'I'll be all right; Robert's there.'

'No!' said Miranda. *'No!'*

Stella must not go out alone into that dark, spring night. It was dangerous; Stella did not realize how dangerous!

But Stella only pulled away from her clutching hand and moved towards the door.

Miranda gave it up. 'All right, then; but I'm coming with you.'

Stella turned, relief and a tense anxiety on her white face. 'No, 'Randa! You keep out of this. Robert was right — we've let you in for too much already. You stay here and lock yourself safely into the drawing-room until I get back.'

'Don't talk nonsense!' said Miranda, hurriedly getting into a coat. 'If you go, I go! I'm not going to let you go running off by yourself. It isn't safe. Besides, I promised Robert that I'd keep an eye on you. Come on — have we got a torch?'

'Yes. But——'

'I'm not going to argue with you darling,' interrupted Miranda firmly, 'but if you think for one moment that I'm going to be left alone in this house, you're crazy!'

Stella laughed a little hysterically. 'All right then — on your own head be it!'

She turned away to unbar the door, and a little chill wind breathed against Miranda's cheek. She turned her head, puzzled, for the front door was still shut. And it was only then that she noticed that the tiny, narrow window alongside the door stood open to the night air.

The window was no more than a slot in the wall; a narrow slab of thick plate glass in a steel frame, that opened inwards and had probably been placed there so that anyone pressing the doorbell could be seen from inside, and letters, small parcels, or messages could be taken in without the necessity of unlocking the door.

229

Possibly it had been a useful and necessary precaution in the days of the Nazi régime, and even now Frau Herbach, the cook, would peer anxiously through it before admitting a visitor.

It was seldom opened and it had certainly not been open when Robert had left — of that Miranda was quite sure, for she had watched Stella lock and bar the door and neither of them could have overlooked an open window directly beside it. But Frau Herbach had left before dark, and there was no one in the house except herself and Stella. Then who had opened it?

The window was too narrow for even the smallest child to squeeze through. Yet supposing someone had thought that by reaching in an arm they could unlock the door? It was not possible, for the window opened to the left and even a double-jointed person could not have touched so much as the edge of the door. But someone standing outside might not know that . . .

Stella pulled back the last bolt, and turning saw Miranda's fixed and frightened stare.

'What is it? What are you looking at?'

'The window,' said Miranda, in a shaking whisper. 'Did you open it?'

Stella shook her head. Her eyes were wide and terrified.

'Someone did. It wasn't open when you shut the door after Robert had left.'

Stella licked her dry lips: 'Perhaps – perhaps the catch is loose and the wind blew it open.' She caught at Miranda's arm. ''Randa, you don't think — you don't think——?'

Miranda said: 'I don't know. Shut that door again and wait here a minute.' She turned and ran back across the hall.

'Where are you going? *Miranda! Where are you going!*' Stella's voice rose to a scream.

'I'm going to get Robert's revolver!'

A minute later, panting and breathless, she was back again, the heavy service revolver in her hand.

Stella shrank back at the sight of it. She looked as though she

230

were going to faint. 'Wha – what are you going to do with it?' she whispered.

'Heaven alone knows. But it may come in useful. We can always wave it at anyone we don't like the look of!'

Stella looked from the ugly weapon to Miranda's face, and broke into sudden hysterical laughter. The glazed look of terror left her eyes and they glittered with excitement. 'I never thought of that gun,' she said.'Dare we use it if – if——'

'Of course,' said Miranda, with a confidence she was far from feeling. 'Any idiot can pull a trigger. We'll fire first and ask questions afterwards. At the worst they can only bring it in as justifiable homicide! Let's go.'

There was a misty halo about the moon and once again the little chill wind that drifted through the branches of the trees threw slow-moving shadows from the nearest street lamp over the walls of the house and the path that led to the garage.

The lilac bushes made a dense pool of blackness about the garage door, and as Stella switched on the torch and fitted the key into the lock, the bushes stirred and rustled and a twig cracked sharply in the shadows. It's only the wind, Miranda assured herself desperately. It's only the wind!

She kept her back to Stella and the garage door, facing the dark tangle of the lilacs with Robert's gun in her hand, and said in an urgent whisper: 'Be quick, Stella!'

'I'm being as quick as I can; it's stiff.' The key grated in the lock and a moment later the hinges creaked complainingly as Stella pushed the doors wide.

Once again a twig cracked in the darkness, and a shadow that was not thrown by the street lamp slipped across the narrow path near the house and merged with the deeper shadows of the walls . . .

Stella opened the car door and switched on the headlights. A blaze of warm light filled the garage and drove back the blackness from around the doors, and in the noise of the engine the small night noises were swallowed up and lost.

231

'Get in, 'Randa.' Stella backed the car out into the road and turned it in the direction of the city.

As the purr of its departure died away down the quiet road, a figure that had been standing in the deep shadow formed by an angle of the wall ran lightly up the path towards the hall door. It paused for an instant and looked intently at the open window, and then slipped through the door that Stella had forgotten to lock, and closed it again.

A moment later, had there been anyone in the empty house, they might have heard the faint click of the telephone receiver being lifted softly from its cradle, and the sound of a number being dialled.

Miranda sank back against the car seat breathing quickly as though she had been running. The palms of her hands were wet and clammy and she put the revolver down carefully on the seat beside her and rubbed them mechanically against her coat.

Now that they had left the house she was asking herself questions; foolish, frightening questions to which there were no answers.

Who had opened the window by the hall door, and why? Had there really been anyone among the shadows of the lilacs by the garage, or was it only the wind or a prowling cat? Why had Colonel Cantrell only wanted to see Stella, and not her, Miranda, as well? Was it really Colonel Cantrell who had telephoned, or someone who wanted to get Stella out of the house? She would not have recognized his voice.

Miranda said suddenly: 'How do you know that it was Colonel Cantrell who telephoned? It may have been someone pretending to be him.'

Stella turned her head to look at her and the car swerved a little on the road. 'I didn't know. That's why I told him I'd ring him back.'

'So you did: I forgot that. Then it must be all right.'

'Of course it is,' said Stella impatiently, her eyes on the road again.

But was it? Supposing it was possible for someone to use Colonel Cantrell's telephone? Someone who might have reason to know that he was out? And yet if anyone had wanted to get Stella out of the house, why had the window been opened? That looked more as though someone had intended to get in.

Yet another idea — a cold, horrible idea — slid into Miranda's mind. If Stella had gone without her, she, Miranda, would have been left alone in the empty house. Had someone intended that, and had she spoiled some carefully laid plan by insisting on going with her?

Miranda shivered and shut her eyes tightly, as though by doing so she could blot out the ugly pictures that were tormenting her: and instantly she saw again, as if it had been flashed on some screen of the mind, the open window by the hall door.

That window ... if only she could stop being frightened and think clearly for a minute, it could tell her something. She did not know why she should suddenly be so certain of that, but she was certain. There was something simple and obvious about that open window that shouted itself aloud, but she could not hear it because fear was scurrying to and fro in her brain like some terrified animal in a trap.

Miranda became aware of darkness and opened her eyes to find that Stella had switched off the headlights and that the car was cruising slowly down a long, tree-lined road, sparsely lit by two widely distant street lamps that made only small pools of light in the long stretch of moonlit darkness.

There were no lighted windows behind the screen of trees, but against a night sky made luminous by the lurid, reflected glow of the city's lights, rose the black outlines of ruined walls and gaping, eyeless windows.

The car slid softly to a standstill, and in the brief moment before Stella switched off the side lights, Miranda caught a glimpse of a pair of rusty iron gates that were vaguely familiar.

There was a soft click and the engine was silent. The dashboard light vanished and they were sitting in darkness.

233

Miranda felt Stella shiver beside her and then open the car door and slip out quietly into the road. She stood there for a moment, listening, the glow from a distant street lamp drawing a faint gold aureole about the dark outline of her blond head.

Miranda scrambled out of the car and stood beside her. 'Where are we?' She had meant to speak aloud, but the words came out as a whisper. And even as she spoke them, she knew where they were. 'This is the Ridders' house! Stella——!'

Stella turned her head: 'I know. He said I was to come here.'

She turned her head again, listening; peering down the dark, moon-splashed road, and said in an urgent whisper: 'There isn't anyone here is there? Can you see anyone else? Any car?'

'No,' Miranda caught at Stella's arm: 'Let's go back! I don't believe that anyone else is here. Or if they are, it's a trap. Stella, don't!'

Stella jerked away her arm and said: 'He told me not to be afraid. I was to walk up the path and into the house, and I would understand when I got there. You can stay here if you like, but I'm going.'

She turned towards the gate and Miranda said: No — wait! Stella, wait for me!' She groped about in the darkened car. 'I can't find the gun.'

'It's all right,' said Stella, 'I've got it.' They were still speaking in whispers.

The iron gates squeaked open under Stella's hand, and Miranda passed through and stood beside her in the black shadow of the laurels, fighting a terrifying conviction that they had been followed.

Clouds had drifted over the moon, but the glow of the night sky silhouetted the gaunt shell of the house above them and they could neither see nor hear any sound or sign of movement. The house and the ruined, weed-grown garden were silent and deserted. A breath of the night wind stirred the laurels, making the lacquered leaves click and rustle, and Stella clutched at Miranda's arm and shuddered.

'Go on,' she whispered.

They moved out of the shadow of the laurels down the sunken path towards the house, their feet stumbling among a tangle of weeds and broken paving stones, and it seemed to Miranda that the wind died away and the night held its breath to listen to them, and that every shadow held an unseen watcher ...

The clouds thinned and faint, watery moonlight filled the garden as Miranda reached the bottom of the short flight of stone steps that led up to the empty, gaping doorway, and took one hesitant step upwards. She could hear Stella's quick breathing a pace behind her and the heavy beating of her own heart. She took another step upward, feeling for it with her foot. Her eyes were becoming accustomed to the uncertain light and the face of the house was clear above her. The empty doorway yawned on black-ness and beside it a fragment of broken glass in a narrow, slotted window gleamed palely in the faint moonlight.

Miranda reached the top step and her groping hand touched a circle of rusted metal in the centre of which lay a smooth, shallow knob of china; the doorbell of Herr Ridder's house.

For a fleeting, hysterical moment she wondered what would happen if she pressed it? Would some mouldering bell tinkle a shrill summons in the black depths of the ruined house, and bring the ghost of a housekeeper called Greta Schumacher, who had also been Mademoiselle Beljame, to peer suspiciously through that narrow slotted window before opening the door?

The window!

Miranda's hand fell to her side and she stood quite still.

The window! Of course, that was the answer! That was what had nagged at her brain. Not from the outside — that was impossible. From the *inside*! Someone had opened the window from the inside. But that could only mean——

She turned quickly, her back to the blackness of the empty doorway.

'Stella! *You* opened that window, didn't you? That was where the draught came from! No one else could have done it.'

She heard Stella catch her breath in a gasp. 'What window? Why should I open it?'

'To reach the bell. You wanted to reach the bell——'

Miranda's voice died suddenly and her eyes stared down at the thing that Stella held in her hand.

Stella's hand was not shaking any longer. It was quite steady, and the moon, sliding clear of the clouds, glinted on the barrel of Robert's revolver.

Miranda lifted her eyes slowly and looked into the face of a stranger. A white, haggard mask with lips drawn back over the teeth in a purely animal grimace below wide eyes, glittering and enormous. She could no more mistake the look on that face than she could have mistaken the hate that she had once seen on Mrs Leslie's. It meant only one thing — *murder*.

Stella laughed. A gay, clear, cold-blooded little laugh that echoed strangely in the hollow shell of the house. She said: 'You gave me the idea yourself. You thought it was the phone bell. I could have done it in the house, of course, but there might have been traces. And you are too heavy to carry. This was so much simpler.'

She laughed again, and said: 'I know you so well you see! I knew if I could make you overhear a telephone conversation you'd fall for it. I did it very well, didn't I? If I'd said someone wanted to see us both you might have been suspicious. But because I pretended it was only me, and that I was frightened, you rushed into the trap and I got you here without any bother at all!'

She sounded as naïvely pleased with herself as a child displaying its first efforts at handicrafts.

Miranda tried to speak, but found that she could not. Her mouth was dry and there appeared to be a constriction about her throat. She could only stare at that ashy-white, unfamiliar mask as though mesmerized.

Something in her petrified immobility seemed to infuriate the older woman. She said shrilly: 'You thought you'd been very clever, didn't you? *Didn't you!* Pretending you thought you'd left your bag in my car, so you could sneak back to the garage and take a look at the speedometer to see how many miles I'd done. You and your "freak memory for numbers"! I didn't know that I'd left a smear of green paint on that door handle, but you saw it, didn't you? You were spying on me in my own house! Spying on me, and trying to get Robert away from me. Letting him kiss you in front of me! That's how sure of yourself you were! Well, you won't get him! Neither you nor that two-faced slut, Sally Page! Once I've got the money I can get him away from the Army and from her. And no one will ever know what happened to you. You'll just disappear and they'll think you've run away because you're afraid of being arrested!'

She paused for breath, gasping and shaking with rage, but only one word of the incomprehensible tirade made sense to Miranda.

She struggled with a nightmare sense of suffocation and said thickly: 'Paint — then it was you who——'

'Oh yes,' said Stella, her voice once more childlike and casual. 'I drowned her. I waited for her by the pool and hit her with the spanner. It was quite easy, and there was no one about. She'd tried to kill me, you see. She wanted to keep all the money for herself. She deserved to be killed.'

Miranda said numbly: 'What money?'

'The diamonds, of course,' said Stella, impatiently. 'They're here — in this house. That's why I had to bring you here. It was easier if you came with me. And then you actually insisted on bringing a gun with you!'

She laughed again and for a moment the barrel of the revolver wavered and Miranda took a step towards her.

'Oh no, you don't!' said Stella, sharply. 'Turn round. Go on — turn round and go into the house. I couldn't miss you at this range, so don't try and do anything silly.'

'Stella, you can't!' gasped Miranda. 'Don't you understand? It's too dangerous. You *know* no one is allowed inside these houses! Colonel Leslie said so ... he said they could fall down at any

237

moment, and that it was even dangerous to go anywhere near them. He said . . . he said . . .'

'*I* said you were to go inside,' said Stella. 'And you'll do as I say!'

Her voice was the voice of a stranger — as changed as her face — and Miranda turned obediently and walked through the gaping doorway into the silent house. Nothing made sense any more. This could not possibly be real. It was only some fantastic and melodramatic nightmare from which she would presently awake.

A torch flashed on behind her and the thin, yellow pencil of light played on the rubble-strewn space that had once been a hall, and a dark ruined archway beyond.

A cold ring of metal pressed against Miranda's neck and she walked forward, following the beam of the torch that Stella held in her left hand. They passed through a gaping doorway and then another one, into a room where the moon peered down from a roofless square above them. A curving flight of steps, choked with debris, descended into blackness and Miranda groped her way down them, following that inexorable bar of light, into what appeared to be part of a ruined, vaulted cellar, with other cellars opening off it.

Loose bricks, rubble and bomb debris slid and clattered under their feet, every step dislodging miniature landslides that continued to rattle down even after they had reached the foot of the stairs. The crash and patter of falling odds and ends filled the darkness with echoes, so that it almost seemed as though not two, but ten or a dozen people were descending in Indian-file to the ruined cellar, following the two women down . . .

Moonlight lay in one small, cold patch at the foot of the broken steps, but in the blackness beyond and around them the torch light seemed to gather strength.

Stella said: 'Now take off that bracelet and hand it to me. No, don't turn round!'

Her high, gasping voice reverberated hollowly around the unseen, empty spaces, and a Greek chorus of ghostly voices repeated *'don't turn round...turn round...round...'* And once again there came a soft, ominous clatter of falling debris——

Miranda's fingers fumbled with the stiff clasp, but the instinct of self-preservation was strong enough to keep her own voice calm and reasonable: 'You can't use that revolver, Stella, because if you do, you'll die too. The noise and the explosion, in a ruin like this, will be enough to bring the roof down on us — and the walls as well. If you fire, you may kill me. But *you'll* be buried alive!'

But it was no use. Stella was beyond the reach of reason, and though she must have heard that deadly rustle and fall of displaced rubble, it conveyed no warning to her obsessed brain. Her voice shot up and she said: 'If you think you can frighten me, you're wasting your time. Stop talking and give me that bracelet!'

If I turn quickly, thought Miranda, I might be able to knock the torch out of her hand ... she couldn't do anything in the dark. She's never fired a gun in her life. She'd miss except at short range. If the torch went out I'd have a chance ...

But she could not do it. She seemed to be gripped by a deadly inertia that prevented her body from obeying her will; it could only obey that high, unnatural voice that was, unbelievably, Stella's.

The bracelet slipped off her wrist and she held it out behind her and felt it taken.

'Now go and stand over there.'

Miranda moved forward again and turned, her eyes dazzled by the full glare of the torch.

'I told you not to turn round!' cried Stella, shrilly. 'I won't have you looking at me! I can't do it while you look at me!' Her voice broke suddenly into a high, childish babble: 'It's not my fault! I can't help it! You shouldn't have spied on me. I wouldn't have touched you if it hadn't been for that. But you'd have told. And I won't hang for Mademoiselle. I won't! And you tried to get Robert, so it serves you right ... it serves you right!'

She lifted the revolver in a shaking hand; and as she did so Miranda saw a movement in the blackness behind her.

239

There was someone else in the cellars. Someone who had followed them down. Two people — three——

'No one will know!' gabbled Stella. 'No one found the diamonds, and no one will find you.'

She steadied the wavering revolver, and a hand came over her shoulder and twisted it out of her grasp.

'I'll take that please, Mrs Melville,' said Simon Lang gently.

Stella screamed. A high, horrible scream like a trapped rabbit, and the torch fell to the floor and went out.

Someone brushed past Miranda in the dark, and then the blackness was rent by a flash of flame and the crashing reverberations of a shot.

Miranda heard Simon say savagely: *'You bloody idiot!'* and then there was another sound; a slow, ominous mutter like a growl of thunder; and a slither and rumble of falling stone.

The vaulted darkness was suddenly full of dust and torch beams and someone was shouting: 'Get on up those stairs!' and someone else had caught her arm and was dragging her, stumbling and running across the uneven floor and up the slippery, broken steps and through the rubble-strewn, roofless rooms to the safety of the moonlit garden.

The rumble grew to a roar and the gaunt black shell of the house appeared to sway and dissolve against the night sky as one wall leaned tiredly inwards and slowly, very slowly, collapsed upon itself.

The ground shook as though it had been hit by an earthquake, and for a minute or two the moonlight was thick with dust and mortar and flying splinters of stone. And when the garden was silent again only one wall of the house remained, and a gasping voice was saying over and over again: 'I tried to get her, sir, but she twists away and runs back. She twists away and runs back ... I tried to get her ...'

18

'It was the German, of course,' said Simon. 'I should have remembered that a continental cop is apt to be a bit quick on the draw. He imagined that she could escape and fired at her. But you can't go loosing off firearms in a building of that description without asking for trouble.'

Miranda said: 'Was she — was she alive?'

Simon looked down at her and glimpsed something of the horror that lurked behind the small white face.

He looked away again and spoke in a completely matter-of-fact voice.

'Yes. For a time. Long enough to make some sort of a statement. It was the best way out for her, you know. She knew it too. The last thing she said was: "I never thought I'd live to be grateful to a German."'

Miranda's mouth twisted and she bent her head hurriedly over the suitcase to hide the fact that there were tears in her eyes.

Over two days had passed since the night that Stella had died, and although Miranda had been questioned and asked to make and sign statements, and been interviewed exhaustively by a number of persons in authority, she had not spoken to Simon until this morning, when he had walked unannounced into her bedroom at the Lawrences' house and found her kneeling on the floor packing a row of shoes into the bottom of a suitcase.

Simon said dryly: 'There is no need to be sentimental over her just because she's dead. She wasn't an admirable character. She connived at one murder and committed another. And would have committed a third if we hadn't prevented it. It's her unfortunate

241

husband you can be sorry for. This has just about broken him up. He loved her very much: more than she knew, I think. I hear he's going home on compassionate leave.'

Miranda nodded without speaking, and Simon looked down at the bent head and the hands that were attempting to wrap a shoe in tissue paper and bungling the job because they trembled so, and realized that talking might ease that intolerable strain. He sat down on Miranda's bed and said in a casual and conversational tone: 'When did you realize that it was Mrs Melville?'

Miranda dropped the shoe onto the floor and sat back on her heels.

'It was the window,' she said. 'The little window by the front door in the hall was open, and I knew quite well that it hadn't been open before. It scared me stiff, because I knew that there was no one but Stella and myself in the house, so I thought that someone must have tried to get in. I couldn't stop thinking about it. And when I saw the window of the Ridder house I suddenly realized that of course it couldn't *possibly* have been opened from the outside. It could only have been opened from the inside. And I knew just when it had been opened, because the draught from it had blown into the drawing-room. But Stella had been in the hall then, and she would have seen if anyone else had been there. So she must have opened it herself. And then all at once I remembered that the doorbell and the telephone bell sounded alike, and I – I don't know why, but I had a sudden picture in my mind of Stella reaching out and pressing the bell, and then going quickly to the telephone. And I blurted it out, and——' Miranda stopped and gave a hopeless little shrug of her shoulders.

She picked up another shoe and began to wrap it mechanically in paper, but her hands were steadier and presently she spoke again, and without lifting her head.

'Simon, why did it have to happen? I don't understand!'

'What is it you don't understand, dear?'

'Anything! Anything at all. It's all such a ghastly muddle.'

'Not now,' said Simon. 'We've sorted it out by now.' He leant

242

back against the bed-head with his hands behind his head. 'Lottie helped us there. Lottie and Wally.'

'*Lottie!*' Miranda turned swiftly: 'Why how could she——'

'Ssh! Don't interrupt. Mademoiselle, who was Frau Schumacher, thought that Brigadier Brindley might possibly have recognized her, and when he took those sleeping pills she saw her chance. She took one herself you remember; intending, I'm fairly certain, to give it to Lottie. But Lottie poured her hot milk down the back of the basin while Mademoiselle was out of the carriage for a few minutes.'

Miranda said quickly: 'So she wasn't asleep after all!'

'No. She only pretended to be. She was still awake when her governess left the carriage that night, and she saw her come back. She saw something else as well. Mademoiselle had worn a pair of black gloves, and when she returned to the carriage she rinsed those gloves in the basin and the water turned red.'

Miranda caught her breath in a hard gasp. 'But why didn't she tell?'

'For a very simple reason — from a child's point of view,' said Simon. 'She had been told so often that hot milk at night made her sleep that she was afraid to admit that she had not slept, for fear that it would give away the fact that she had thrown away her milk instead of drinking it! All the same she did tell someone: she told Wally. And then a little later she told her stepmother — that was just before Mrs Melville walked into your room at the Berlin hostel and found her governess rifling your suitcases.'

'So you were right about that! Was it my bracelet she wanted?'

'It was. And for a very odd reason. We all thought that she and her husband murdered the Ridders for the sake of the diamonds, but it turns out that they knew nothing whatever about them. They had planned the murder for the sake of the money and the jewels alone. They knew there was a safe in the cellar, and had once seen it open; but they thought it only contained special wines. They had no idea that it concealed a second safe.

'Herr Ridder had mentioned on arrival that night that he had

243

managed to acquire some Napoleon brandy, and he carried it directly down to the cellar. They must have killed him when he came up. When they came to strip his body they found the bracelet with the Egyptian charm.'

'Why did they keep it? Did they think it meant something?'

'No. They threw it in with the other stuff merely because it had to be removed, since Herr Ridder was known to have worn it. Schumacher escaped to England, where he died, but Greta Schumacher was left behind and ended up in a concentration camp under a false name. And in that same camp she met someone she knew: a distant cousin, Rosa Müller, who with her husband, Kurt, used to be called in to help as extra staff whenever the Ridders entertained — Rosa as parlourmaid and Kurt as footman-cum-waiter ...

'The Müllers had no idea why they had been arrested, for the Ridder story was not public property at that time — or for some considerable time afterwards — but I presume it was known that they worked regularly for Herr Willi and his wife. Poor Kurt was interrogated on arrival and died in the process: apparently he had a heart condition, and had been poorly for some time. Because of their kinship, the two women, Greta Schumacher — or whatever she was calling herself then — and Rosa Müller naturally gravitated together, and one presumes that Greta swore Rosa to secrecy in the matter of her identity, and cooked up a good story to account for it ...

'They liked to talk over old times together, and one day, in the course of conversation, Rosa told how her husband, who had been helping clear up after a late party at the Ridders', took several unopened bottles of wine back to the cellar, and surprised Herr Willi opening a safe in the back of the one in which he kept his special wines. He'd already opened the back of that safe; and was fiddling with the dials of an inner one: reading off the numbers, or the code or whatever, from a small, oddly shaped key attached to a chain bracelet. When he heard Kurt he whipped round so that his back hid the safe, and told him off like a pickpocket. Fortunately, Kurt had the sense to play the idiot-boy so convincingly that it all blew over, but Willi's fury had scared him so badly that he didn't even dare tell his Rosa about it until over a year later — by which time Hitler had marched into Poland and the incident didn't seem in the least important——

'Greta certainly didn't think anything of it. She had always known that Herr Ridder had a wine safe built into a wall in the cellar, and if there was a second safe concealed behind it, she supposed that he kept his top secret documents there. And since she was not interested in official documents, she never gave it another thought. Until Brigadier Brindley came out with that talk about the diamonds, and you told him about the Egyptian charm — and actually handed it around so that everyone could have a good look at it! It was only then that "Mademoiselle Beljame", née Greta Schumacher, remembered cousin Rosa's story and started putting two and two together; and came up with the right answer.'

'Was it really a key?' demanded Miranda, leaping womanlike from the general to the particular: 'And have you found the diamonds?'

'It was. And we have — though we had to shift a mountain of rubble to get at them. There were two keys to that safe, and your charm incorporated both of them. The stem of the ankh fitted into a tiny slot that opened a thick slab of steel at the back of the outer safe, and behind it were three sets of combination locks that worked on that series of hieroglyphics that were engraved on the back and front of the charm. Very ingenious. What's more, it still works. If it hadn't, I suppose we'd have had to blow the safe open. Which wouldn't have done the contents much good.'

Miranda said: 'How did you find out about all this? About Rosa Müller and Mademoiselle — I mean Greta Schumacher? Is Rosa still alive?'

'No. She died in the camp about a year later. The information came from Mademoiselle. She told Mrs Melville. And Wally Wilkin, in his role of Dan Dare, Detective, was hiding under the bed!'

'What!'

' "*What*" indeed! You know, it will always rile me to think that between them those two kids knew almost everything there was to know, right from the start, and kept it under their hats because Wally wanted to play a lone hand and solve the case without the help of the "grown-ups". And that I was fool enough to give him such a telling off for snooping that he shut up like a clam.'

'But why on earth should Mademoiselle telh Stella?' demanded Miranda.

'That's where Lottie comes in. Lottie had told Mrs Melville about Mademoiselle's doings in the night, and Mrs Melville, horrified, had rushed along to your room to consult you. She caught the governess going through your boxes and told her that she was going straight to the police.'

'But why didn't she, Simon?'

'Because Mademoiselle bribed her silence. Being desperate, she told her the whole story and offered her a half share in a colossal fortune to hold her tongue.'

Miranda stood up suddenly and went over to the window to stand with her back to Simon, staring blindly out into the garden.

'*Stella* did that? For *money*?'

'For Robert,' corrected Simon.

Miranda swung round. 'What do you mean?'

'It's rather an involved story,' said Simon slowly. 'We got part of it from Mrs Leslie.'

Miranda said quickly: 'Mrs Leslie hated her! You can't go by that.'

'She had her reasons,' said Simon gently.

'Robert?'

'No. Johnnie Radley. Stella's first husband. When Radley returned to India after his first leave, Stella refused to go back with him. She disliked the East and all foreign countries, so she tried to eat her cake and have it. But it didn't work out that way. Radley got fed up with a wife who preferred what she termed "civilization" to him. He was hurt and lonely, and he fell in love with

246

another girl and asked Stella for a divorce. She wouldn't hear of it; and finding no way out, he volunteered for a particularly dangerous mission and was killed. The girl — who was young and impressionable and very much in love — shot herself when she heard the news. She was Norah Leslie's sister.'

'Oh!' said Miranda on a gasp. 'I see. Then that was why ... Go on.'

'Stella posed as a heartbroken widow, and after the war she met Robert. But Robert was different from Johnnie Radley. She was in love with Robert. Really in love.'

'I know,' said Miranda, almost inaudibly. 'I was thinking about that only the last — the last morning, and that Stella would die for him if she had to.'

'She did die for him; indirectly. She was prepared to risk death by hanging rather than lose him. When Robert was sent abroad she would have gone with him, but was not allowed to. She became terrified that history would repeat itself and that because she could not be with him he might leave her for someone else. She was older than Robert, and that didn't help. Then, on the journey out here, she realized that he knew Sally Page rather too well, and it frightened her. She began to see that she must live Robert's life or lose him, because they could not afford to leave the Army and live at Mallow ...

'Mademoiselle's story and her offer came at just the right moment. The sight of Sally Page and the way she had looked at Robert had scared Mrs Melville badly, and the news that the regiment was to go to Malaya put the lid on it. Money was the only way out. A lot of money, that would enable her to live at Mallow and keep Robert with her.'

Miranda said with a bitter little laugh: 'And I thought it was Sally! Did you know that? I worked it all out.'

'Did you? Why?'

'Several things. I remembered that just after Mademoiselle left to look for Lottie's bear, Sally went off to telephone someone and that she was away for simply ages. Quite long enough to do what

they say Stella did. And then – then on the morning after Mademoiselle's body was found, Andy and Sally were given a lift by the
Leslies because their car had run out of petrol, and Andy made
a great fuss about it. He insisted that he'd filled up the tank only
a few days before and that Sally must have been using it a lot since
then: and – and I wondered. I thought perhaps she'd been using
it up seeing Robert, and that Mademoiselle ...'

Miranda sketched a quick, impatient gesture with one hand,
as though brushing away a too persistent fly, and changed
course abruptly: 'And then there was the time when she spilt the
sherry ...'

She paused for so long that finally Simon said: 'I'm not with
you; what sherry, and who spilt it? Mademoiselle?'

'No. Sally. It was the morning after Mademoiselle's body
had been found, and most of your team had dropped in for a
drink.'

'My *what*?' exclaimed Simon, bewildered.

Miranda's pale face was suddenly pink. 'I'm sorry. It just
slipped out. I'd forgotten you wouldn't know about that.'

'About what, for heaven's sake?'

' *"Lang's Eleven"* — there were eleven of us, you see. — Suspects,' translated Miranda, as Simon still looked puzzled. 'The
ones in that sleeping-car coach from Helmstedt to Berlin. Two
Melvilles, two Marsons, two Leslies, two Pages, Mademoiselle,
Mrs Wilkin and myself.'

Simon laughed and said that he hadn't considered Mrs Wilkin,
but that she was right about the rest, and would she please go on
about Sally and the sherry?

Miranda's flush deepened and she said hastily: 'It sounds very
silly now, but she spilt some on a chair and mopped it off with a
face-tissue that she took out of her bag and threw away afterwards
into the fire, but it missed and fell inside the fender instead. And
after they had all gone I began to pick up some petals that had
fallen on the floor, and I noticed the face-tissue: it was an Elizabeth Arden one, and that gave me a horrid shock, because there

had been an Elizabeth Arden tissue on the floor of Mademoiselle's room on the day that——'

She saw the expression on Simon's face and said quickly: 'You knew about that?'

'Yes. Mrs Melville put it there. She'd borrowed one from Sally.'

'*Stella* did? But why?'

'Because Mrs Page used them, and she wanted to throw suspicion on her. She reasoned the way you probably did: that some people might think that Sally Page had a motive for getting Robert's wife out of the way — the people who thought that Friedel had been killed in mistake for Mrs Melville. But it was Mademoiselle who killed Friedel — in mistake for you.'

'*Me?* Why me?'

'She was expecting you to go over to the Leslies' — she wasn't in when you cancelled that, remember? I imagine she only meant to knock you out and steal the bracelet, thereby doublecrossing Mrs Melville. But she hit harder than she intended, and Mrs Melville was convinced that her governess had meant to murder her ...

'She palmed that toy of Lottie's, sent Mademoiselle off on a wild-goose chase, and went after her in the car. All very simple. It was late evening and the numbers of cars with British zone licence plates are not taken, nor are the cars stopped. But she didn't reckon on the green paint.'

Miranda said: 'Did she — did she get some on herself?'

'She couldn't very well avoid it, after sliding both Mademoiselle and her bicycle into the water. She got it all over her gloves and smeared a little on the car door in the dark. She didn't notice it until she got home and hadn't any idea where it came from. But Wally knew. He was snooping through the garage window when she arrived back and he saw her pull off her gloves and look at the green stains. She fetched Mademoiselle's bottle of turpentine, and cleaned off some that was on her wrist, and burnt the gloves.'

'Robert spilt the turpentine,' said Miranda slowly.

'Did he?'

'Yes. I – I even thought once that he might have arranged it with Sally.'

Simon looked a question.

Miranda said: 'I – I thought that she, Mademoiselle, might have seen them together, or found a love-letter, or something of the sort, and tried to blackmail them. I had a horrid moment or two before I realized that Robert couldn't possibly have done it — not in a million years. Robert's not — he isn't ...'

'Ruthless enough?' offered Simon.

'*Yes*. He's too easy-going, and I don't think that anything has gone really deep with him. Until now. Poor Robert! Did you know that he's going to send in his papers and use his gratuity to turn Mallow into a home for handicapped children? The Leslies are going to help him run it as soon as Colonel Leslie retires ... one of their boys is a spastic. I didn't know that. It's to be called the "Stella Melville Memorial Home" ...'

Miranda shivered and pushed her hands into the pockets of her skirt to hide the fact that they were trembling again. She said: 'You knew it was Stella, didn't you? You knew all the time.'

'No. Not for a long time,' admitted Simon.

'When did you know?'

'Not until the very last day, I'm afraid. I knew that someone in the house must be involved when I heard that the governess had come back in the night and left that china bear and removed some of her belongings. I was sure it wasn't true; because though no one had heard her, the front door was locked. And that type of door will only lock from the outside if it's banged fairly hard. It seemed to me more likely that for some reason of their own, someone inside the house had faked that return and just slipped the latch. You see both the back door and the french window were bolted at night. And there was no key missing. I checked on that.'

'When did you begin to think it was Stella?'

'When I mentioned the green paint,' said Simon soberly. 'I saw her face in the glass, and I was sure. There are some expressions you cannot mistake.'

250

'No,' said Miranda in a low voice, and shuddered. She pushed the thought away from her and said quickly: 'You told me as much as you dared, to try and put me on my guard, didn't you?'

For the first time since she had known him Simon looked disconcerted. 'Well — not exactly,' he said.

'Why, then?' demanded Miranda, surprised. 'Was it because——' She checked herself and coloured.

Simon laughed. 'No, dear. It was not for the sake of your *beaux yeux*. It was because you are one of the many exceptions that prove the rule. Where your feelings are concerned you are a darned bad actress, and I wanted you to know too much in order to ensure that you would behave in the guilty manner of one who knows too much!'

Miranda flushed angrily and her chin went up with a jerk. 'And why should you want me to do that?'

'Because I needed proof. I thought that if Mrs Melville could be brought to believe that you knew more than you should, she might be goaded into showing her hand.'

'Thank you,' said Miranda in a voice that trembled in spite of herself.

'I'm sorry, my sweet. It was a rotten trick to play on you, but I needed evidence and I had only theories and guesswork. I didn't know then about Wally. And even now I doubt if the unsupported stories of a nine-year-old boy and a girl of seven would have been accepted in court: a good lawyer would have made mincemeat of them. I didn't know that Mrs Melville suspected you already. But I knew that she was afraid of you.'

'Of *me*?' said Miranda astounded. 'Why should she be afraid of me? I'd always been fond of her.'

Simon examined his fingernails with careful attention and said without looking at Miranda: 'Robert.'

Miranda coloured hotly. 'But that's absurd!'

'Is it? There was a time when I myself wondered if there might not be something in it. You could have wanted money and Robert. The two went together.'

251

Miranda whipped her hands out of her pockets and clenched them into a pair of admirable fists. She seemed to be having some difficulty with her breathing. 'You dared! You actually dared to think that I . . .'

'Calm down, darling. It was only a theory — one of many. But he had a habit of putting an affectionate arm about you on every possible occasion, and——'

'He *is* my cousin!' interrupted Miranda stormily.

'Oh, quite. All the same it put you under suspicion when Friedel died; and it upset his wife. Besides, you were too pretty and too young, and Mrs Melville began to fear the constant contrast that your youthful charms offered to her more mature attractions. She was, in the words of an ex-cook of my mother's, "in a state". What with her unbalanced passion for her husband, a dislike of foreigners and foreign countries that amounted to a phobia, jealousy of Sally Page, suspicion that you were also on the way to an affair with her Robert, and the conviction that her governess had intended to murder her, she cannot have been quite sane. That's the kindest view to take of it, anyway.'

Miranda said helplessly: 'But even if you are right, why should she want to kill me? There was still Sally.'

'Oh, it wasn't that. I thought you knew. From your own account of that night, she told you herself.'

'She said something about spying on her, and – and a speedo-meter. I didn't understand.'

Simon looked at her curiously. 'Then you didn't notice anything about the car on the night that Mademoiselle disappeared?'

'No. What was there to notice?'

'She was convinced that you had, and that there was only one way to make sure that you didn't eventually tell someone. It seems that you went down to the garage that evening just after she had got back from the swimming-pool, and that there were three things you might have noticed. First, that the engine was still hot although the car was supposed to have been back well over half an hour. Secondly, that the handle of the door on the driver's side was smeared with green paint — she cleaned it off next day with petrol, still without knowing that it had any connection with Mademoiselle. And lastly, that the speedometer had clocked up a higher figure than it should. You evidently made some idle remark during supper that night about always remembering numbers, and a guilty conscience suggested to her that you were hinting that you had spotted it.'

Miranda said bitterly: 'Then she had it all planned!'

'Oh, no,' said Simon gently. 'She was afraid of you giving her away; and then when her husband left that night, he kissed you. That's right, isn't it?' Simon lifted an interrogatory eyebrow.

'Yes. But it was only . . .'

'It was only the last straw. She told us that it all jumped into her mind then and there. Her husband had gone out and there was no one else in the house. But the next day there would be a resident batman. If she could just get her hands on the bracelet and the diamonds, and dispose of you at the same time, it would all be over and she would be safe. If you disappeared, suspicion might point to you. And if you were never found you might be supposed to have bolted behind the Iron Curtain. But she had to get you out of the house and just where she wanted you without fuss. And then she remembered that the doorbell sounded like the telephone. She was nearly off her head with fear and jealousy, and the cunning of near lunacy suggested it all to her in the space of a few minutes.'

Miranda said stormily: 'And you knew what she might do — and you let me go through all that – that horror! You're nothing but a cold-blooded, scheming . . .' She searched for a word and failed to find one sufficiently opprobrious for her purpose.

'You weren't in any danger,' said Simon mildly. 'I'd run Wally to earth by then, and had a pretty clear idea of the form. The place was crawling with cops and you were more or less under observation from the second you walked out of the front door. You see we couldn't be sure where she was heading for — though we had a shrewd idea. So we had to tail you. Once you got to the Ridders'

253

house, we knew we were right; and after that we were practically on your heels. Fortunately for us, and thanks to all that loose rubble, your descent to the cellar was so noisy that we were able to sneak down behind you without any trouble, and, after listening to what she had to say, step into the picture in a nice melodramatic manner at the last moment.'

'And I suppose,' said Miranda furiously, 'that it didn't occur to any of you that she might have pressed the trigger a second before you got it away from her?'

'It wouldn't really have mattered very much if she had,' said Simon, placidly.

Miranda stared at him unbelievingly: rigid with a sudden sense of outrage that had, illogically, nothing whatsoever to do with her terrors of that past night.

Simon observed her reaction with a half smile. There was a gleam of complete comprehension and a warm, dancing malice in his eyes.

'One of the things I like about you, Miranda,' he remarked gently, 'is that you are so beautifully uncomplicated. Don't worry, my darling. I wasn't being callous about your personal safety. I only meant that I had taken the precaution of unloading that weapon and removing all live ammunition from the house, just in case of accidents.'

'*Oh!*' said Miranda explosively. 'Well if you're quite sure that you've said all you want to say, I think you had better go! I've got a lot of packing to do. And I don't know what you mean by walking calmly into my bedroom in the first place, and I'm not your darling!'

'Aren't you?' said Simon softly. 'Well I won't argue the point, but you are wasting your time over that packing. You'll only have to unpack it all again. As for my walking into your bedroom, I'm afraid you will have to get used to it. I understand it is one of a husband's privileges.'

'Oh!' said Miranda again, on a long breath: 'You – you're very sure of yourself, aren't you?'

'Very,' agreed Simon placidly. 'I generally get what I want.'

'Miranda,' said Mrs Lawrence, walking briskly into the room a few moments later, 'do you know if Captain Lang has left yet, or ... Oh, I'm so sorry!'

She retreated hurriedly and closed the door.

'Well, really!' said Mrs Lawrence, addressing the empty landing, a bundle of laundry, three regimental prints of unusual hideousness and her immortal soul: 'You wouldn't think that after three murders and ... Oh well, perhaps they are right. Life is more important than death.'

She shrugged her shoulders tolerantly and went downstairs to explain to her cook in what she confidently imagined to be German, that *der Herr Polizisten Capitan Lang* would be remaining to luncheon.